Praise for

Karen Eisenbrey's
A Quest for Hidden Things

"This tale is built on two very powerful things—great storytelling and beautiful prose. The author writes each scene with such rich detail it transports you into the action. It's a classic fantasy adventure with a touch of cozy. I loved the intrigue and the unexpected twists and turns. Highly recommend! Karen is a fabulous writer. *A Quest for Hidden Things* is my favorite read so far this year."

-JL Henker, fantasy sci-fi author and host of the *Women Fantasy Authors* YouTube Channel

"*A Quest for Hidden Things* deftly interweaves multiple timelines and multiple points of view in a charming and magical coming-of-age tale. ... As Crane and Ketty grapple with their own magical abilities, blossoming romance, and the repercussions of generational trauma, they discover a greater mystery looms and with it a threat that could annihilate their villages and beyond."

-M.K. Martin
author of the *Survivors' Club Chronicles*

"Because Karen Eisenbrey already developed this universe in her *Daughter of Magic* trilogy, reading this prequel series feels like coming home to a richly conceived world of magic, beauty, tenderness, and misconceptions overcome through grace. This is the universe I want to live in."

-Benjamin Gorman
author of *The Convention of Fiends* series

A Quest for Hidden Things

Karen Eisenbrey

Published in the United States by
Not a Pipe Publishing Ink-Corporated L.L.C.,
www.NotAPipePublishing.com

Trade Paperback Edition

ISBN-13: 978-1-956892-59-8

Cover Art by Michaela Thorn
Cover Design by Benjamin Gorman
Map by Karen Eisenbrey and Steven E. Scribner

Dedication

With gratitude to Nan H., who has believed in Deep River almost as long as I have, often with better faith.

None of this would have happened without you, Nan.

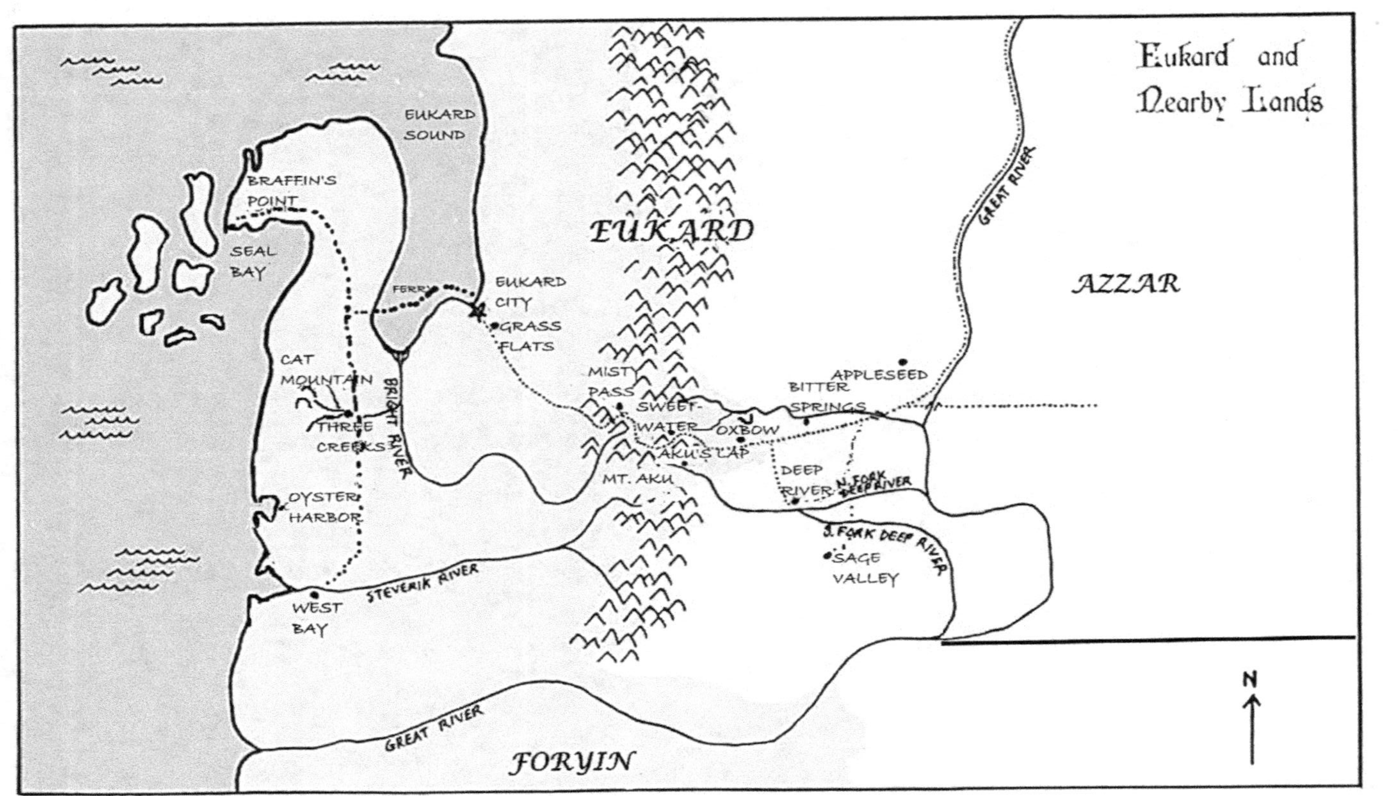

Eukard and Nearby Lands
EUKARD
AZZAR
FORYIN
EUKARD SOUND
BRAFFIN'S POINT
SEAL BAY
FERRY
EUKARD CITY
GRASS FLATS
CAT MOUNTAIN
THREE CREEKS
BRIGHT RIVER
OYSTER HARBOR
WEST BAY
STEVERIK RIVER
GREAT RIVER
MISTY PASS
SWEET-WATER
OXBOW
AKU'S LAP
MT. AKU
BITTER SPRINGS
APPLESEED
DEEP RIVER
N. FORK DEEP RIVER
S. FORK DEEP RIVER
SAGE VALLEY
GREAT RIVER
N

CHARACTERS

(In alphabetical order; major characters in **bold**)

- Alna (AHL-nuh), wife of Kryg (age 39)

- Ati (AH-tee), wife of Yshna, stepmother of Sunnea (age 41)

- Brettif (BREH-tif), son of Tiek and Breff, twin brother of Tibreff (age 0)

- Briato (bree-AH-tow), weaver, husband of Keena, father of Tiek, Kiat, and Brynnit (age 39)

- Brynnit (BRIH-niht), youngest daughter of Briato and Keena, sister of Kiat and Tiek (age 8)

- Chamokat (chuh-MOH-kaht), Aklaka Listener (age 17)

- **Crane, wizard, son of Stell (age 17)**

- Docna (DOHK-nuh), daughter of Marna and Docken, sister of Mardo and Kennen (age 7)

- **Elic (EH-lihk), Crane's best friend, teacher in Deep River, son of Sudi and Ohme, brother of Jagree, (age 19)**

- Eslo (EHS-low), innkeeper in Misty Pass, father of Ketty (age 46)

- Farl, miller in Deep River, husband of Lynka, father of Rynk and Foli (age 40)

- Jagree (JAG-ree), apprentice blacksmith and stable keeper, son of Sudi and Ohme, brother of Elic (age 11)

- Jelf, Keeper of Records in Deep River, Stell's uncle (age 60)

- Keena (KEE-nuh), wife of Briato, mother of Kiat, Tiek, and Brynnit (age 38)

- Kennen (KEN-ehn), son of Marna and Docken, brother of Docna and Mardo (age 3)

- **Ketty (KET-ee), apprentice midwife/healer in Misty Pass, daughter of Eslo (age 17)**

- Kiat (KEE-aht), daughter of Briato and Keena, twin sister of Tiek, sister of Brynnit (age 18)

- Knot (naht) see: YRAE

- Kolma (KOHL-muh), Stell's neighbor, wife of Toli, mother of Liko and Tolik (age 39)

- Kruff, healer in Misty Pass (age 70)

- Kryg (Krihg), potter in Deep River, husband of Alna (age 42)

- Lalik (LAH-lihk), Ketty's childhood friend, wife of Darys (age 18)

- Liba (LEE-buh), wife of Sinth, mother Silib and Senri (age 40)

- Lynka (LIN-kuh), wife of Farl, mother of Rynk and Foli (age 39)

- Mardo (MAR-doh), son of Marna and Docken, brother of Docna and Kennen (age 5)

- Marna (MAR-nuh), wife of Docken, mother of Docna, Mardo, and Kennen (age 27)

- Myn (old) (Mihn), mayor of Deep River, father of Mynna and Young Myn (age 50)

- Myn (young) (Mihn), son of Old Myn, brother of Mynna (age 6)

- Mynna (MIH-nuh), daughter of Old Myn, sister of Young Myn (age 19)

- Nari (NAH-ree), traveling merchant, lover of Eslo (age 42)

- Ohme (OH-mee), blacksmith, husband of Sudi, father of Elic and Jagree (age 41)

- Senri (SEHN-ree), son of Sinth and Liba, brother of Silib (age 6)

- Sinth, carpenter in Deep River, husband of Liba, father of Silib and Senri (age 40)

- Soorhi (SUR-ee), past teacher in Deep River, uncle of Yrae (deceased)

- **Stell, innkeeper in Deep River, mother of Crane (age 36)**

- Sudi (SOO-dee), midwife, Stell's best friend, wife of Ohme, mother of Elic and Jagree (age 40)

- Sunnea (soo-NEE-uh), daughter of Yshna (age 18)

- Tibreff (TEE-bref), son of Tiek and Breff, twin brother of Brettif (age 0)

- Tiek (TEE-ehk), wife of Breff, mother of Tibreff and Brettif, sister of Kiat and Brynnit (age 18)

- Trilmi (TRIHL-mee), midwife in Misty Pass (age 60)

- **Yrae (EAR-ay), wizard on Mount Aku (age 38) (see also KNOT)**

- Yshna (EE-shna), tailor, husband of Ati, father of Sunnea (age 40)

A Quest for Hidden Things

Chapter I. An Ordinary Day

Yrae soared on eagle's wings in the sun-warmed air. Below, a stone-gray torrent sprang from a glacier and zig-zagged down Aku's slopes. The great bird followed as the stream leaped over cliffs in glittering cascades and gathered the offerings of smaller creeks. It grew into a river, winking up at Yrae through thick forest. The rugged valley broadened, and the river slowed and deepened. A dam of mud and debris checked its eastward flow. The eagle circled above, inspecting, while the river turned southeast, carving a new channel, flowing across the open plain, a shining green ribbon of life.

Below the dam, Yrae floated above a dry gully through grassland and sagebrush, past rippling fields and a village of low, stone houses: Deep River, named for that vanished stream. The villagers didn't know where their river had gone. They never asked.

Eagle-Yrae circled above the tallest house. He had visited many times over the years in this form. He came to watch the boy. But someday — someday soon — the boy would come to Yrae.

Deep River

The pump screeched as Crane worked the handle to draw water for the day. Across the road from the inn, shutters thumped as the blacksmith opened the windows of his forge. All around, the waking village of Deep River prepared for a new day. An ordinary summer day, with no hint anything would ever change. The morning air was sweet with the baked scent of dried grasses. Fitful gusts of a chilly breeze made Crane wish for his coat, but it was sure to grow hot before the morning passed.

The sky above shimmered red, a strange effect Crane alone could see. Something magic, he guessed, though it never *did* anything. He had learned as a child that no one liked to hear him talk about it. He recalled learning to write and spell, completing simple sentences like *The sky is _____.* When Crane filled in *red*, Teacher Soorhi called him imaginative. Most of the other children laughed, not in a nice way. And that was before any of them knew he would be a wizard.

Crane looked again, past the red shimmer at a cloudless blue sky. A meadowlark trilled the beginning of a children's song, adding its call to the squeak and sigh of the old pump.

With an echoing gurgle, rusty water gushed from the spout. Crane continued pumping until the water ran clear. The flowing water reminded him of last night's dream: flying, an eagle, and a river running with clear water. He'd never seen a real river, but he knew that was what he'd dreamed. He struggled to recall more. A river, a sense of hidden danger. And a voice, calling his name.

The bucket overflowed onto his foot and banished the dream in a cold, wet rush. His mind on his task once more, Crane filled a second bucket and lugged both under the tangle of rose brambles that arched over the door to the Blue Heron Inn.

The empty common room was fragrant with the day's first baking. A great stone fireplace dominated the room, though it wouldn't be lit until fall. Tall ladder-back chairs and two long tables stood on the swept wooden floor, waiting for suppertime. Small square tables lined the walls under the large front windows. The only activity was in the kitchen, where Mama prepared breakfast for two over a small cooking fire.

She looked up as Crane joined her. She had been looking up at him since he was fourteen years old. He doubted he would ever get used to towering over her. And at seventeen, he was still growing.

He carried the buckets to the corner behind her and emptied them into the big keg there. The routine action, the tables and chairs, his mother cooking — it could have been any morning in his life, all alike. And yet, as sometimes happened in the early morning, Crane had a vision of life as it was not: the empty river channel flowing with water; the empty inn peopled with guests; the empty place at table filled by a father. A father he'd never met.

These dreamy visions departed as quickly as they had appeared, leaving Crane with only a sense of longing, and an unanswered question. That was the story she never told.

After breakfast, Crane fed the chickens and gathered eggs, then watered and weeded the vegetable garden. Chores completed, he found his mother kneading bread dough for the second baking, her hands and apron dusted with flour.

"Anything else you need?" he asked.

"Not now, but there should be firewood to chop later."

Crane stuffed a heel of bread into his pocket and filled his tin water flask. It held a pint and had a flattened shape to fit into a large pocket or hang on a woven strap over his shoulder. Mama's name, Stell, was scratched into the bottom.

"All right, then. See you later, Mama."

Across the road, a shirtless little boy waited in front of Aunt Sudi's house, his pale skin flaming with sunburn. The midwife provided care to all who needed it. Though not kin to Crane's family, Sudi was like a sister to Mama and had always been 'Aunt Sudi' to

Crane.

"Morning, Senri," Crane greeted the boy.

Senri grinned. "Do me a magic!"

Crane glanced around to make sure no one else was looking, then drew a small amount of power. Warmth rose from his core and flowed to the fingers of his left hand. He reached behind his back and produced a stem of fragrant purple lupine. The blossoms became a cloud of blue butterflies that fluttered over the boy's head. A pretty, useless illusion, amusing to children. Senri clapped his hands and tried to catch the butterflies before they vanished.

"Looks like you got too much sun yesterday." Crane winced in sympathy. Though no stranger to burns, his darker skin didn't react as obviously to the sun's rays. He had stopped wondering why no one else in Deep River shared this protection. "Are you going to see Sudi? She has a salve that's as good as magic."

Senri nodded. "I'm waiting for Mama. She won't run!"

"Senri, what do you think you're doing?" Senri's mother strode up. Liba's thin face looked even more pinched as she pursed her lips and glared at Crane.

"Good morning, ma'am. I was just recommending-"

"We don't need advice from *him*." Liba took Senri's arm and steered him away from Crane. The interaction was common enough, it didn't offend him ... much. He allowed himself secret pleasure at seeing them go into Sudi's house. Behind Liba's back, Senri turned and gave Crane a little wave.

Every morning, Crane took a long walk to nowhere in particular to refresh his mind before tackling the frustrating task of teaching himself magic. This morning, he walked east down the dusty road that ran through the village. The day was already warm, the sun beating down from a cloudless sky. The wind rose as the sun climbed higher, but Crane enjoyed the stiff breeze on his face.

He nodded a greeting to two neighbor women who chattered in an open doorway. They stopped their conversation and peered suspiciously at him as he passed.

"Fine, who needs folks?" Crane muttered.

Past the school, he left the road and followed a footpath through yellowing grass, down to the dry, stony riverbed. The boundary of his world. The old folks called this place The Ford and described it as the easiest place to cross. But cross what? Dry stones? The ground showed no marks of a recent crossing. Crane had never ventured up the other bank. He gazed across, at once curious and reluctant. A long, gentle slope rose toward the sky, showing no sign of cultivation.

Though he stood in the open air, Crane had the sensation of standing at a wall, under a low, invisible roof. This gentle pressure turned him westward, to walk along the riverbank. The wind at his back blew Crane's long hair into his face and distracted him from his questions. He drew a cord from his pocket and tied it back out of his face.

Crane!

"Who's there?" Crane called. Only the wind answered.

Away from the ford, the banks rose above the dry river, sheer walls of gray rock and soil streaked with rusty orange and white. The river bottom grew thickly with gray-green sagebrush and yellowing bunch grass, revealing the hidden water deep below the ground. It was hard to imagine water had ever flowed at the surface.

Crane's path now took him behind houses and under the few scattered trees that grew in the village. He'd been told the tree behind the school was a cherry, though he'd never seen it bear fruit. Behind his own house, he came under the welcome shade of a big cottonwood. Crane looked up through the soft, white-bottomed leaves to the remains of a treehouse he and his friend Elic had built when Crane was nine. They'd had so many plans and schemes back then. He couldn't remember any details now. The treehouse had never been more than a platform of boards and branches. Now it was a trash pile in a tree.

How could we let it get like that? he wondered. *First chance I get, I'd better ... but no, we're men now. No more treehouse for us.*

Beyond the shade of the tree, the small kitchen garden thrived. There would be plenty of carrots, turnips, and herbs for the winter. Chickens clucked and pecked, untroubled as Crane walked among them. He passed the remains of another tree, a broad stump with wilting daisies growing in a hollow at its center. Though

Crane had never seen the tree alive, he knew the story of how his great-grandfather had planted it when the village was first settled, and how it was cut down the winter he was born. He tried to imagine its cool shade, nearly impossible in the late-morning heat.

Crane walked until he reached a lone pine tree with a dead top, as far from town as he'd ever been. He checked for snakes, then sat in the tree's scanty shade on the bank of the dry river. He ate his bread, washing it down with water. His fingers brushed the engraved letters on the bottom of the flask. He didn't know when Mama would have needed to carry water with her. She rarely traveled farther from the inn than Aunt Sudi's house across the road.

Upriver, a distant aspen grove formed an indistinct patch of green, shimmering in the heat. It turned brilliant orange and yellow in fall, the colors clearly visible from this distance. Crane had never been that far from home. Had Mama? Not likely.

As Crane walked back through the village after lunch, he wished he could take wing like the eagle circling high overhead. The soaring raptor stirred something in Crane's mind, but the stubborn memory refused to open.

By noon, few villagers were out, though Crane suspected any number of busybodies watched through windows along the way. Brynnit, the weaver's youngest daughter, played with an orange kitten in front of her house. She stared at him with wide eyes and a hint of a shy smile. Then her mother appeared and rushed the child inside, leaving the kitten mewing at the door. Crane walked on, disappointed. Children didn't fear him. They appreciated his illusions.

Farther up the road, Crane recognized the little girl's older twin sisters as they walked toward him. Kiat and Tiek were a few months older than Crane. They had all been in school together as young children, though the girls had refused to associate with Crane then. He hadn't spent much time around them since he was ten and joined the morning class of older boys.

Tiek had married the previous summer and moved to her husband's horse farm. She had returned to town recently to stay with her parents, near the midwife, as she awaited the birth of her first child. It was hard to believe her small frame could support her swollen belly. She moved slowly and leaned on her sister. Kiat gave Crane a piercing glance and whispered something to Tiek. Tiek looked up and froze, then slowly crossed to the other side of the road, though it meant a longer walk in her uncomfortable condition. Crane tried not to watch the sisters, but he sensed four people avoiding him, not three. Did Tiek know she was having twins? Even if she didn't, she wouldn't want to hear it from him.

The Village Hall was a larger version of most of the houses in town. It had the same walls of rounded river rock above a shallow earthen cellar, and a slate roof. It had the only door with an actual lock, though Crane didn't know why. There was nothing inside worth stealing. Maybe the lock was meant to safeguard young people from their own foolishness. It had failed to protect Crane.

At this time of day, the door was unlocked. With a sigh of relief, Crane entered the cool meeting room. Sunlight sparkled through dust motes onto the long table in the center of the room, the old wooden chairs, the rough benches.

"Good day, my young friend," old Jelf called from the library, a smaller room at the end of the Hall. Jelf held the position of Keeper and had charge of Deep River's historical records, to which he added each day.

"Hello, Jelf." Crane leaned against the library's doorframe. Four shelves held assorted volumes that included the logs of events and daily notes on crops and weather. Behind Jelf's desk, a glass-fronted case displayed the village treasures, heirlooms whose families had died off and left them behind: a faded and fragile weaving; a set of tiny glass bottles in a rainbow of colors; a collection of seventeen ballads in an antique script and obscure musical notation no one could read anymore. Nothing anyone would bother stealing.

"Good walk this morning?" Jelf asked. "I imagine it's good thinking time."

Crane sighed. "There's so much I don't understand, no matter how often I read it. But some things get clearer when I'm away from the books." He blinked as his eyes adjusted to the dimmer light inside the Hall. "On a hot day like this, though, it's good to get out of the sun."

Jelf leafed through the old logbook in front of him until he reached the page he sought. Crane glanced at Jelf's work. The faded writing was almost illegible.

Jelf smiled. "Where did your rambles take you today?"

"I walked out along the river as far as the ..." He frowned. "Everybody talks about *the river*. Where's the water?"

Jelf looked at Crane as if from a great distance.

"Gone."

"Well, obviously, but gone where?"

"Just ... away." Jelf's voice trembled. He dropped his gaze back to his work.

"All right. I didn't know rivers could do that. I didn't mean to upset you."

"You didn't." Jelf smiled up at Crane and shook his head. "It's not something I think about. I don't know about other rivers. That's what ours did. But it happened before you were born. How would you know?"

"Now I do." Crane stared at the old Keeper, who still seemed unnerved by the subject. "I suppose I'd better get to work."

"What will it be today?"

"I'm almost finished with the dark green one. Have you got anything I haven't already seen?"

Jelf rose from his desk and searched the shelves. He pulled out two heavy volumes, one bound in tattered green, the other in black, and dropped them onto the desk with a thud and a puff of dust. He shook his head. "There you are, the last big one. So, when are you going to show me something?"

"Not anytime soon. I'm not ready yet." *I'll never be ready.*

But something tugged at Crane's heart, a call to ... he didn't know what. Only that it was important. He'd have to *get* ready.

Chapter 2. Swamp

"You won't show me anything?" Jelf teased. "The young ones love your tricks, you know."

"That's all they are. Tricks. When I'm confident I can show you something real — and not do any damage — I'll let you know."

The old man patted Crane's shoulder. "There's no rush. At least someone's getting some good out of the books."

"I don't know if I'd say that. Have you ever read these?" Crane flipped open the cover of the black book. He laughed without humor. "*Magical Combat.* That'll be useful."

"I've taken a peek or two," Jelf admitted. "Impossible to make anything of them, though."

"They're not always helpful, but I wouldn't call them impossible."

"That's because they're meant for you, not me."

Crane looked at the open page again. The first time he had opened one of these books, the whole page had been a jumble of syllables that looked familiar but made no sense. As soon as he tried to read it, the syllables instantly rearranged themselves into logical sentences. Did Jelf mean they didn't do that for him?

"I admit, I've never heard of any wizard learning his trade solely from books," Jelf went on.

Crane heaved a discouraged sigh. "What else do I have? I need a wizard to teach me. Teaching myself? Talk about impossible!"

"Yes, it was poor planning of old Lok to die before you were born, and not even leave us an apprentice." Jelf grew serious again. "Perhaps these books will help you learn enough to use your gift to serve Deep River."

"I'm not sure anyone cares except you and me, but thanks, anyway."

The old man chuckled. "If you'd like to procrastinate, I could use your help. My old eyes aren't what they used to be, and I'm having trouble making out an entry."

Crane walked around the desk and peered over Jelf's shoulder at the logbook on the table. "What is it?"

"It's an old census — a count of everybody in the village and all the farms nearby," Jelf explained. "I hadn't thought of it in years. I remembered it when I was working in my garden this morning. Something about that kind of mindless work brings back old memories of when things were ... different." Jelf paused and rubbed his forehead. He shook himself. "Look, here's your grandparents. Stoli was my best friend."

Crane studied the faded entry: *Stoli and Telna - innkeepers*. He recognized other names on the page, tradesmen and farmers now, listed here as the children of people he didn't know. His mother's friend Sudi was listed as the infant daughter of Greelin and Elika. Crane remembered Elika, but Greelin was gone long before his time. He laid his finger lightly on his grandfather's name. "I remember Grandpa Stoli, a little. I never knew Grandma Telna. Where's my mother's name?"

"She was born later. This census was one of the last things my father did before he died."

"He was Keeper before you?" Crane had never considered there may have been another Keeper in all of Deep River's history. How could he have missed something so obvious?

"Yes, and his father before him," Jelf replied proudly.

Crane laughed. "And his father before him, I suppose."

"Why, no, there would have been none before my grandfather. He was one of the founders."

Crane blinked, speechless at the thought of a time before Deep River was settled. In his heart, it had always stood just as he knew it now. But his mother's voice echoed in his memory, telling a story: *Once upon a time, a long time ago, before the founders came, when giants roamed the land ...*

"My father taught me to read and write so I could

follow him as Keeper. That was before we had the school," Jelf said. "Now here's the entry I'm having trouble with. Can you make out the number?" He pointed to an entry labeled *Swamp* at the bottom of the page.

Crane peered at the faded writing. "It looks like a three, crossed out. Then there's a four, but that's crossed out, too, and then a two. No names. Was he counting people there?"

"He must have been. I'd forgotten all about this. He must have gone back more than once and got a different answer each time. I suppose he wanted to make sure they were living there, not merely camping."

"What does it mean by 'swamp'?"

"A wet, boggy place." Jelf continued to peruse the census.

"I know what a swamp *is*, but where?"

"Oh. You wouldn't know, would you? When there was a river, there was also a swamp." Jelf waved eastward. "Straight out that way, a couple hours' walk, I guess, for a fit young person."

Crane pictured the route and walked it in his mind. "You mean the Bone Trees?" At Jelf's uncomprehending expression, he clarified. "It's what Elic and I call them — that spooky place with the dead poplars and those old chimneys with no house."

"Sounds right. You've been there?"

"Sure, we used to go there a lot when we were young. The lone pine was the farthest west our mothers would let us go, and the Bone Trees were the farthest east. I walked out there last week, but I didn't stay long. It felt ... haunted."

"Haunted? I guess it could be."

"What, you think those people died there?"

"That might explain why the numbers changed. I'm just speculating."

Crane shivered. "Why would anyone live in a swamp?"

"I'm not sure. Many years later, I thought to repeat my father's census. When was that? Before you were born, anyway. For some reason, I never finished, but I did visit the swamp. You never saw so many mosquitoes! It must have been a miserable place to live, with the bugs and the noise."

"Noise?" Crane asked, baffled. "When I was there, it was too quiet."

"Well, yes, now. Then? So many birds! Calling, squawking, quacking, pecking — what a din! No people lived there anymore but it was a lively place. More kinds of ducks than I ever knew existed, and a heron, like the one on your sign. Even some cranes." Jelf smiled and raised an eyebrow. "You've probably never seen one."

"I have a picture. Soorhi gave me a drawing of a gray one, and I pinned it up in my room."

"Well, that's better than nothing. We used to have all kinds of water birds stopping here on their migrations. I remember flocks of gray ones feeding in the swamp and the irrigation ditches. And once, I was lucky enough to see a whooper — much bigger, and white as new snow." He sighed, then shook himself as if waking up. "Listen to me go on! I hadn't thought of any of this in years."

Crane scanned the census again. "Is there a wizard listed?"

"No. We've rarely ever had more than a healer living

here, and often, not even that. Used to get itinerant wizards passing through from time to time, though not lately."

"Then where did these books come from? Who was Lok?"

"Wizard Lok retired here for the dry climate. We didn't ask much of him. He helped as he could. He didn't take apprentices after he came here. When he died, the village kept his books. I guess they'll be yours when you want them."

"*If* I want them," Crane muttered.

"What was that?" Jelf asked, his hand to his ear.

"Nothing." Crane read more names. "Jelf, I never knew you had a wife!"

"We were newly married then." He cleared his throat. "Teel and I were together almost twenty years, so I guess I shouldn't complain. But she and her sister Telna both died too young."

"Her *sister* Telna? My grandmother?" Crane's knees wobbled and he leaned on the desk for support. "You're my ... you're Mama's uncle?"

"And yours. Well, great-uncle."

Crane had always regarded Jelf as something like a grandfather. He'd had no idea they were family. "You never told me."

"I assumed you knew," Jelf said. "Your mother never mentioned it? Well, she has plenty to think about. She probably figured you knew, too."

Crane didn't know what to make of this. Then he saw it as if he were there: a woman who resembled Mama, not old but wasted with illness and bedridden, and the healer Elika by her side. A golden-haired girl who could only be Mama, no older than Crane and overflowing with life, told a story that brought a smile to the sick woman's pale lips. Jelf cleared his throat and the vision scattered.

"Mama looked like her aunt," Crane said.

"Yes, she ..." Jelf frowned. "Since when do you read thoughts?"

"I'm ... not sure. I didn't do it on purpose."

"That's all right. I did ask you to show me something. And Stell does look like Teel. Too much for me to look at her. That's why I stay away, but I've always done what I could to help her. Eventually, that meant helping you."

Crane had a new thought. "Let me work with you."

"What? Why?"

"You said yourself you followed your father as Keeper. You have no children, nor an apprentice. Who will take over when you can't do it any longer?"

"Crane, this isn't suitable work for one of your abilities. Two generations of villagers read and write now. Any one of them could do it. If it even needs doing anymore."

"But would they want to? I *want* to do it!"

"Do you?" Jelf asked gently. "Or do you want to give up your studies now that they've become frustrating?"

"They've always been frustrating! All I want is to learn from *someone*, not a book."

"I appreciate your offer." The old man rose and rested his hand on Crane's shoulder. "There's no one I'd rather teach. I don't think what I can teach you is what you need to learn."

"So, I have to be a wizard? I don't get a choice?" Crane carried the two books out to the long table in the meeting room, where he could study and not disturb Jelf further.

Jelf followed him as far as the doorway. "The magic chose you. Does it bring you no joy at all?"

"It draws me. I can't *not* come here to read. And sometimes I lose myself in it. Other times ..."

Jelf chuckled. "Would it help to know everyone has those times? But if it draws you, turning away won't free you. It will only pull harder."

"When did you know I had it?"

"The same time you did," the old man said with a fond smile. "Or don't you remember?"

"Hah!" How could Crane forget, when he had the scars to remind him? He was twelve, and all the boys were playing Dares. Crane felt lucky to be included, though he dreaded the actual dare. Most of the feats were physical: climbing to the roof of the Village Hall, crossing a bull's pasture. Elic, the leader, had proposed a different kind of challenge for Crane.

"Sneak into Jelf's library and read a page from a spell book." They had all shivered with a spooky thrill, but Crane remembered a strange calm when he accepted the dare. That evening, Elic distracted Jelf before he could lock the door, and Crane crept in at sunset to select a book at random. He let it fall open and quickly memorized a brief spell. To prove he'd done it, he had to say the spell for the other boys when they met in school the next day. Speaking the powerful words without understanding, he terrified everyone by setting fire to his own hand.

"I still have nightmares." Crane flexed his scarred fingers. Even five years after the accident, he could neither straighten them all the way, nor close them tightly. That hand had no fist. "I was lucky Soorhi didn't lose his head. He leaped clear over his desk, extinguished the fire with his bare hands, and wasn't even hurt. I never saw an old man move so quickly."

"I always wondered whether the old fellow might have had a bit of magic himself," Jelf mused. "We all recognized you for what you were then, and you've never had to sneak in here since."

Crane was silent a moment, remembering. A long, painful recovery had followed the immediate panic of the fire, his burned right hand slowly healing while he learned to do everything with his left. Even as the pain abated, he had encountered the equally painful rejection by his fellow villagers. Many of them had always treated him with suspicion. Now he had given them a reason.

"I didn't see Soorhi's name on the census."

"No. He hadn't come yet."

"He wasn't from here?"

Jelf chuckled. "I don't know where he was from, though I ended up his closest friend. He appeared one day, to start a school. He said he'd had a vision: someday, someone in Deep River would need to know how to read. He was right, as always. And maybe he even knew who that person was. His way was to teach everyone, just in case." He paused, smiling. "There was surprisingly little resistance, considering he was a stranger."

Crane considered this story. "A stranger. That's odd. No one ever comes here."

"Not anymore, they don't. But Soorhi did. He was ... compelling. There were a few who didn't think the older boys should go to school after they'd started apprenticeships, and others objected to the girls. There was especially strong resistance to mixing boys and girls in one classroom. Soorhi understood how adolescents might distract each other from schoolwork, so he worked out a compromise we still use today. Imperfect, but it works well enough."

Crane nodded. Boys over age ten attended school in the morning; girls of all ages and the smaller boys, in the afternoon. Students began when they were ready and attended as long as they — or their parents — liked. "It's hard to imagine another way."

"We became accustomed to it quickly. And to Soorhi, though he never quite belonged." Jelf sighed. "I miss him."

"I do, too."

Crane felt Soorhi's absence most at times like these. The teacher had possessed broad knowledge, and a talent for engaging his students' interest in any subject. Even during the last years of Soorhi's life, when his apprentice had taken over most of the beginners' lessons, Soorhi had continued to instruct the older students. Crane especially enjoyed his lessons about the natural world. Soorhi knew the uses and characteristics of every tree, flower, and herb the students could name, and many they'd never heard of. He could even distinguish similar specimens by scent.

Crane wasn't sure what use he might make of such knowledge but learning it had been an enjoyable challenge. In contrast, his study of magic, conducted on his own, was almost always a struggle, with no one to explain or demonstrate the things Crane didn't understand. Maybe Soorhi could have helped in this area. It was too late to ask him. Crane was on his own.

Chapter 3. Daydreams

Misty Pass

Ketty did her morning chores after breakfast, tidying the kitchen and common room of the Fogbank, sweeping the loft and any of the private rooms that had been occupied. The handful of overnight guests had eaten breakfast before departing on the morning coach. Ketty and her father took advantage of the few quiet hours to make their inn ready for the evening, when many locals joined travelers for supper and drinks. She gathered used bedding and lugged it downstairs for airing or washing, then remade the beds fresh.

She paused and leaned on her broom in front of the painted map of Eukard that hung in the common room. The map was her father's most prized possession, aside from the inn itself. How Mama had laughed as she teased him for letting the governor's mapmaker trade it for five nights' lodging and meals, when he had plenty of coin to pay. But Papa had taken a shine to the beautifully detailed and colored map. He never regretted his trade, though he hadn't left Misty Pass even once, content to hear about other places from travelers who passed through. It was enough for him to know where a town was on the map. Not for Ketty. She dreamed of the day she might visit these places for herself.

She traced the road with her finger, from Misty Pass down to the lowlands to the west. What would it be like to visit Grass Flats, so near Eukard City, the capital? It was almost too much to imagine visiting such a grand place as the city itself, though Ketty's mother had come from there. Was that reason enough to visit? Maybe, though it would have been nicer with Mama to show her around.

To the east, the road passed a place called Sweetwater, which was much nearer and sounded inviting. Ketty let her eyes wander on new adventures, away from the main road.

"I don't remember seeing this one before," she muttered. "Deep River? Sounds like a pleasant place, at least for the Dry Side." She was sure she'd never met anyone who came from there. She wasn't eager to travel to that desert region, though it would certainly be a change from her home in the wooded mountains.

She wasn't in a hurry to leave home. She loved the forest, and working with Papa at the Fogbank exposed her to an endless parade of interesting people from all over Eukard. Did she want to be an innkeeper her whole life, though? It was enough for Papa, but Ketty had other talents he knew nothing of.

"Ketty!" Papa called from the kitchen door. "Come lend a hand."

She hurried through the kitchen and out to the back porch as her daydreams scattered. Papa waited with a ruffled white hen under his arm.

"Lily hurt herself somehow," he said. "I'll hold her if you'll clean her up."

"All right. Give me a moment." Ketty returned to the kitchen for soap, a rag, and a basin of warm water. "Where is she hurt?" she asked when she came back outside.

Papa turned the bird, keeping a firm grasp on her legs with one hand and pinning her wings with his arm and body. Blood stained her breast, and she was missing a few feathers. A small gash still oozed. Ketty gently cleaned the wound and the surrounding feathers. Ketty wasn't fond of a whole flock of chickens. They were noisy, smelly, and disorderly. But a single hen was no problem. She recognized Lily as one of the young hens who had just started laying. Worth keeping alive and safe.

Although Ketty was happy to collect the eggs and pluck and cook a bird for supper, the flock was Papa's responsibility—feeding them, securing them in the coop at night, letting them out in the morning, keeping their fence in good repair. He always named his laying hens with flower names, the way fine city folk used to name their children before working people adopted the fashion. Ketty smiled to think how those fine folk would feel about the fashion coming down to chickens.

"It doesn't look bad," Ketty said.

"I got to her before the others could start pecking," Papa said. "She can stay in the crate while she heals."

The crate was a private coop he'd built on the porch to shelter sick or injured birds while they recovered. He placed Lily inside and passed Ketty an empty water dish to fill. When she returned with it, he was scattering a handful of feed. Once the hen was provided for, he latched the hinged cover.

"I'm off to fetch ale," he said. "It'll be a warm one today. Maybe two kegs so we don't run out of drinks."

"I was thinking of serving bread with cold meat, cheese, and fruit, rather than heat up the place cooking a hot meal." Ketty had run the kitchen side of things since she was twelve — almost five years now.

"That's my smart girl," Papa said. "Don't ever leave, or I don't know what I'd do!"

"Not any time soon," Ketty assured him. She wasn't in a hurry to get married, probably the only way Papa imagined she would leave home. Her childhood friends had already taken that plunge, though. Some had even left Misty Pass. If Ketty married someone local, she could keep working at the inn.

Neither of those were the future she wanted, but how could she leave Papa alone? And not only with all the work at the Fogbank. The two of them were all the family either had ... except Papa's useless Uncle Scadi. If Ketty ever left Misty Pass, it wouldn't be on a lark. She would have a good reason.

When Papa had gone, Ketty returned to the chicken crate and unlatched the cover. Lily muttered and clucked to herself. Ketty scooped her up, grasping her feet the way Papa had taught her. She tucked the hen under her arm and stroked her with tingling fingers.

"Sh sh sh, it's all right." Ketty brought one finger to the wound she had cleaned. It would heal on its own in a few days. Under Ketty's touch, the bleeding stopped, and the edges of the gash knitted together. She stroked the place until there was no longer any sign of injury.

Ketty returned the hen to the crate and latched the cover. She sank down onto the step and wiped her brow. Healing left her drained, but a little rest and she'd be fine. As fine as Lily now was. There was no need to tell anyone what she had done for this chicken, or the other injured animals over the years. Especially not Papa.

He could never know his little Ketty had a gift for healing. For magic.

Chapter 4. Magic

Deep River

Crane picked up the dark green book. He hadn't marked his place, but it opened to where he'd left off, a few pages from the end. Just getting this far was an accomplishment. Not only did this volume concern advanced magic, most of which he didn't understand, the book itself was so decrepit, several pages were missing. The text often broke off in mid-sentence at the bottom of one page, only to resume in the middle of another subject entirely on the next.

Although Crane doubted he had retained much, he was determined to read to the end. A late spell snagged his interest. It concerned transformation into animal form. The spell itself, though longer than anything else he'd learned, seemed simple enough. A note in the margin read, *Transformation will occur only when you know it can occur.*

"Thank you. That's a great help." Crane had grown used to such opaque instructions, and studied the page, anyway. This was the first hint he'd found that his dreams of flying might be more than mere dreams. Even two readings of the whole section didn't make clear how to choose which animal you wanted to become. The instructions described the method as almost identical to a technique he didn't remember reading about. Not surprising, considering how many pages were missing and how much he had probably forgotten. Once again, useless.

He memorized the spell, anyway ... for another day. Although he took care not to speak it aloud or even let his lips move, his heart thudded, and his mouth went dry. He closed his scarred hand by reflex. Without the correct technique, the words alone were probably powerless. He didn't dare take a chance. Every new spell he learned evoked a similar reaction, but transformation seemed especially dangerous. As dangerous as fire, if not more so. Do it wrong and he could turn into anything. Maybe permanently.

Crane turned the page. The final section of the book covered instructions for crafting a magical staff, which also seemed pointless. He shoved the green book aside and opened the black-bound one. Magical Combat. To his surprise, he soon found himself immersed in the subject. It didn't have any direct application, but magical combat was at least something new. And by contrast, the text was refreshingly straightforward. He was engrossed when the door banged open and Elic rushed in.

"Crane, are you almost done?"

"Shh, I'm reading."

Elic dragged up a chair and flopped down across from Crane. "You're always reading. How many of those spell books are there?"

Crane glanced up from the text. Elic was a year older than Crane, shorter, broader, and this late in summer, almost as dark. A wild cloud of brown curls topped his grinning face.

Crane pushed hair out of his own face and retied the cord to hold it back. "So, Teacher, you think I read too much?" Elic had been an unenthusiastic student at first, only to mature into Soorhi's successor by the time he was eighteen. He had recently moved from his parents' home to the teacher's house behind the school.

"No. I guess we could use a village wizard, and you're the closest we've got. But I hardly see you anymore!"

"Sorry. I have so much to learn, and not long to learn it."

"Since when?"

"Since ... I don't know. Something's pushing me."

"Where to?"

"I'm not sure. Maybe it's pulling me. I don't think I'm getting anywhere. I'm afraid to try the fire spell again ... or anything else that might be of use. What good are little illusions?"

Elic laughed. "I don't know, the skunk in the council meeting was pure genius. It had smell, even!"

"You would remind me of that." Crane laughed, too, in spite of himself.

"That meeting wasn't going anywhere. It needed to be broken up."

"Tell Mama. I had extra chores for a week."

"Worth it," Elic said. "You do need to work on your control. Remember when you were trying to learn levitation with rocks?" He rubbed his forehead. "I still have a dent here."

"One more thing, on top of everything else." Crane clenched his teeth and thumped his fist on the tabletop. "I have this sense I'm supposed to *do* something, but what? I'm trying to prepare. How can I when I don't know what I'm preparing *for*?"

Elic raised his eyebrows at this outburst. "I'd help if I could."

"This is something I have to do myself. I mean, you won't always be there."

"Where will I be, then?"

Crane ignored the interruption. "The real magic ... I can feel it, inside me. How do I unlock it?"

"With a magic wand?" Elic balanced his chair on two legs. "Don't wizards always carry a wand or a staff or something?"

"In stories, but I've never seen ..." Crane stared at Elic. He grabbed the green book again. It flipped open to the last spell: crafting a wizard's staff. He read with renewed interest.

The wizard's staff focuses and magnifies his power ...

Crane tried to read, but Elic's fidgeting made it almost impossible to concentrate. His thoughts leaked out and invaded Crane's attempt to study. It came as no surprise Elic was thinking about his sweetheart, Sunnea. He'd been devoted to her since he was six. A new element excited his imagination.

Finally, Crane looked up from his book. "Out with it. What's so important?"

Elic laughed uneasily. "Come with me to Mam and Pap's, and I'll tell you."

Crane closed the book. "Jelf, I'm going now. I'm borrowing the green one, and I'll go on with the black one tomorrow."

Crane and Elic went out together into the hot, bright afternoon. A basket of produce waited next to the steps. Elic picked it up and they set off toward Elic's parents' house.

A glint from the dusty road caught Crane's eye. He spoke a single delighted syllable, and a dark pebble flew up ... straight at his head. He ducked and stuck up his hand to catch it, grimacing as the translucent stone smacked into his palm.

"Agate." He held it out for Elic to see.

"Not as big as mine." Elic's most prized possession, Crane knew, was a honey-colored agate the size of a hen's egg. He'd dug it out of the riverbank when he was eleven.

"But the color! Have you ever seen such a deep red one?"

"Fine, it's beautiful. So, what did you learn today? Anything useful?"

Crane stashed the stone in his pocket. "Maybe, for once. I was reading about combat spells."

"Combat? You?"

"You asked." They had been scuffling for over a dozen years, and Crane almost never managed to land a blow. "Hold still. I'll demonstrate."

Elic set down the basket of produce. "This won't hurt, will it?"

Crane laughed. "I read some things I wouldn't want to try, but this one sounded safe enough." He tucked his book into the basket, then flung out his arm and spoke a single word.

"Oof!" Elic doubled over as if he'd been punched and stumbled backward several steps. He sat down hard in the dust, gasping for breath. "What was that?"

"A repelling charm. What do you think? Useful?"

"In a fight, maybe." Elic held out his hand. Crane grasped it to pull him up, but Elic pulled Crane to the ground. "Magic is all well and good. I prefer two strong arms and the element of surprise."

The two wrestled in the middle of the road, neither quite prevailing. Elic had the advantage of strength and skill. Crane's longer limbs kept him constantly struggling. Elic finally pinned Crane and was beginning to count when someone giggled. Elic paled, then reddened. He released Crane and clambered to his feet.

"Sunnea. Hi. Um, good day, Mynna." Elic brushed the dust off his clothes. Black-haired Mynna smiled broadly at his greeting and squeezed her friend's arm. Golden Sunnea dimpled shyly and blushed. A loop of gold glinted from each girl's right earlobe, a sign they were ready and allowed to entertain suitors. Sunnea had received hers in the spring, Mynna a few months before that. They didn't acknowledge Crane until he raised his hand in greeting. They put their heads together, whispered something, and hurried away without a word.

"Sorry, Crane. I wish they wouldn't act that way. Well, Mynna's always like that, isn't she? To everybody, I mean. So important because she's the mayor's daughter, as if anyone cares. Sunnea, though … she's not …" Elic's babbling trailed off as he watched the girls walk away.

Crane watched them, too, and sighed. "I think I'm cursed."

Elic drew a ragged breath. "Not … just you."

Crane snorted a laugh. "What's that supposed to mean? You've never had trouble with girls."

Once again, Crane was party to Elic's thoughts. This time, they weren't clear or obvious. They slithered away like garter snakes in tall grass, and he struggled to speak. "Not … me. Us. Deep River."

Crane faced Elic directly and gripped his shoulders. "What are you talking about? Who told you we're cursed?"

Some of the heaviness lifted. "Soorhi," Elic said. "He called it 'Yrae's Curse'."

"Like Yrae the Mad Wizard in Mama's stories?" Crane released Elic and started walking again. "He's not real."

Elic picked up the basket. "Soorhi believed he was.

Jelf, too."

"Fine, but what made them believe there was a curse, or that he was involved?"

Elic shrugged. "They had to call it something. Doesn't it sound like something an evil wizard would do?"

"I guess." Crane paused and Elic bumped into him. "Jelf said the river went away. Is that part of it?"

"Part of what?"

"What do you mean, part of what? Part of the —"

"I've decided to ask Pap to talk to Yshna," Elic interrupted.

Crane blinked. He smiled as he took in Elic's words. "Does Sunnea need her father's permission? I thought she was of age."

Elic grinned. "She is, and has already accepted me, if her father gives his blessing."

Crane had a nagging sense they'd been talking about something else, something important. But this was important, too. "Does she really want to marry a schoolteacher?"

"Why wouldn't she? The job comes with a house, it doesn't make me dirty or smelly, and I'm unlikely to be killed or injured at my work. Not to mention I'll have the harvest season free."

"Also, she knows you're good with children, especially rascally little boys."

"Having been one myself, I'm an expert."

"Then I wish you a whole family of them!" Crane slapped Elic on the back. A new thought sobered him instantly. "Will she ... allow me in the house?"

"I'll insist," Elic said.

Elic flinched as a dust-gray female bluebird fluttered her bright blue wing plumage in the road in front of them. Too late, he pretended he hadn't been startled.

Crane laughed, but not at Elic. He pointed at the bird. "There's magic for you. Sky out of dust."

Elic shook his head. "Crane, your moods shift quicker than the weather these days. At least you're smiling again."

Chapter 5. Aunt Sudi

The sun's glare blinded Crane, but his feet knew the road, and there was nothing new to see. Elic had told him something new. What was it? An insect opened scarlet wings and clicked away in front of them, and the thought flew with it. A dog let loose a half-hearted woof from under a porch. A ball rose above the rooftops and dropped back, the laughter of unseen children floating higher than their ball.

As they reached the blacksmith shop, Elic's brother Jagree, a sturdy, freckled boy of eleven, ran out to meet them. A magpie perched on his shoulder, its long tail feathers hanging down his back.

"Jagree!" it croaked.

"I didn't know you still had your bird," Crane said.

"Maggie isn't *mine*. She visits when she feels like it. She must remember me."

Crane could easily believe that. A year or two earlier, Jagree had found the injured bird and rescued it from scavengers. His tender care had returned it to health. Now the big black and white bird stared at Crane. With a croak that sounded almost like his name, it took wing. Crane and Jagree watched it flap away.

"Is Pap at the forge?" Elic asked.

"No, he's out. Why?"

Elic, usually so confident, turned red under his tan and didn't speak up. Crane stepped in to help him out. "I need him to work on our pump. It doesn't just squeak; it shrieks."

Jagree grinned. "I can fix it for you. I'll head over as soon as Pap's back. Mam's in the house, if you want to wait."

"Good, I have to drop these off, anyway." Elic shifted the basket and moved toward the door.

"Mam!" Elic called into the house. "I've brought a surprise."

"Is it the garden stuff you promised?" Plump, dark-haired Aunt Sudi wiped her hands on her apron as she turned toward the door. "I don't know what's wrong with my garden this year. It won't —"

"How are you, Aunt Sudi?"

"Crane! How wonderful to see you! You never come around anymore," she scolded.

"I know. I've been ... well, not working hard, but studying hard."

"That's work, love. You boys always did know when I was baking. Have some cake?"

Crane and Elic sat at the familiar old table. Growing up, Crane had been in and out of their house almost daily, playing with Elic and absorbing Sudi's talk — equal parts chatter and sound advice. Elic didn't live there anymore, so Crane no longer dropped in the way he used to.

The kitchen was stifling, though the window and both doors stood wide open to the breeze. Irresistible aromas of honey cake and rising bread dough filled the hot air.

"Why are you baking in the hottest part of the day?" Elic asked.

His mother laughed as she cut thick slices of cake and poured three mugs of tea. "I was up half the night tending a case of false labor. I took a nap this morning, and it threw off my whole schedule! I had hoped it wouldn't be as hot today. In any case, I'm nearly finished." She peeped under a towel at a pan of rising dough. "At least the dough rises faster in hot weather. In it goes." Heat blasted from the cookstove's oven as she slid the pan in and closed the door.

"I knew it, Crane," Elic said as she set the plates on the table. "You always were her favorite. She gave you a bigger piece."

"Now, he needs it more. Look at him! He's a twig."

"Not anymore." Crane rolled up his sleeve to reveal a long, brown arm, lean but strongly muscled. "Carrying kegs from the brewer's is finally paying off."

Elic rolled up his sleeve to arm wrestle. His hand was as brown as Crane's, his arm pink above the wrist.

Aunt Sudi cut in as they gripped hands. "None of that with food on the table! Will you boys never grow up?"

Two purring cats twined around Crane's legs. The long-haired gray sprang onto his lap and rubbed her face against his. "Hello, Ashy." He stroked the cat's back and scratched her head.

A half-grown black and orange kitten leaped from floor to tabletop in one graceful bound.

"Embers, no!" Embers ignored Aunt Sudi's order and sat on the table to wash. When she tried to push the cat off the table, Embers crouched, immovable. "Cats. They never listen."

The door to the forge opened and Jagree poked his head in. "Pap's back! Hey, Ashy! Embers, get down!" Both cats thudded to the floor and followed Jagree.

"I'll be right out." Elic finished his last bite of cake and rose from his seat. "Coming, Crane?"

"No, I'll stay here and catch up. Good luck."

Elic smiled nervously as he followed his brother.

Aunt Sudi watched Elic leave the kitchen and sighed. Crane caught flickers of her thoughts, the way he had with Jelf and Elic. *A grown man, and practically a married one, too. Where did the years go?* He wasn't sure when this business of hearing people's thoughts had started. No more than a week ago, though. He'd never tried it on purpose, but when someone near him felt something strongly, he couldn't help overhearing.

Aunt Sudi turned to Crane with a smile. "I swear, Crane, you're taller every time I see you. Seems only yesterday you were no bigger than Jagree."

"I should come around more often," Crane apologized.

She waved this away as she wrapped the loaf of cake in a clean towel and set it on a shelf in the corner. "You don't want to be sitting around with an old woman. Now, a young woman, maybe."

He laughed. "Name one who would have me." He sipped his tea.

"Maybe no one here," she allowed. "You've got your charms, though. Maybe you need to find a girl wizard, if there is such a thing. I guess you'd have to look elsewhere for her."

Crane almost choked on his tea. "Look *where*?"

She opened her mouth, then closed it again without answering. Her thoughts had gone blank. "Look around! Any girl would be lucky to have a smart, hard-working fellow like you."

"Thank you, Aunt Sudi. You've always been good to us."

"And why not?" She wiped up flour and stacked mixing bowls and spoons for washing.

"I don't know why not. The others must have some reason." She'd know he meant the other mothers of the village. "They're all sort of sniffy with Mama, and they act like I'm ...well, they give me this look." He demonstrated Liba's pursed-lip, nose-in-the-air expression, and Aunt Sudi cackled. "Like I fell out of the sky."

"You're not *that* strange. You arrived in the usual way." She sat across from him with a sharp knife and cutting board. She drew Elic's basket of vegetables between her feet and examined the produce.

"Then what is my problem?"

Aunt Sudi studied a bunch of carrots. "They don't know you. Or her."

"But why not?"

She looked him in the eye. "I guess you have a right to know. It started long before you came along. When we were young, a few of our friends envied your mother."

She didn't name names, but they spilled from her thoughts: *Keena. Ati. Sullea.* Keena was Kiat and Tiek's mother. Crane didn't remember Sullea, Sunnea's mother, dead for fourteen or fifteen years. Ati was Sunnea's stepmother.

"Fellows they were interested in only had eyes for Stell," Sudi went on, "though she was the youngest of our group and didn't even have the courtship ring."

Crane nodded to show he understood. It was an old courtship ritual. Usually between the ages of sixteen and eighteen, a girl started wearing a little gold ring in her right earlobe, as Mynna and Sunnea now did. In the usual course of things, she would see at least one suitor until she received a marriage proposal. If the engagement was approved by both sets of parents, she and her betrothed each added a ring in their left earlobes, to signify they were promised to each other. So, a girl with one earring was formally available for courtship. A girl with two, or none, was formally off-limits.

"These so-called friends of ours spread gossip about Stell — so pretty and lively, and working at the inn, among all those strangers, and no mother to watch out for her."

Fire exploded in Crane's guts, and he half rose from

his seat. "How can you say such a thing?"

"I didn't say *I* believed it!" Aunt Sudi drew a deep breath and gave him a little smile, which he returned sheepishly and sat back again. She shook her head slightly and cut off the feathery green carrot tops. "Have you ever seen such beautiful carrots? Seems a shame to cook them."

"Don't."

"You're right, they'd be refreshing on a hot day, just as they are. I still need to kill and pluck a chicken." She dabbed at her brow with her apron and pulled a cucumber from the basket.

Crane sighed, and after a long silence, asked, "So it's not about … my father?"

She studied him for a moment. "Yes and no." She sliced the cucumber. "He didn't help."

"Was he that bad? Did he die dishonorably or something?"

Sudi raised her eyebrows. "What makes you think he's dead?" She fetched a small bowl, filled it with cucumber slices and carefully poured vinegar over them.

"He's alive? Where is he? *Who* is he?"

Sudi laughed. "Slow down! Now think about it: does your mama act like a widow? Or like she's waiting?"

"Waiting for what?"

"For her lover to return, maybe?"

"Lover? Weren't they married?" Crane asked.

"Think, Crane," Sudi said. "Think about your mother's ears."

"Her ears?" That didn't make sense, until suddenly it did. "Oh. Her ears."

"She doesn't wear any earrings, does she?"

"No."

"And she never has." Aunt Sudi let the significance sink in.

Crane had never thought about it before. Perhaps because it was right there in plain sight, not hidden at all. No earrings, and no sign they had been removed.

"Now, marriage isn't required to have a child," Sudi said. "My parents never signed the book, did they?"

"Then what's the difference with us?" Crane asked. He wanted to know the truth, though it was embarrassing to think of his mother in these terms. Of himself. But if Mama wouldn't talk about it, Aunt Sudi was the next best source.

"My father was *here*. People knew they were together," Sudi said. "While *your* father ..."

"But who was he?"

"No one from around here. What has she told you?"

"Not much." He pursed his lips. "I stopped asking her about him long ago. She never gave me the same answer twice. I started to think maybe I never had a father."

Aunt Sudi laughed. "I'm sorry, Crane, I'm not making fun of you. I give you my word as a midwife, everybody has a father, even if they don't know who he is."

"Sometimes I think even she doesn't know."

"What did she tell you?"

"When I was small and asked about him, she used to tell me stories."

Aunt Sudi smiled. "She would."

"She told me the old tales, and I was never sure whether she was changing the subject or trying to tell me something about him. He was all mixed up in my mind with the kings and heroes; shepherd boys and millers' sons. And after she told those stories, she always sang the same song. Only the tune, but it sounded sad, even without words. I always thought it was about him."

"I know the song you mean," Aunt Sudi said. "No one remembers the words anymore. It must have been one of those sad ballads; probably older than the stories. Does she still sing it?"

"Not lately."

"That's too bad. She has such a sweet voice. Anything else?"

"When I was older, she told me he'd gone far away and couldn't ever come back. I thought she meant he was dead. You know the way adults talk to children when someone has passed. She never talked about him again. That was years ago. She thinks about him, though." He gazed into his empty mug. Aunt Sudi refilled it.

"How do you know?"

"She gets this funny little smile on her face, as if she has a secret." He smiled himself.

"How do you know she's thinking about him?"

"I just know."

Aunt Sudi nodded. "You're probably right. I've seen her secret smile, too. When she learned you were coming, and again when you were here."

She got quiet as memories overtook her. Crane took advantage of her distraction to get himself a second piece of cake. He caught scraps of her thoughts — Mama as a young woman, pretty but tired and sick, then surprised at the midwife's news. He recognized the secret smile. Her whispered words didn't make sense:

"So it was real."

Aunt Sudi shook herself and tried to look annoyed about the cake theft. Crane shrugged and grinned.

"Let me tell you what little I know. Your mother and I were always good friends. After her mother died, when Stell was twelve or so, my mama looked out for her, and we got to be like sisters. Such good times we had! We'd go to dances at the Village Hall, and up in Oxbow and Bitter Springs —"

"You went places?" Crane frowned. "Nobody goes anywhere."

Aunt Sudi stared at him a moment. "That's ... true. But was it always?"

"Always for me. Don't you remember?"

"Sometimes I do. I don't know, I rarely think about it. With you here, though ..." She smiled at him and continued her story. "We did then. Stoli wouldn't let anyone court Stell, but she could go to dances and enjoy herself."

Crane took a large bite of cake as he tried to imagine such odd ideas as *dances* and *other towns*.

"I had my own sweetheart then, my Ohme. We got married and had Elic. Maybe I wasn't paying enough attention to Stell. No earring, no fellow, but out of nowhere, she was with child."

Crane dropped his fork onto the table. "And no one had any idea?"

"I can't imagine she'd tell anyone and not tell me. If she had already accepted someone, they would have hurried up the wedding. There would have been winks and nudges and comments on how big the baby was for coming so early, but that would have been it. Even if she hadn't accepted anyone, her father could have rounded up all her admirers and persuaded one of them to step up. As it was ..."

Crane had trouble finding words. "I always figured I was the only one who didn't know."

Sudi patted his hand. "I was mystified, especially when you didn't resemble anyone here. I thought it was kind of sweet. Like one of her stories. The others, though ... it confirmed their old gossip. They never got over it, and they passed it on to their children."

"You stood by us." Crane didn't trust his voice above a whisper.

"How could I not? Close as sisters."

"People ... fear me. I don't understand why. Even Elic does, a little."

"People often fear what they don't understand." Sudi opened the oven and let out a cloud of fragrant heat. "Even your mother is afraid of your magic."

"You're not."

Aunt Sudi thumped the bread's top crust and listened carefully. She removed the bread from the oven and tipped the fresh loaf out onto her work counter next to the cookstove. "My mother had a talent for healing. Nothing like your gift, of course, but still ..."

"I haven't done anything yet. What makes you think I have anything great?"

She smiled. "Someone told me so, someone with eyes to see."

Crane puzzled for only a moment before he grinned, too. "Soorhi, again. Why is he so much on everyone's mind today?"

"It was a year ago he left us."

"I can't believe I forgot," Crane said. "I wonder why Elic didn't mention it."

"I expect he's trying not to think of it. And he has other things on his mind."

Crane picked up his fork again. His appetite for cake had returned. "I interrupted your story, something about your mother."

"Yes, Mama was midwife before me. Unlike me, she had some magic. It helps me understand you."

"Because the magic is ... familiar?"

"And you're familiar. I helped Mama the night you were born, so I've known you from the start. I saw you come into the world." Aunt Sudi wiped her eyes with the corner of her apron. "I put you into Stell's arms. She couldn't take her eyes off you, and she couldn't stop crying, except to say, 'I'll call him Crane.' She didn't explain why, but I never saw a woman so happy."

"Happy? You said she couldn't stop crying."

"Yes, happy, and I was happy for her. At that moment, I didn't care who your father was."

"You didn't ask?"

"Oh, I asked. She never answered. So, I stopped asking, same as you. Not my business."

"The men don't shun her," Crane observed.

Aunt Sudi hooted and slapped the table. "They most certainly don't! When you were just a little fellow, Yshna even asked her to marry him."

"But you said she never even had the courtship ring."

"After a certain age, a man might overlook such formalities. She must have refused, because the next thing we knew, he was keeping company with Briato's sister, Ati." Aunt Sudi made a wry face.

"I wonder why Mama said no."

Sudi shook her head. "I don't know. I told her, 'Stell, marry one of them. A boy needs a father.' She wouldn't listen to me."

The angry flames surged again. "I don't want *a* father; I want *my* father."

"Hush, dear, I know. She does, too, or she would have settled long ago for someone else. Although I also thought she should give you a sister or brother. Interesting to imagine — if she'd married Yshna, Sunnea would have been your sister, which, if things go the way I think they will, would eventually have made Elic your brother."

Crane sipped his tea to calm himself. "You did that already."

"So I did. You and Elic were inseparable."

"And you defied all the women in the village, didn't you? Standing by us."

"If they wanted to be smug and petty, I couldn't stop them. But I do what I like. I always have, just the way my mother taught me." She chuckled softly. "I can get away with it because they need me. And there were you two boys, close as brothers, as you say. That sealed it."

Crane frowned as he thought. "Elic always made sure I wasn't left out. The other boys included me grudgingly, but they did it. Because of him."

"I know. I remember once, when he was a little thing, six or seven, he came home in tears when they said he shouldn't play with you. I asked him, 'What do you want to do, Elic?' and he said, 'Crane is my friend, and I'll play with him if I want to. And if anybody doesn't like it, I'll knock him down.'"

"He did, too! He saved me from a miserable childhood." Crane laughed, though he fought against tears. "Why is your family the only one with any sense?"

"Hah! I like that. We formed a helpful habit; the others formed a hurtful one. That's all. You'll show them, one day."

"You think so?"

She thought a moment. "I hope so. You have a gift, a heavy load for a young person. I hope you'll find a way to open it up and use it well. I think most of us want you to find your way."

"How am I ever going to do that?"

"Spread your wings." And her voice echoed in his mind, *Fly away.*

"I need to talk to you more often."

Aunt Sudi laughed. "Time to catch that chicken." She got up and went to the back door.

Just then, a child dashed in at the front, long brown braids swinging. Brynnit, the girl Crane had seen that morning with her kitten. "Ma says it's time."

Aunt Sudi faced her, hands on hips. "Is she sure, now? I was up with your sister all last night, for nothing."

"She said you better come now." The little girl glanced at Crane. He smiled at her. She quickly looked away, but not before she returned a hint of a smile.

"All right, get on back home and tell them I'm on my way," Aunt Sudi said, and the little girl darted away. "Wouldn't you know it, just when I'm about to get supper. You live another day, chickie. At least it's not the middle of the night."

She closed the back door and crossed the kitchen to

disappear into one of the bedrooms. She returned with a large leather bag, packed with the tools and herbs of her trade.

Crane stared after the young messenger. "I can't believe Brynnit's that big already."

"Eight years old, and already a good weaver, Briato says."

"It can't be Tiek's time yet," Crane said. "I just saw her."

"I know, at least three weeks early." A worried frown creased Aunt Sudi's brow.

"Is it more difficult, delivering twins?" Crane stood up to leave.

"Oh! Is it! I could tell you stories ..." She stopped, her face suddenly pale and serious. "What do you mean?"

"I sensed it when I saw Tiek and Kiat earlier today." He paused at Aunt Sudi's troubled look. "But I could be wrong. This is your area, not mine."

She shook her head. "You have a sense for hidden things, Crane. I'll trust you on this one. No wonder she's early." Aunt Sudi added a few more items to her bag, then turned to Crane with a smile. "Care to assist?"

"I'm no healer."

"So you say. Well, you'd better get home to help your mama, anyhow. You may see my menfolk over at the Heron tonight. They're not likely to get supper here."

Chapter 6. The Staff

When Crane returned home, the empty common room was ready to receive supper guests soon. The front windows stood wide open to the breeze. The lamps were filled, polished, and trimmed.

In the kitchen, Mama stirred something savory in a pot over the fire. A honey-gold rope of hair hung down her back, ending in a tassel of golden curls shot with silver. Although not yet old, she wasn't the girl from his vision anymore.

"Smells good in here." Crane hugged her from

behind.

She turned to him with a warm smile. "What did you learn today?"

"How to knock Elic onto his backside."

"I suppose that could be ... useful." She didn't sound convinced.

To amuse her, Crane waved his hand and transformed the rough floorboards of the common room into a flowering meadow, with a sparkling stream meandering between the tables. The lamps erupted with fountains of multicolored butterflies fluttering up through the heavy beams to the high ceiling. "How's that?"

"Pretty, but not useful." She smiled and stood on tiptoe to kiss his cheek. The illusion dissolved into the air.

"I'm on my way to sweep, then. Do you need anything else? Anything *useful*, I mean."

"The woodcutter delivered the firewood. You don't have to chop it all now, but enough to cook with."

Crane stepped into his bedroom to leave the spell book on his bed. He grabbed the broom and dustpan from the corner and headed for the stairs. He paused on the first step. "Remind me again why I'm doing this. We haven't had an overnight guest in ... how long?"

"Better to be ready for guests we don't have than unprepared for guests we don't expect."

"If you say so."

Crane wiped sweat from his neck and forehead and ran up the steep wooden steps three at a time. A narrow gallery overlooked the common room below. He opened the six doors and found the guest rooms stifling. The windows faced south and let in plenty of light. Pleasant in winter. In summer, these rooms were ovens.

Crane opened all the windows and began sweeping up the dust. He wished he could have done it in the morning, when it was cool, but there would have been little point before the wind died down. He had swept yesterday, but the fine, dry dust sifted in through cracks around the windows, all summer long. Keeping the place up and customers happy was an endless round of similar tasks. Mama was equally good with people and housekeeping; she made the job look easy. Crane had to work at it. If he couldn't make a wizard of himself, he'd be doing this job for the rest of his life. Still, it was a pleasure to use muscles after the frustrating hours of study.

Guests we don't expect. She didn't mean supper guests. They always had enough of those to keep the business alive, if only just. Crane couldn't remember ever having an overnight guest in summer. In winter, when a snowstorm had buried the roads, a lost traveler might wander in and spend the night before being shown the correct way. Even that hadn't happened in a long time.

Mama took pride in the tidy rooms, so Crane did a thorough job on each one. A large open space was partitioned into five cubicles, each furnished with a narrow straw tick on a wooden pallet. Crane's grandfather had added doors for privacy, though the partitions could be moved to create larger spaces if needed. Which they never were.

The "best room" had real walls and was the same size as Crane's room below it. It had two chairs, two windows at the southwest corner, and its own small hearth and chimney. Even Crane's room was warmed only by the back of the brick oven. The bed was as large as those in the family rooms downstairs — wide enough for two and long enough even for Crane. He finished sweeping, then plumped the pillows and fluffed the featherbed, as if someone would soon sleep there.

He paused to gaze out at the mountain and the dry riverbed, a mirage of a puddle wavering in the cracked earth. A heap of unsplit firewood lay in the yard below. Crane closed up the guest rooms, returned the broom to its place, and went out the back door, past a dwindling woodpile.

In the shade of the big cottonwood, Crane set a chunk of firewood on the chopping block, raised the ax, and swung it down hard. The length of pine split with a satisfying crack and a pungent resiny odor. He soon got into an enjoyable rhythm and kept at it longer than he'd planned, in spite of the heat. He didn't chop all the wood, but more than enough for a few days' cooking.

As he chopped and stacked the wood, lost fragments of the day came back to him. Jelf had said something about routine work helping him remember when things were different. What did that mean? Before the river went away? Aunt Sudi had spoken of visiting other places, which nobody did now. And Elic had told him ... something new. The thought was sliding away, water through his fingers. All three of them had said it was easier to talk about these things when Crane was there. He should be able to hold onto a thought long enough to look at it squarely. He built a mental dam to hold it back. What had Elic said?

Deep River was cursed. It seemed unlikely, but that was it. He'd called it ... Yrae's Curse. If there was a curse, maybe that was why Deep River needed a wizard. And to be a wizard, Crane needed a staff.

For that, he would need a different kind of wood than the pine he'd been splitting. He put the ax away and hurried inside. Mama stood tying on a clean apron. She no longer looked weary. She had unbraided her hair and brushed the shining curls into a golden cloud around her head and shoulders. Crane didn't understand why she wore her hair loose in the evenings when she had the most work to do. The most she ever said about it was, "Oh, they seem to like it."

Crane dodged past her and into his room. Where was it?

"What are you looking for?" she called after him.

"Nothing."

Crane closed his door to look behind it. The object he sought wasn't there. He could picture it, a long walnut branch, seasoned but unfinished, given to him years ago by Sinth, the carpenter. He remembered that story without anyone telling him. It came from the big nut tree Crane's great-grandfather had planted when he came to Deep River. The tree was stressed by drought (*and the loss of the river?*), and damaged in a windstorm the winter Crane was born. It was cut down and the wood used for Mama's rocker, Soorhi's desk, and the big table in the Village Hall. The big branch had been too nice to burn, so Sinth had given it to Crane to play with when he was old enough. He had ridden it as a hobbyhorse, vaulted fences, and poked at things. When and where had he seen it last?

When he had outgrown it as a plaything, his mother had suggested making it into a broom handle. Crane had hidden it … somewhere. He could almost see it. He dropped to the floor and reached under the bed, between the mattress and the frame. Yes, there it was. He pulled it out and stood up with it in his hand. It was near his height with a nicely balanced heft. It had been too tall and heavy for a child to use as a walking stick, but now it suited him perfectly.

"Crane?" Mama called. "Could you fetch more water before supper?"

He closed his eyes and breathed deeply to calm his impatience. He laid the stick next to the book. That project would have to wait.

Crane went out to the pump. True to his word, Jagree had already fixed the squeak. Under the clear water, a layer of dark grit swirled at the bottom of each bucket. A typical occurrence in late summer, when the water level in the well dropped. Crane had turned to go back inside when a muffled cry drifted from the weaver Briato's house, across the road and two houses west. The doors and windows stood open. The air surrounding the house churned with pain, but also life. Crane reached toward the house with his mind, his spirit, toward the center of that pain and life, to ease the pain, encourage the life. A baby's cry startled him back to himself.

"She has Sudi. What would she need with my help?" But he smiled to himself and tucked away the feeling of life breaking forth.

so I haven't been out much. I'm better now, though. Time to let folks know."

"You're happy about it?"

"I am. And terrified, but mostly happy."

"And how does Darys feel about becoming a father?" Ketty asked.

"He is thrilled," Lalik replied. "He's already building a cradle."

"Well, you're building the baby. The man needs something to do."

"Might I ask what you are doing at the midwife's house?" Lalik asked with a sly grin.

"I'm here to cut rosemary," Ketty said. "It was good luck meeting you. I wish I could spend more time, but ..."

"No, you have plenty to keep you busy, running the inn and everything."

"Papa runs it," Ketty corrected. "I help out."

Lalik crossed her arms. "You cook and serve from sunup to sundown, and then clean up afterward. That's a lot more than *helping out*, and I hope Eslo knows it."

"He always says he doesn't know what he'll do if I leave home." Ketty frowned. "*When* I leave home. Someday, I will."

"Wherever you go, they'll be lucky to have you. And we'll be sorry to see you go."

Ketty hugged her friend goodbye and opened the gate into Trilmi's garden. The rosemary was hard to miss, a sprawling, overgrown shrub. She clipped the fragrant sprigs and imagined how they would flavor roast meat and soups. It was tasty either fresh or dried. She wouldn't have to worry about using it up quickly.

Trilmi joined her when the basket was half full. "Take

all you want! It's good for more than cooking."

"That's how I plan to use most of it. I wish I knew some of those other uses," Ketty said.

"I use it to treat headaches, and it helps prevent infection," Trilmi replied. "My mentor thought it could lift a low mood and sharpen memory."

"Maybe it lifts a low mood because it makes the kitchen smell so good." Ketty clipped a few more sprigs to add to the pile in her basket. "Speaking of kitchens, I need to get back. Thank you for all this."

"Thank you for pruning my shrub." Trilmi grinned. "I'm happy to talk about herbs anytime."

Ketty waved as she let herself out by the gate. Learning about medicinal herbs wasn't magical healing. It wasn't nothing, though. Papa couldn't object to something so homely and practical. Ketty could feed her curiosity without leaving home ... yet. But she couldn't keep her secret forever.

Chapter 14. Saying Goodbye

Deep River

Crane entered the Village Hall with a sense of finality and looked around the familiar room. He knew every stone, floorboard, table, and chair, and yet he saw them now as if for the first time, or in a new way. He would miss things he had never noticed. With a sigh, he walked to the closed library door and knocked.

"Who is it?" Jelf called irritably.

"Crane."

After a moment of shuffling and thumping, the door

flew open and Jelf appeared, all traces of irritation gone from his face and voice. "I wasn't sure I'd see you today. What'll it be?"

"Nothing, Jelf. I've come to say goodbye. I'm … going away."

The old man raised his eyebrows. "Going away where?"

"I've decided to follow Yrae's Curse to its source. But I wanted to say thank you first."

"Oh. Well, you're welcome. I was happy to be a help when I could." Jelf furrowed his brow. "How did you learn about it? I think I wanted to tell you, but I couldn't. Been reading minds again, have you?"

Crane smiled and leaned back against the big walnut table, brother to his staff. "No, but you weren't the only one who wanted to tell me. I guess I put it together for myself, out of little things people managed to spit out. Before, I couldn't think about it. Now I can't think about anything else. So I'm going to find Yrae, and I leave tomorrow."

"You're a brave fellow. Don't go looking for a fight."

"I promise you, I'm not. But I want to understand the curse, and break it, if I can. Who better to seek than the wizard responsible? And who knows? Maybe I can take the curse back to him!" Crane laughed, a hollow, unconvincing chuckle.

"I'll miss you, my boy. I guess it's about time one of our young people left home. It's been too long. Wait here." Jelf disappeared into the library for a moment, and returned with a small, thick book with a pale green cover, a faint pattern of leaves all over the front. He placed it in Crane's hands. "Most of Lok's old books are falling apart, but this one is small enough and in good enough condition to travel. Perhaps you can learn from it while you journey and come back able to serve your village."

Crane stared at the small book in his hands, a volume of healing charms and uses of medicinal herbs. "I can't take this," he said, stunned. "What if I ... what if I don't come back?"

"You will. You'll have to return that book! Now off with you."

"Thank you." Crane's voice broke with emotion. "I won't forget this."

He returned to the inn to find a sturdy knapsack on his bed. Mama had kept her promise. She busied herself with such meaningless tasks as rearranging chairs, wiping up invisible dust and spills, straightening jars of spices.

"Mama!" Crane cried at last. "Sit down a moment. You're making me tired, just watching you."

"I can't sit down now. If I sit down, I'll cry. I can sit tomorrow."

He caught her hand as she swept past and pulled her close to him. "Mama, I have to do this."

"I know." Her tears dampened his shirt. "I always knew this day would come, ever since ..." She squeezed his scarred hand. "I was lucky to keep you as long as I did. But, oh! You men, always leaving, and all I can do is stay here and wait. I hate it! And who will help with the inn?"

"I'll come back," he murmured into her hair. "I'll be back before my birthday." It was an impulsive promise that felt like a contract as soon as the words were out.

Mama nodded, snuffling. "I'll ask Ohme if he can spare Jagree a few hours a day, to help with the heavy work." She clucked softly. "I wish you had better clothes for your trip."

He laughed and kissed her. "These are fine! No one is going to care about a few patches. I wish my new boots were finished, though; there isn't much left of these." He extended a foot to display a comfortable but shabby boot.

"Didn't I tell you? I picked them up yesterday when you were out playing with your stick. Your coat, though-"

"Coat? Mama, it's summer!"

"It won't be summer forever. And in the mountains, it will be cold at night even now."

How does she know about mountain weather? The thought was gone before he could voice it. "The coat I have will have to do."

"That rag? It was already too small for you last winter, and it's in shreds."

"I don't have time to have a new one made. You can't stop me from going."

Mama bit her lip and looked hard at him. "No, I have something else for you." She disappeared into her bedroom, and he heard her open the blanket chest that stood at the foot of her bed. When she returned, she held out a heavy woolen cloak, dark gray with a large hood. "This was your father's. He left it here."

Crane took the cloak from her. Holding a tangible token of the man's existence, hope and longing overwhelmed him, mingled with anger and sorrow. He rubbed the rough, warm fabric between his fingers. Though clearly not new, it was clean and neatly patched, and long enough even for Crane. "He left it for me?"

"How could he when he never knew about you? He probably forgot it in his hurry. I put it away and kept it all these years."

"Which of us were you keeping it for?"

She looked down at the floor, her old secret smile briefly flickering across her lips. "I was a silly girl. Now it is yours. May it warm you well." She smiled bravely. "One more thing — give me your moneybag."

Crane pulled the bag out of his pocket. The few remaining Eukardian duls clinked as he handed it to her. He rarely needed to buy anything, but kept coins handy in case, since he had nothing useful to trade. He supposed she would add a few more. She preferred money to barter, which made sense in her business. Her customers didn't always have what she needed, when she needed it, and it was easier to store coins than pigs or chickens. Every coin in Deep River had probably circulated through the Blue Heron at least once.

Mama climbed up on a stool and took a small crock from a high shelf. She set it on the table, removed the lid and proceeded to scoop handfuls of silver duls into the moneybag.

"What are you doing?" Crane protested. "I can't take so much of your money! You might need it."

"This isn't mine, it's yours. Your wages, if you like. I've put aside a little every week, for years."

"Surely I won't need money —"

Mama cut him off. "You never know. I'll give you food to take, but how long will that last? Do you know what to eat in the woods?"

"Well, no ..."

"If you have money, you can buy what you need in some village or from a farmer or what have you. Take it; I'll feel better." She returned the bag, bulging and heavy with more wealth than Crane had ever known.

"All right, then. Thank you."

Supper that night was the usual gathering. The people, the talk, the food: everything was the same as always, except Mama smiled at Crane more than usual, and kept patting him whenever they passed.

Elic came in, and as soon as he had been served, he stood and raised his mug. "Attention, everyone. Quiet, please. No, Crane you're not getting away." He grinned and grabbed Crane's sleeve. "Now, listen, everyone. This night is unlike any other. Tomorrow, our friend Crane is … is going away."

The announcement was met with stunned silence. Crane had never known this many men to be this quiet when there was plenty of ale at hand.

Elic continued his speech. "So, are we going to let him sneak off, or are we going to give him a party?" The crowd roared approval, and Elic pushed Crane into a chair. When Crane tried to get up, his friend handed him the mug of ale. "Drink, friend. No work for you tonight."

Elic tied on an apron and helped Mama serve, while Crane sat, embarrassed but pleased, the guest of honor in his own house. The crowd sang songs, bought round after round of drinks, and offered advice, though none of them knew anything about travel.

"Now, you be sure and watch out for bears," an old farmer offered, sitting down next to Crane. "There's bears out there can eat a man in one bite." He chomped at the air. His lack of teeth diminished the ferocity of the gesture.

"There's no such thing as a bear that big," Briato, the weaver, argued. "What you need to remember, my boy, is to mind you don't walk into quicksand. Why, that stuff will make you think it's solid ground, and then suck you right down."

"There's no such thing as quicksand," another voice broke in. "What you have to watch out for is giants ..."

Elic kept refilling Crane's mug, and Crane kept emptying it. His outlook grew rosier, if fuzzy around the edges. He listened to his mother telling every tale she could remember about a hero on a journey, and it was all he could do not to laugh. He didn't feel heroic. But it didn't matter.

What did matter was that this rowdy crowd of rough, ordinary, hardworking folk had always made sure he and his mother had a decent living. Though Grandpa Stoli, long ago, would have protected her from the likes of them, all of them were like family to her and to Crane. They had protected her from the more real dangers of poverty and ill opinion. They would continue to do so when Crane was gone.

The party finally broke up well after midnight. Nobody stayed to clean up, so Crane ended up doing some work that night. He bumped against the kitchen table as he carried a stack of mugs to be washed.

"Careful," Mama warned. "You're a little drunk after all that ale."

"It's not strong."

"You've never had that much before. Be sure to drink plenty of water before you go to bed. Might save you a sore head."

Crane downed two mugs of water to humor her. He stumbled to his room and dropped into bed, asleep as soon as he lay down. Come morning, he would leave everything he'd ever known. But Mama was safe. Crane slept easy.

Chapter 15. Leaving Deep River

Deep River

Crane's plan was to set out at first light. He hadn't counted on Elic's little party. When he woke to the usual kitchen clatter, the sun was already up, and the aroma of fresh bread filled the house. His mouth was dry, but at least his head didn't hurt.

Crane fetched water as usual. When he returned to fill the keg, Elic sat at the table.

"I didn't expect you today," Crane said. "You won't talk me out of going."

"Wouldn't think of it." Elic grinned. "I'm going with you." He reached behind his chair and hefted a knapsack from the floor.

"No, you're not. This isn't your quest."

"I have nothing better to do." As if Elic were tagging along on a casual stroll. "And what kind of friend would I be if I didn't at least walk with you a day's journey?"

Mama intervened before Crane could argue further. "I think it's a fine idea. Crane, sit down and eat. Who knows when you'll have a proper meal again? You, too, Elic." She gave them a large, hot breakfast. While they ate, she busied herself with unnecessary tasks, refolding towels and washing clean dishes.

After Crane had finished his breakfast, he returned to his room and shoved his feet into his new boots. "These boots are too big," he called.

Mama joined him and knelt to feel his toes. "Not much, and your feet aren't finished growing. Wear two stockings in the meantime."

He took her advice, though that made the boots uncomfortably snug. He packed a change of clothes, his father's cloak, a sharp knife, and Jelf's book in Mama's old knapsack. She gave him a generous wedge of cheese and five small loaves of bread, wrapped in a napkin and warm from the oven. At the last moment, Crane added shaving things, though it was hard to imagine he might meet anyone who would care. He filled his water flask and slung it over his shoulder. He tied a rolled-up blanket to the knapsack, and his packing was complete. He shouldered the pack and joined Elic at the door.

Mama handed him his staff and stood on tiptoe to kiss his cheek. "Back before your birthday, remember.

Bring me something."

"Bring you something? What do you mean?"

"I expect it's ... different, where you're going. Not like here. It would be nice to have a token from somewhere else. It's been so long ..."

Crane wondered what souvenir he could bring back from the land of his dream. How could he bring her a forest, a mountain, a river? "I'll try."

She kissed him again and stepped back, drying her tears on her apron. He swallowed his own sadness and forced a smile onto his face as he closed the door between them. Leaving home? It didn't seem real.

"So, this way?" Elic turned toward the road.

Crane shook his head. "Do you know where the road goes? I don't." He pointed with his staff toward the dry river channel. "This way." He set out walking, and Elic fell in beside him. Crane didn't speak, but his heart warmed to have his friend with him. He paused when they reached the blackened stump.

"You have my permission to pass this place." Crane gestured with his staff as if opening a gate.

Elic gave an exaggerated bow and walked on. "How do you even know which way to go?"

"Dreams. And ... a feeling."

Elic whistled. "I guess I'll have to trust it. I wish I could go the whole way, though! This is probably the only time I'll leave Deep River."

"You could leave if you chose." Crane had to work even to hold onto the thought. They were talking about something that had never seemed possible.

"Yes, but why would I choose? I don't have a *feeling* to lead me anywhere. And besides, I'm getting married."

"Lucky you." Crane wasn't sure which circumstance he considered luckier.

It turned into a pleasant day for walking. The sun shone at intervals among passing clouds, and the air was comfortably dry, with a light, cooling breeze. The travelers spoke little. There was nothing that needed to be said between the two old friends, and it was enjoyable simply to walk along together, not yet far from home, anticipating unknown adventures.

Crane's new boots called attention to themselves at first. Besides the snug fit, they were stiffer than their worn-out predecessors. Not bad. Different. As he adjusted to the new feel, he appreciated the thick soles protecting his feet from the uneven, rocky ground, though his toes were crowded by stockings and stiff leather.

The riverbed itself was so overgrown with sagebrush and yarrow, it was difficult to recognize as a riverbed. Still, it should have been an easy matter to follow the bank. The two friends had to repeatedly detour out of sight of the guiding channel, around eroded places and clumps of brush along the bank. Crane's unerring sense of where he needed to go always led them back and onward.

Near midday, Crane stopped to take a drink and pointed ahead of them. "Woods, like in my dream. This is farther from home than I've ever been." He turned and looked back at Deep River, tiny in the distance, a gray smudge against gold and brown. Then he faced forward again, awed and excited that he was about to leave the familiar behind.

A large bird gave a harsh cry and rose from a tree at

the fringe of the woods. As it glided nearer, Crane recognized the long tail and black-and-white plumage. The magpie fluttered down onto Elic's shoulder. "Ek!" it croaked.

"It said my name! That's the first time."

"Thank you for the scouting ahead," Crane said to the magpie. It regarded him in its solemn manner, then bobbed its head courteously. "Go on back to town, tell Jagree we haven't been eaten by bears yet." As if it understood, the bird flapped into the air and away toward Deep River.

With a grin at Elic, Crane took his first step into the unknown. Nothing changed. He walked on the dry grass and stony soil, like what he trod on every day. But now his quest had truly begun.

They hiked for an hour or so in the sparse forest of pine and scrub oak before they stopped for lunch. They kicked aside the hard little acorns and sat on the cushioning pine needles to eat. Crane broke a loaf of his mother's bread in half. The sour, yeasty aroma gave him a brief pang of longing for home, but he was too hungry and excited for it to last. He passed half the loaf to Elic and tore into his own share.

As Elic finished his lunch, he pointed upstream. "What is that?"

Crane followed the gesture. "I've been wondering, too. Do you hear water?"

"Let's investigate." Elic gathered his pack and stood. "Ow," he groaned. "Do your legs ache as much as mine do?"

Crane grimaced. "Yes. And my toes hurt. Did you notice we were climbing?"

"Not until I looked behind me just now." Elic's grin turned into a wince.

They stretched and shook out sore muscles as they continued slowly along the streambed. The slope felt steeper than it had, and Crane's pack weighed on him as if it were loaded with heavy stones. Every step was an effort, like trudging through deep, wet snow.

Crane turned to Elic to comment on how the rest break hadn't done its job. Elic was not at his side. Crane spun to face back the way they had come, nearly falling in his haste to find his friend. Elic walked briskly away from him, toward Deep River.

"Elic!" Crane called. "You're going the wrong way."

Elic stopped, shoulders slumped, but didn't turn around. Crane jogged downhill to join him. It was so easy. What were they thinking, going that other way? He closed his eyes and tried to remember. He was ... going into the mountains. To ... find someone. Yrae. To break Yrae's Curse.

Crane opened his eyes and looked up through the branches at the sky. The glittering red network hung overhead, closer than before. He rested a hand on Elic's shoulder. "It isn't time to go back yet. We're on an adventure, remember? A quest."

"It's too hard," Elic whispered.

"Not for you. And if you're with me, not for me, either." Crane gently turned Elic to face the right direction again. "It isn't only our sore muscles slowing us down. Yrae's Curse weighs heavier here than it did closer to home. We have to fight it."

Elic nodded. Crane stayed close by his side as they covered the same ground again. They made it a few steps farther than Crane had reached on his own before Elic slowed and stopped, bent over with his hands on his knees.

"I can't," he puffed.

"*We* can."

Back when Crane didn't know what the curse was, he had always let it turn him aside. Now he pushed against it, refusing to let it force him back. At the first step, his boot seemed to have a long taproot deep in the ground, unwilling to move. Crane slowly lifted one foot, then the other. The more he pushed, the less the curse resisted.

"Follow me," he said. The pressure lessened. Elic straightened and walked forward at Crane's side.

The sound of rushing water grew louder ahead of them. They broke through the trees near a massive dam of mud, sand, stones, and debris. Above the dam, a broad river flowed down a wooded valley, out of the mountains. Diverted by the dam, the river bent and ran off to the southeast.

"It's our river," Crane said.

Elic stared at the dam. "How did that get there? Did somebody make it?"

"It doesn't look built, does it?" Crane said. "At least now we know what happened. The river was blocked by this pile of mud and changed course. I wonder if it happens a lot, with rivers." Crane studied the dam. It wasn't hiding anything other than more mud and sticks. "Maybe it isn't part of the curse. Didn't anyone ever bother to check?"

He gazed back the way they had come, and then followed the flowing water with his eyes. The bend from the old channel to the new was slight, and he could look from one to the other with no effort. Yet that angle resulted in enough distance that the people of Deep River couldn't see what had become of their river. On the hillside across the dry channel, a stand of aspens quivered in the slight breeze. The shining stream rushed past this grove, tumbled down from the woods, and flowed out across a rolling plain of pale grasses and gray-green sagebrush. Trees and bushes lined the river's banks, marking its course into the hazy distance. Far away, Crane thought he could make out a thread or two of smoke. He couldn't tell whether it came from a village, a lone house, or some sort of camp. It was true — there were people outside Deep River.

"It looks so pleasant and peaceful," Crane sighed. "If I've taken the curse away from Deep River, I don't want to carry it back again. I could give up this quest and find a life down there." He nodded toward the distant plume of smoke.

"It looks exactly like home." Elic gripped Crane's shoulder and turned him around. "You're not going into exile. After you break this curse, you're going home."

Chapter 16. The River

Crane turned his back on the scene and took a step toward the flowing water. He fell to his knees in the damp sand, dizzy and stunned, as if a weight had unexpectedly lifted from his back. In a fit of inexplicable giddiness, he laughed out loud. Elic sank down next to him, also laughing.

"What's so funny?" Elic gasped.

"I don't know." Crane glanced up, then stared at the clear blue sky. Blue, with no red shimmer. He shouted with joy. "We've escaped! We're not under Yrae's spell anymore!"

They continued along the river, talking and laughing as all the stifled plans and suppositions of a lifetime bubbled to the surface. Periodically, one would burst into song, and the other would join in, making up ridiculous verses for familiar songs until they were laughing so hard, they couldn't continue. Sore feet and aching muscles were forgotten in their newfound freedom. Crane couldn't stop himself from looking up through the trees at the sky, a blue sky finally free of the annoying net of glowing spells.

The sun shone low as they made camp. Crane removed his boots and stockings and soaked his cramped feet in the cool river. Then he used magic for the first time all day to light a small campfire.

"I was wondering if I'd ever get to see you do that," Elic said.

Crane laughed. "Finally, I can do one thing right." He put water on to boil. "I'm glad you thought to bring a kettle and mugs." He unpacked bread and cheese for supper. Elic added tea and dried apples from last fall's harvest to the meal.

"Take the tea and a mug with you," Elic offered. "And the kettle. I've got another at home. Mam said this one is made for travelers."

"It's still hard to believe our mothers used to go places," Crane said. "Easier now, though."

"How far do you suppose we've come?" Elic asked as they ate their meal.

"My legs say a hundred times whatever you guess." Crane stretched out, wiggling his bare toes. "It isn't only the distance. We've walked into a different world."

After supper, they lay wrapped in cloaks and blankets and stared up at the first stars. Elic said, "I have never felt so happy and peaceful in my whole life. I feel ... it's hard to describe. I feel ... free. Is that what the curse is? Being trapped, and not even knowing it?"

"I guess so. I've never seen the sky clearly before, just the sky and nothing else." Crane drank in the twilight overhead. "I'm sorry the curse is still on Deep River, but now I'm glad it wasn't on me."

"If you can break the spell, I'll be happy to have had a part in it." Elic sounded half asleep already. "I want to feel like this on my wedding day. I want Sunnea to feel like this."

Crane chuckled. "You two will manage whether the curse is lifted or not. It would be a nice wedding present, though, wouldn't it?"

"Well, if you don't succeed, at least now I have a reason to think about leaving Deep River."

Crane smiled and watched his friend fall asleep. He lay back and gazed up at the stars twinkling overhead. The hardest part of the journey lay before him, but he felt calm and almost content. For the first time in his life, the boy from Deep River fell asleep to the sound of running water.

The weary travelers woke early, forced from their beds by the cold air, the hard ground, and the sun's rays slanting through the trees.

Crane groaned as he threw off his blanket and tried

to sit up. "What did we do yesterday? I can't move without aching."

"It's not what we did. It's what we *over*did." Elic stretched gingerly.

"I felt so good coming up from the dam; now I'm paying for it. Maybe this is the curse!"

Elic laughed. "Come on, it'll help to move around. Brr!" He shivered as he stood up and made a dash for the river.

The air was cold and the river water colder as they washed their faces. Now fully awake, they ate a hasty breakfast and broke camp.

"You're sure you won't come with me?" Crane teased his friend. He rolled up his blanket and hung the tea kettle from his pack.

"It's a tempting offer, now that I know what I'll be missing. But I'm not quite as free as I once was."

"I know. Safe journeying, my friend."

Elic chortled. "Don't worry about me! I'm just going home. You be careful."

"I'll try." Crane couldn't bring himself to laugh at Elic's joke. In saying goodbye to Elic, he was taking leave of everything he'd known. He had no idea what came next.

Elic clasped Crane's hand. "Don't get into too much trouble without me." He looked away for a moment, and then met Crane's eyes again. "Do what you have to. Come home afterward and tell us the story."

Crane pulled Elic into a final embrace. They shouldered their packs and Elic set off down the river, whistling. Crane knew he had his own path to follow but stood and watched Elic walk away. When he was almost out of sight, Crane had a vision of his friend walking into darkness. "Elic!" he called. Elic turned to wave and smile from a distance, even as the premonition slipped away like a dream.

Chapter 17. The Forest

When Crane could no longer see Elic in the distance, he turned and set off upriver, following the pull that had brought him this far. The terrain wasn't much steeper than before but felt like a vertical climb at first. Every muscle ached, from his neck to his feet. Hiking with Elic the previous day, Crane had carried his staff jauntily. Now he leaned on it as he put one foot in front of the other. Wearing only one pair of stockings, he could at least wiggle his toes. If his legs ached this much at the beginning of the day, he could only imagine how much he would suffer before he camped for the night. He had enough food for only two or three days, though. Going nowhere wasn't an option. And the pull felt stronger. He had to be close.

His stiff muscles loosened as they warmed up, but his feet slid and rubbed inside their too-big boots. He tried walking gingerly to prevent further rubbing. It didn't help, and his legs suffered the strain of every awkward step.

After so many years with an empty channel, the sight and sound of rushing water distracted Crane from his discomfort. The river served as guide and companion as he followed it up the valley. It wasn't the same as having another person by his side. He and Elic had talked little before they reached the dam, but this journey felt very different now that Crane was alone.

I really am alone now. I thought I knew what that was like.

As he hiked, voices whispered, almost obscured by the sound of his own crackling footsteps. He paused to listen, alert for concealed danger. Ever since Aunt Sudi had pointed out his sense for hidden things, Crane had tried to pay attention to it. The only sounds were the breeze in the trees, bird calls, and the murmuring river. The voice of the forest.

Still, a warning nagged at the edge of Crane's consciousness, as if he glimpsed a threatening movement from the corner of his eye. When he looked for the threat, he couldn't find it anywhere. He shook his head and continued.

Creeks crossed Crane's path on their way to the river — some mere trickles, others wide, rushing streams. He stepped from rock to rock and crossed slippery logs without hesitation. He had always been sure-footed, and he knew he couldn't look back.

Crane hiked through the morning, leaving the dry pine woods behind. The way grew steeper, and the river ran narrower and wilder the higher he climbed. A gurgling sound in the thick undergrowth announced another creek before Crane saw it pouring over stairsteps of rock to reach the river. There was no easy crossing over the wide stream, but the swift water wasn't too deep to wade.

Crane sank onto a rock to take off his boots and stockings. The balls and heels of both feet were blistered and rubbed raw. He shed his pack and unslung his water flask. This was as good a time as any for a lunch break. After a long drink, he took out a hunk of bread and bit into it with enthusiasm. Even a day old, Mama's bread tasted like a feast. While he chewed, he gazed about him, finally able to spare attention to his surroundings. He gazed in awe at the massive tree trunks and dense canopy overhead. The forest floor where he sat grew thickly with ferns, flowers, and seedling trees. Crane had heard of forests in stories. He had never understood until now what the word meant.

Everything — the rocks, the tree bark, the soil, even the light — was green. It *smelled* green. All around Crane were tree species he had never seen before. Within arm's reach was a massive tree with flat, reddish bark, fibrous under his fingers. He picked up a graceful fan of scaly needles and crushed them under his nose.

"Cedar," he whispered, echoing a voice in his head. He touched other trunks, other branches, and knew them, as if each tree introduced itself by name: alder, hemlock, maple, fir.

He could only assume he had learned these names in school. Old Soorhi had extensive plant knowledge from his mysterious past. Crane could imagine no other way he would know these things, though the voice in his head did not sound like Soorhi.

It's all there in my memory, Crane said to himself. *Funny, though, how the names popped up so quickly, after all these years, as if I were meeting old friends.*

He gazed up into the dizzying canopy. None of Soorhi's descriptions and drawings had prepared Crane for the immensity of the great forest trees. He pictured the pine he had destroyed, the cottonwood behind the Blue Heron, and Elic's apple tree. Crane had thought them tall. He never would again.

With a flash of black and white tail feathers, a large gray bird swooped down and stole the crust from his hand. "Hey!" Crane protested, though he had to laugh at the bird's boldness, so like Jagree's magpie friend. It sat on a low branch across the creek and mocked him by eating its prize in full view.

The sound of his own shout startled Crane, too loud for the surroundings. The forest was not silent, but quiet, full of small sounds. As he ate part of his cheese, carefully guarded against winged thieves, Crane listened to the forest. Flowing water murmured and splashed; alder branches squeaked against each other in the light breeze; birds warbled, squawked, and scolded; insects buzzed. He heard no more whispered warnings.

Crane stretched his legs and rolled his trouser legs past the knee. He got to his feet with a barely stifled whimper, shouldered his pack, and hobbled down the creek bank. The icy water took his breath away, then numbed his sore feet as he stepped carefully across the gravelly creek bottom. Upon reaching the other bank, he knelt and filled his water flask.

He rested only long enough for his legs and feet to dry, though he was sure he could have slept if he let himself. But it was only the middle of the day, and he suspected he had much farther to go. With regret, he pulled on both pairs of stockings — he had learned that lesson — and his boots. He got to his feet and continued his journey. He now paid more attention to the place he passed through. The deep shade was pleasantly cool even on this hot day. He could almost forget his sore feet as he gazed in wonder. The giant trees had stood and would continue to stand for hundreds of years.

The sense of hidden danger broke through again. Crane looked around warily, though he couldn't see far through the dense forest. The landscape, only moments ago new and fascinating, now felt like a trap. Crane halted and gazed up at the distant forest canopy. Where the trees grew thickest, he could barely glimpse the sky. The treetops swayed. Then the treetops were still and solid ground swayed. The sense of menace increased. Crane stumbled backward and stepped in a small burrow. His right foot bent painfully under him.

He twisted and flailed to stop his fall, only succeeding in landing on his side on a cushion of moss and needles. His head lay among lacy ferns. His staff dug into his ribs. He shrugged off his knapsack, rolled onto his back and stared up at the distant, swaying treetops. He couldn't blame them for his fall, though they had contributed. It was his own fault. He didn't belong here.

Crane's ankle protested when he tried to stand. He flopped back onto the ground. He didn't know where he was, and neither did anyone else. He didn't know anything. Except that this quest was over.

A gap in the canopy framed an eagle that circled overhead. Unless it was a vulture. Crane dragged himself into a sitting position against a fallen log and tried his best to look alive. His ankle throbbed.

The whispering took up again at the edges of his hearing. Crane couldn't understand any words, but imagined an unseen watcher asking, *Who do you think you are?*

"I'm a … I'm *supposed* to be a wizard."

Some wizard. What a foolish idea to set out on this quest alone, following a pull, a call. The call of his enemy. But someone had to break Yrae's Curse. There wasn't anyone else.

And now it wouldn't even be him.

For all Crane knew, Yrae had lured him out here, away from Deep River, to kill him before he could break the curse. Clever Yrae — he didn't even have to do the deed himself. Even uninjured, Crane doubted he was a match for the hidden danger he imagined lurking in every shadow. Unable to walk, let alone run, he would be easy prey.

Better to get out of this forest. In Deep River, he could rest and heal before trying again. Maybe persuade Elic to come with him the whole way. How many days might it take to limp back home? He wouldn't run out of water until he passed the dam. His food supply was severely limited, though, and he was in no shape to forage. Even if he could remember what was safe to eat. He probably wouldn't starve, but it would be a miserable trek. And humiliating to return home so soon after the sendoff they'd given him. Would he really have the nerve to try again? Having come this far, maybe it was better to keep going.

Then he saw the danger, not hidden at all. Everywhere he looked, great logs littered the forest floor. Ancient, moss-covered humps with young trees and ferns growing out of them. More recent casualties, like the one he leaned against, with sharply broken ends or uplifted roots attached. So. The forest giants didn't stand forever. Like sure-footed Crane, even they could fall.

Death by tree was not something he had considered before. *Is that better or worse than being eaten by a bear? Either way, I'll never get to do anything.* These gloomy thoughts filled Crane with such regret, he wished he'd never started this quest. But there was no going back now. *Anyway, at least I left home this once. If I can, I must go on.*

He couldn't move. "I must go on," he repeated aloud. With strengthened resolve, he tried again to stand. His right foot wouldn't bear his weight. He sank back down, tears of pain and frustration springing from his eyes. This was more than a twist. It hurt enough that Crane feared a serious sprain. A minor enough injury at home, with Aunt Sudi to patch him up and Mama to fuss over him. Not here, on his own.

Crane crawled back to where he'd dropped his pack. Maybe he could travel on all fours until his ankle was better. Needles and cones pricked his hands, stones bruised his knees, and holding his staff while he crawled even a short distance was awkward and exhausting.

There must be something I can do! he fretted. *I wish I were a healer.*

He leaned against a cedar trunk and closed his eyes to control his mounting panic. An image bubbled up in his mind: Jelf's hand, holding a small, thick book. Crane sobbed with renewed hope and dug into his pack to find the book. Although he had learned a few healing spells from one of the other books, he'd had no luck making them work. This book was new to him. It couldn't hurt to try. He flipped through it without daring to hope, noting fever charms and headache remedies. He was about to give up when he came to a charm to ease sprains and swelling.

The handwriting was more ornamented than he'd seen before, but clear and legible. He imagined the healer who wrote this book was a woman like Aunt Sudi's mother Elika. How long ago had she written down these spells? More important, how good a healer was she?

Crane started to remove his boot. He yelped when he bent his injured ankle. The boot had to stay on. He leaned against the tree and gritted his teeth until the pain subsided to a throbbing ache. He placed his hands on either side of the injured joint and read the words off the page while pushing power through his fingers. Maybe it was wishful thinking, but the pain lessened. Crane repeated the charm until dizzy from using his power. The ankle was better, if not completely healed. He flipped through the pages until he found something about blisters. He tried the charm, but it had little effect. Either it didn't work, or he was out of magic.

Temporarily, he hoped.

Crane stood and leaned heavily on his staff. With that support, he could walk with only a slight limp. He gave silent thanks to the unknown healer who had written the book.

His attention returned to all those fallen trees. Crane swallowed the lump in his throat and recalled a spell of protection he had once studied. He muttered it as he walked, hoping he remembered it correctly. He jumped at every noise in the forest, from snapping twigs to the loud drumming of woodpeckers. He saw only chipmunks and birds.

And the trees stood.

Chapter 18. Hidden Things

The morning's pleasant shade turned hot and close by mid-afternoon. A cooling breeze stirred near the water. The air swarmed with biting flies and mosquitoes. The protective spell had no effect on them if it worked at all. Crane's face and hands were soon lumpy with bites.

Anyway, it takes my mind off my feet. He swatted bugs away as he stopped again to renew the charm on his ankle. It helped, but the relief didn't last. Not the charm's fault. He lacked talent as a healer. Still, it was better than nothing.

A loud, repeated trill rang out from a branch above.

A black bird with bright red shoulders took off and flew ahead. The bird was going his way, so Crane followed and soon emerged into a wide clearing with a large pond at its center. The blackbird perched on a cattail and sang his three-note song.

Small, pointed stumps surrounded the pond, which had formed behind a small dam of sticks that slowed the river. As he watched, a plump, brown-furred animal splashed into the murky water. A ... beaver. As with the trees, he knew this animal, though he had never seen one before. Had Soorhi spoken of them? Dragonflies darted above the surface of the pond, while swallows swooped after insects. Ducks paddled along, lifting their tails to the sky as they dabbled for food. Crane had only seen ducks in flight, passing over Deep River on their migrations. Now he laughed aloud at a family of half-grown ducklings that disappeared one after another, only to reappear in another place.

His laughter broke off as a large white bird stepped into view. Tall and graceful, it waded with deliberate steps and dipped its long bill into the water. It turned toward its human namesake and spread wide, black-tipped wings.

Crane dropped to the ground in awe and watched the crane he had never expected to see. This was not the smaller gray kind from the drawing on his wall. Jelf had implied it was rare to see one of these big white ones, and Crane felt honored. He forgot his pain and fear, studying the graceful, confident bird. Finally, though, he had to tear himself away and continue hiking.

Above the beaver dam, the churning river was gray with silt. The terrain grew more rugged, and the undergrowth denser. Crane walked close to the water rather than fight through brambles and brush, though the river's rocky bank grew steeper and increasingly difficult to climb. Crane trudged on until a roaring waterfall finally brought him to a halt. Spray cooled his face, and rainbows danced off the wet, mossy rock walls. It was beautiful, magical ... and impassable. He looked up at the sheer rock cliffs, perilously slick; and then into the dense, impenetrable forest.

"Where now?" he asked aloud. He leaned back against a boulder and gazed around in frustration. He took a swig from his water flask, nearly empty now. One more thing to worry about; he didn't like the look of the silty river water.

Hidden things, he thought. *Nothing could be more hidden than a path through this forest.* He backtracked several paces to a place where he'd seen hoof prints in the damp sand, and another, partial print he couldn't identify. More like a paw than a hoof, though it could as easily have been a human foot. But if deer could get down to the water, he should be able to climb up into the forest.

Near the tracks was a low spot where Crane managed to scramble to the top of the bank. He poked his staff into the thick tangle of berry brambles, looking for a way through. He tried to shove his way into a place where the thorny vines grew thinner. He sprang back, his hand already itching with nettle stings. He forced himself to be patient. His search finally revealed a break in the ferns and brambles. He squeezed through. The berry thorns caught at his sleeves and scratched his face and arms. At last, he emerged from the berry patch, back under the shade of the trees. A narrow path ran parallel to the river, leading upward.

Even an animal path was better than none. Crane followed it above the waterfall. He continued muttering the protective spell, his imagination filled with falling trees and other dangers he had never considered before. The trees here looked even more ancient, their branches and roots weirdly tangled. Massive mats of roots uplifted where huge trees had fallen. Crane imagined wild beasts living in the hollows of those great trunks and hurried on.

The sky was bright overhead, but the sun had dropped out of sight behind the mountains. Crane stepped across a small, clear stream running down to the river. Near this creek five huge firs and cedars grew intertwined into one mass. Crane lit a campfire nearby and heated water for tea. He thanked Elic for this small comfort, though camping that evening was a lonely affair, with none of the laughter and wonder of the previous night.

He opened his pack, appalled at how little food remained after only two days. *It sounded so simple, following a dream*, he thought. *There are all these things I didn't foresee*. As if on cue, his ankle throbbed again. He murmured the charm, which he now knew by heart. It gave some relief, and he turned his attention to his rumbling stomach. He hated to cut so deeply into his meager supplies, but he couldn't go on if he starved himself. "I'll find something," he said at last, and broke the remaining loaf of bread in two. He also divided the rest of the cheese, though it no longer amounted to more than a few bites. Half he ate, half he put away. When that was gone, he'd have to trust his luck.

After supper, Crane climbed up into a snug alcove in the clump of trees and sat with his back against one of the trunks, muttering protective spells, alert to danger. As he gazed up at the twilit sky, a small bat fluttered out of its roost in the deeply grooved bark of a fir. The tiny creature was soon joined by more of its kind, swooping and darting after mosquitoes. Crane broke off his spellcasting to watch. He chuckled. "Thank you, little friends." He soon dropped into exhausted sleep.

Crane flew on great, white wings. Another flew beside him; he saw the fierce eye and cruel beak of an eagle. He drew back from it, fearful. The eagle turned its head and looked at him, and for a moment it had a human face with a human smile. Then it was the wild bird of prey again. Crane no longer feared the eagle. But there was still fear, of something else he couldn't name.

Yrae soared over the forest on eagle's wings, then returned to his hidden mountain dwelling. The boy was on his way. He followed the pull with unerring accuracy — a testament to his power, and to Yrae's. Even injury didn't stop him. Soon, at long last, they would meet.

Chapter 19. Giants and Phantom Pains

Crane woke at dawn, cold, cramped, and sore. He hadn't slept well enough to feel rested, but there was little chance of going back to sleep. A chipmunk scratched and nosed at his knapsack.

"Good morning, thieving rascal." Crane opened the pack and offered a morsel of bread. The little animal stuffed the food into its cheek and waited for more. "Sorry, I'll be on scant rations myself today." The chipmunk bounced away, barely touching the ground. Crane laughed at it and at himself. "I have been a fool, if the worst I have to fear is you and these ferocious insects. Perhaps there is no danger at —"

A figure emerged from the forest, higher up the little stream. In form, it appeared to be a man, though like no man Crane had ever seen. Crane scrambled down from his perch. It had been years since he had looked *up* at another person's face. This face was darker than his own, though no older, to judge by the scanty growth of whiskers on the chin. The towering stranger wore deerskin clothing and a woven hat like a shallow basket. His black hair, longer than Crane's, hung in a braid down his back. He stood perfectly still while Crane gawked at him, as much a part of the forest as the trees and shadows.

Giant. Crane stared in stunned silence, too startled to be afraid. *The stories are true. There are giants in these mountains.* Yrae was real, giants were real ... Would he also meet dragons and monsters on this quest?

He'd parted from Elic only a day ago. It seemed much longer since he had seen another person. He hadn't expected to meet anyone in the middle of this trackless forest, and certainly not a mysterious giant.

They gazed at each other in silence until the newcomer spoke, a rapid series of clicks and guttural syllables. Crane shook his head. Maybe he was still dreaming. The stranger spoke more slowly, touching his chest and repeating the same group of sounds. "Chamokat." His name? Crane tried his best to repeat the word, and the man smiled. He pointed at Crane, who spoke his own name in a strangled whisper.

"Crane," the stranger repeated. He reached into a basket at his side and pulled out a silvery fish. He put it in Crane's hand, clicked again, and vanished into the forest as if he had never been.

Crane stood holding the fish and stared into the unbroken and apparently uninhabited forest. *Could I follow him? But I have my own path.*

With a shake of the head, he turned his attention to the strange gift he had received. A dead fish? No, breakfast. The trout was freshly caught and cold from the stream. Crane's sense for hidden things guided his knife in slitting the belly, though it was still a slimy, bloody job. He stripped out the insides and cast them off to the side.

Crane lacked the utensils and seasonings his mother had used to prepare the one fish he remembered eating. He lit a fire and made do with a sharpened stick to broil the fish. He could hardly wait while it cooled enough to eat, his stomach growling like a wild beast. At last, he picked the flesh from the bones with his fingers and devoured every flaky morsel, silently thanking his benefactor at each bite.

As Crane washed the fish grease from his fingers, a deep, chuckling bark rattled through the trees. Crane looked around uneasily, half expecting another giant to appear. From high overhead, a raven flapped to the ground. It cocked its head and stared at Crane with one shiny black eye. It walked to the little heap of fishbones, head, and guts, snatched them up, and bore them away. Nothing would be wasted.

Misty Pass

Ketty woke early from a dream of running barefoot over sharp stones. She found no injury and massaged the pain away. Out in the chicken yard, a rooster crowed. Ketty gave up any notion of going back to sleep. She shivered out of bed and dressed quickly in the cold gray light of summer dawn in the mountains.

She braided her hair and tied a kerchief over it that was so faded it was a memory of green. When she was a little girl, Ketty's mother had dressed her in cool shades of green and blue to set off her fiery red hair. She remembered her mother's beautiful dark brown hair, and the subtle red lights in it when the sun shone on her head. To see that sight again, even once ...

Wishing wouldn't bring Mama back or change the color of Ketty's hair. It wasn't even the color she minded, so much as the attention it attracted. But attention meant business. Nothing she couldn't deal with.

Ketty crossed the dark common room to the kitchen. With the skill of long habit, she built up the banked cooking fire and lit the lamps. She paused for a moment to admire her domain, glowing with warm lamplight, and only briefly quiet and empty. There was plenty of work to do before the guests woke, wanting breakfast.

She was humming over a pot of porridge when Papa emerged from his bedroom, stretching his strong arms and scratching his big belly.

"Well, look who woke the sun." He kissed the top of her head.

She smiled at him. "It never hurts to get an early start." There was no need to trouble him with her dream of sore feet.

Ketty expected to spend a routine day cooking and serving meals, cleaning rooms, and dancing away from outstretched hands. In the middle of the morning, her right ankle suddenly flared with excruciating pain, and something tore at the soles of both feet. Blinking back tears, she leaned her broom against the wall and limped to a bench. She sat and removed her shoes. The pain spoke of blisters, bruising, blood; her eyes saw only uninjured feet. Ketty gently rubbed her soles and toes, and the pain faded, though not from her memory. It reminded her of the way she sensed other people's emotions, only more extreme. This was someone else's pain. She was sure it was a message, a warning or a plea for help. But from whom? And why to her? She didn't see anyone else limping or checking their feet.

The Forest

Besides making an excellent breakfast, the fish allowed Crane to save his remaining food, barely enough for a meager lunch. He was happy to refill his water flask from the clear, rushing stream. Much more appetizing than the silty river. He renewed the charm on his ankle and set off, in a less fearful and more wondering frame of mind.

He didn't bother with protective spells this morning. He chose instead to pay more attention to the forest. Everything about these ancient trees was twisted: branches, roots, the bark itself. A few huge trunks, hollow and nearly dead, lifted tufts of foliage high overhead, reaching toward the sun. He passed uneasily under fallen trees hanging over the trail, though they seemed solid and stable, as if they had always rested in that attitude.

For all Crane knew, the forest teemed with more giants, silent and unseen. The one he'd met was harmless, even friendly. There was no reason to fear them. The place was surprisingly devoid of any other large animal life. Though he had seen tracks and heard noises in the undergrowth, he hadn't even seen deer. Chipmunks and birds were everywhere, and insects. The only large animal was Crane himself. All his fears were foolish.

He sipped water as he hiked, saving his food until the sun was high. He ate slowly to make the hunk of stale bread and bit of greasy cheese last longer. His food supply was gone, and he didn't know how much farther he had to journey. The sour, yeasty smell that clung to the empty napkin brought tears of homesickness to his eyes. His stomach wasn't close to full, and his chest felt equally hollow. He had come so far, turning back was not an option. He flicked the tears away and took a long drink to fool his stomach. The trail rose up and away from the river, his faithful guide. He hated to leave it, but there was no other way to go.

Misty Pass

Ketty didn't have time or patience to solve a mysterious message, if that's what it was. But it filled her with restless energy. She completed her chores quickly and started cooking supper early. She enjoyed these rare occasions, as it eased the burden of the supper hour. Made ahead, soup could stay hot on the back of the stove. It would even improve with the extra time. As she cooked, Ketty grew calmer, as if lentil soup and corncakes were the correct answer to the message. She laughed at the ridiculous notion, happy for the first time all day.

The Forest

Away from the water, the insects lessened their attack, and the air cooled as Crane climbed higher, though the afternoon sun shone hot on his skin. Higher up, the forest changed again. The trees were smaller, slender, symmetrical evergreens with branches growing out of the trunk from bottom to top. The trees grew shorter and more sparsely as he climbed higher. On exposed slopes, they lost their symmetry, having branches only on the sheltered side. In places, they were only a little taller than Crane himself, though they had the look of great age. These looked so unlike their tall, graceful counterparts, Crane wasn't sure how he knew they were the same species. It was as if the trees had somehow told him themselves.

He leaned on his staff as he limped along, his feet protesting every step. He spoke to his ankle more than once, but the charm had less effect as he grew wearier. He ignored the pain and trudged on. As afternoon merged into evening, he left the last bit of forest, a few scattered islands of stunted, wind-twisted trees. Above him, bare rock stretched to the top of the ridge. Moss, grass, and wildflowers clung to tiny cracks.

Crane began an eager scramble up the steep, rocky slope. The top was farther away than he'd assumed, but he finally stumbled onto a flat open space. This gave him a sense of achievement, though he had no idea where he had gotten to, other than a long way from home. He turned and looked back over the way he had come. Gazing down at treetops, his brain reeled. *I'm a bird,* he thought, giddy. *If only I could fly the rest of the way.*

Though the sun had not yet set, the depths of the valley were already in shadow. The mountain's snowy peak seemed close enough to touch. Crane yearned toward it, but there was no clear path from where he stood. Beyond it, a range of mountains stretched away to the south, green fading to gray in the distance. A haze of moisture blurred the trees below into a nubbly carpet of green.

The long uphill hike had kept Crane hot and sweating even as the sun sank and the air cooled. Now he shivered in cold and clammy clothes. He unpacked the woolen cloak and draped it over his shoulders, pack and all. Its heavy warmth felt reassuring, like strong hands on his shoulders. In the time it took to wrap himself, the moisture in the air condensed into rivers of fog in the valleys, rippling and undulating as it flowed into all the low places.

Crane's feet demanded rest, and his throbbing ankle could barely support his weight. He was ready to drop and sleep where he stood, too weary even to speak the charm again. The idea of sleeping out was so unappealing, whether on this rocky ridge or in the foggy forest, Crane hesitated to make camp. Maybe he could go farther and find a more protected spot. He peered down into the valley on the other side of the ridge.

Was that a flicker of firelight? Crane blinked and looked again. There it was again, barely a glimpse, much closer than he dared hope. He nearly wept with relief. He didn't know who or what he might find in the light of that fire. But fire meant food, shelter, and comfort, all things he desperately needed. As suddenly as it had appeared, the gleam was obscured by fog. With hope of a refuge, Crane hobbled down into the trees and the ghostly river of mist.

A short time later, he staggered out of the dark and dripping forest into a large clearing. It was lighter here, but wetter. He put up his hood against the soaking mist and took a few steps forward, into the middle of a good, wide road. Ahead of him stood a cluster of log buildings — a small village, though he guessed by the many lighted windows it was a bigger place than Deep River. Here was the source of the welcoming beacon. Crane followed his nose into the village more than his eyes. An enticing aroma reached out from a long, two-story building, solidly built of heavy logs. The faded sign over the door read The Fogbank — Food and Lodging. Crane sighed with relief, and with his last remaining strength, leaned against the door and tumbled inside.

Chapter 20. A Stranger

Misty Pass

Ketty stole a moment while the soup simmered to read one of the tales of adventure and magic. All the stories she'd read so far concerned wizards fighting monsters or boys seeking wizards to help them accomplish an important task. This one was different, about a healer-witch who could follow a dying soul to the Other Side. If she was fast enough, she could bring them back and restore them to life. It was the reverse of the Old Mother Bones tales Ketty had grown up with. She had never read about a healer as the hero; her pulse quickened at this unusual adventure. The Other Side, even without much description, seemed more dangerous than the mountains and islands in the wizard stories.

Ketty reluctantly put the book away and prepared the common room for suppertime. In the middle of this ordinary task, both feet burned with overwhelming pain. She reeled from the suddenness of it, but the scent of lentils cooking revived her. She slid to the floor and leaned back against the wall.

As Ketty wiped tears from her eyes, the front door opened. A tall figure stood silhouetted against the pale, misty light. Or did this person carry their own light? Though the face was obscured, the form looked familiar, and Ketty clenched her fists in her lap. *How dare he come here?* She glared at the man as he hesitated in the doorway.

He didn't look her way as he limped in and dropped onto a bench by the door. He said something in a faint voice that startled her with its youthful tone.

"Mama?"

Now she saw a brown, wiry young man, a disheveled, exhausted traveler. Untidy black hair was tied back off a frowning face, scratched and lumpy with insect bites. The traveler's shirt sleeves were torn and speckled with blood. He wore an old gray cloak, patched and frayed, and clutched a walking stick that shimmered with a strange blue light. It must have been wet, reflecting lamplight.

Ketty didn't know this traveler, and her anger subsided, though uneasiness remained. There was something about him, at once familiar and strange. He stared at her as if he didn't know where he was. He opened and closed his mouth, trying to speak, but unable. Ketty was staring, too. She forced a welcoming smile and climbed to her feet.

"Welcome, traveler." She winced. Her feet ached in protest as she stood. "You're early for supper, but are you hungry?" He nodded and looked relieved. She gestured toward the table. "Please, sit wherever you like."

With great effort, he rose from the bench and shrugged off his cloak and knapsack. He laid them on the bench. He held his walking stick a moment more before leaning it against the wall. He moved like an old man and lowered himself carefully onto the bench at the table.

As he sat, a wave of poignant sadness brought a physical ache to Ketty's chest. She was moved nearly to tears by powerful emotion. It wasn't hers. She drew back from the traveler, and the feeling abated. It was his homesickness she felt.

The stranger glanced around the room, as if seeing wonders. Ketty cleared her throat and regained her composure. "First time stopping at an inn?"

He grinned as if she'd told a joke. "I ... have never traveled from home before." His voice was deeper and more resonant than she would have expected from someone so young, and his smile hinted at kindness and good humor. She thought of thunder and sunshine on a spring day.

"After supper, you are welcome to make your bed in the stable, or here by the fire. Though it will be quieter in the stable."

The scowl returned. "Oh. I couldn't have a real bed, could I? I've slept too many nights on the ground." He grimaced and rubbed his lower back with his hands. "I have money to pay."

"I beg your pardon. I thought ... I mean, you have a bedroll ... Never mind. Yes, you can have a bed." Ketty returned to the kitchen to hide her embarrassment.

"So, girl, where is the innkeeper?" the stranger called after her.

Ketty turned abruptly, holding an empty soup bowl and ladle. "Until my father returns, I am the innkeeper." Girl, indeed!

"Oh," he mumbled.

She accepted this comment as an apology and finished dishing up his food. She set before him a bowl of fragrant lentil soup and a plate of hot corncakes, crisp at the edges. "This will put some life back into you. I expect you're thirsty, too." She drew a mug of foaming brown ale for him.

He drank deeply, then spooned up the soup like he hadn't eaten in days. Ketty understood food was more important than conversation. She left him to his meal. When he had eaten half the bowl of soup, he slowed down and picked up a corncake. He studied it, frowning. He broke off a piece and sniffed it.

He chuckled. "It's like bread. I didn't recognize it."

"I hope it's to your liking."

"I've never liked anything more. I haven't had this kind before."

"In summer, I prefer baking bread on a griddle to heating the oven."

"Smart." He took another swig of ale. "Will you join

me? I've been eating alone for days."

"Just a moment." Ketty took a bowl to the only other guest, a snoring pile of clothes with its head on the table. "Scadi, wake up and eat."

She returned to the stranger's table and sat across from him. She swiped a corncake from his plate. "So. I'm Ketty. Who are you?"

"Nice to meet you, Ketty. My name's Crane."

"Crane. Like the bird? You're not swamp people, are you?" Papa wouldn't like it if he found out she'd fed one of those vagabonds while he was out.

Crane frowned. "I'm from Deep River."

Ketty laughed. "I'd never heard of it until a few days ago, and now here you are! It's on the Dry Side, right? I've often wondered, why would anyone want to live in the desert? There's no water, it's dead."

"Why would anyone want to live in the forest? You can't see more than a few steps in any direction." Ketty was about to defend the beauty of the forest and mountains, but he wasn't finished. "Anyway, it's not a desert. In spring, everything is green, and at harvest time, the fields glow golden. You can see the distinct shape of every hill. The sky is a deep blue clear to the horizon. And the light ..." His eyes shone, and he shook his head as if surprised by what he was saying. "It's not a desert." He bit his lip and blinked rapidly.

Ketty's chest ached again. "You make me want to see it myself." To cheer him and relieve his homesickness, she added lightly, "I don't suppose you care for our wet weather."

"I love the rain. I never get enough," Crane said.

"Spend a winter here, and you'll sing a different

song," Ketty said. He smiled, a smile that warmed her like a fire and drew her gaze. "Is everyone so tall in Deep River?"

"No," he said. "Only me. You know where it is?"

"I've seen it on Papa's map." She tore her gaze from his face to nod toward the large map on the wall behind him.

Crane turned to look at it. "He must be a great traveler."

"No, he's never been anywhere. He likes to find the places his guests come from. He doesn't read, so I help him with the names." Was Crane impressed? He seemed not to have heard, though he got up and limped over to look more closely at the map.

"What's this map of?"

She laughed in surprise. "It's Eukard! Don't you know your own land?"

He stared at her for a moment, uncomprehending. He smiled sheepishly. "Of course I do. I've just never seen a ... such a big map before, that's all. How do you find anything?"

Ketty stood beside him. "Wet side." She slapped her left hand on the left side of the map, which was colored green. "Dry side." She slapped her right hand on the right side, the brown side. "And you are here." She pointed to a dot near the middle. "Misty Pass."

He searched the map until he found and placed his finger on Deep River. He traced a crooked blue line past the dot on the map until it ran into a wider blue line that wandered down the Dry Side from the top of the map and curved across the bottom.

"They need to change that." He allowed his gaze to

sweep back across the map. "What's all this blue?"

She didn't laugh at his ignorance this time. "The sea."

"The sea." He stared hard at it.

The other guest rose and staggered up to Crane. "Flatlander," he muttered derisively, and gave the startled traveler a vicious shove.

"Uncle!" Ketty exclaimed.

Crane righted himself and flung out his arm as he spoke a word Ketty couldn't quite hear. Though Crane barely touched him, Scadi toppled backward and lay unconscious on the floor.

"Sorry," Crane said, and his expression told her he meant it. "I guess I don't know my own strength."

"It wouldn't take much with Uncle Scadi. He's usually drunk, and always disagreeable, poor man. He doesn't like anyone, no matter where they come from. But he's family. We have to take care of him. Here, help me move him." They lifted the limp form and laid him on a broad bench by the fireplace at the end of the room.

When Crane returned to his supper, Ketty started to sit across from him again. She stopped herself and got back to work, though she wanted to keep him talking. She had seen all kinds of people in her short life. Crane wasn't like anyone she'd met. She liked his face, especially when he smiled, and he looked to be about her own age. But that was not reason enough to neglect her work, especially with the supper crowd due any moment. She had never been so drawn to a guest before, and at the same time, so uneasy.

What was it about this strange young man?

Chapter 21. The Fogbank

What was it about this girl?

Crane refrained from reading her thoughts. It wasn't fair to spy that way. Besides, he was exhausted, so maybe it wouldn't work, anyway. As a precaution, he put up a mental barrier as he had with his mother, so stray thoughts wouldn't leak through.

He sneaked glances at Ketty whenever she wasn't looking. It was hard not to notice her, with the fiery red hair. And she cooked a good supper. The plain, hearty fare had renewed his energy and cleared his head. He laughed inwardly at his own confusion when he first arrived, thinking he was at home and this strange girl was his mother. She was small like Mama and had bright hair. Her face had a different shape, its alert expression less dreamy than Mama's. But there was something unusual about her — something missing, or something extra.

When Crane called on his sense for hidden things, he detected only hiddenness, not the thing hidden. She was concealing something, and skillfully. Was she hiding it from Crane, or from everyone?

"I still think you're young to be running an inn," he commented. "You can't be any older than I am."

"Seventeen next week."

"Oh, then we *are* the same age! At least for a few months."

"Papa let me take charge when I was twelve." Ketty set out baskets of hot corn cakes down the center of the table and stacked bowls handy to the soup kettle.

"Your father obviously trusts you. Isn't it dangerous, though? A girl among men —"

"The men who live here know better than to bother me, and strangers don't try anything more than once." She gave him a pointed look.

He swallowed hard. "I ... see."

"So, what are you, Crane?"

"What do you mean?" He wished he hadn't answered so quickly, as if he had something to hide.

"What do you do in Deep River? What work?" She pinned him with an inescapable stare.

He stiffened. "Same as you — I help my mother keep the inn, though she would never leave me in charge."

"Nothing else?"

"Why do you ask?" Crane followed her gaze to his staff. It gleamed softly with a faint blue light only he could perceive.

"When you first came in, I thought you were someone else, a wizard I've seen," she said.

The door opened and a short, sturdy man tromped in, carrying a keg on his shoulder. He was nearly bald and wore a neat white beard. "Evening, Ketty. Ah, an early guest, I see."

"Yes, not only Scadi for a change." She went to help the man with his burden. "Papa, this is Crane, a guest for the night. Crane, my father, Eslo."

"Good to meet you, sir." Crane rose stiffly to his sore feet and stood for a moment before resuming his seat.

"Crane's mother runs the inn at Deep River," Ketty said.

"Deep River?" Eslo said. "Now, we haven't had a guest from down that way since, oh, before you were born, Ketty. Did you ride in, young man? I didn't notice any strange horses in the stable."

"No, I hiked through the forest."

"A long trek through wild country."

"I know." Crane frowned and rubbed his legs.

"We used to get the best apples from Deep River," Eslo sighed. "Do you remember, Ketty? Of course not, it was too long ago. Don't they grow apples down there anymore?"

Crane shook his head. "Water troubles." The mention of apples brought Elic's wise old tree to mind, and a lump rose in Crane's throat. Ketty touched her own throat and backed away.

"Oh?" Eslo said. "Ah. Well, what brings you up this way, lad?" He sat beside Crane.

"Looking for ... someone, sir."

"Whereabouts? Here, in Misty Pass? I know everyone here."

"No, but nearby," Crane said, and waved vaguely toward the north, south, and west. "On the Mountain, I think."

"Not Mountain Folk?" Eslo's eyes narrowed.

Not sure how to answer this question safely, Crane raised his eyebrows and hoped for some help.

"You know, those fierce giants skulking around the forest," Eslo replied with obvious distaste. "Not that I've ever seen one, but I've met many fools who thought they'd go looking."

Crane chose not to mention his encounter with the towering Chamokat. "Oh, no, not me. I'm looking for a ... a hermit."

"Not much better," Eslo muttered. "Never could figure why folks would want to live that way, isolated off in some valley, like they had something to hide." He eyed Crane suspiciously.

"No, I don't know, either ... sir." Crane added his entire quest to the list of things to keep to himself. The longer this conversation continued, the more flustered he became. He was saved by a crowd that filled the room, calling for supper. Crane slid over to make space for them, while Eslo moved off to greet the new arrivals. Crane was about to leave the table when Ketty refilled his soup bowl. He smiled at her, but she had already gone to serve other guests. In any case, it was now too noisy to continue their earlier conversation.

Crane took comfort from the familiar sounds and smells, though it was unsettling to look around at only unfamiliar faces. He observed and listened to the crowd and could soon identify who was a local and who a traveler. There were faces lighter than his mother's and darker than his own, and at least one man near his height, though not as tall as Chamokat. Most of the men wore beards of various lengths, but enough were clean-shaven that Crane did not feel out of place. Crane had never seen such a diverse group. All the world passed through this small town on the way to somewhere else.

Maybe that's our problem. Deep River isn't on the way to anywhere. Maybe I could make a life here ...

The man next to Crane startled him out of his daydream with an elbow nudge to the ribs. "So, stranger, gonna try your luck?"

"Pardon?"

"With her." The man tilted his head toward Ketty. "They say no one's ever managed to lay a hand on her."

Crane watched as she easily eluded several outstretched arms, never losing her smile or dropping plate or cup.

"She does have good reflexes." This game made him uneasy, though he suspected Ketty had nothing to worry about.

"They're just warming up, but so is she! Eyes in the back of her head, I say," the man continued.

Ketty turned and Crane watched the end of her braid, a dancing flame bouncing through the crowd. His head nodded as he listened to it crackle over the dull buzz of conversation.

"You're a stranger here, ain't you? How about we lay

a small wager …Wake up! You'll miss the fun."

Crane jerked his head up, embarrassed to have dozed off at the table. "No, thanks, not tonight. Too tired." He rose from his place and gathered his belongings. He found Eslo in the crowd and said, "You provide excellent hospitality, but I'm near dead on my feet. Ketty said something about a room?"

Eslo snapped his fingers, a sound that carried through the loud talk and laughter. Ketty pushed a standing patron back into his seat. The other guests grumbled. Ketty waved to them and joined her father.

"Please, this way." Ketty opened a door to reveal a steep, narrow staircase disappearing into darkness overhead.

"I'm sorry to trouble you." Crane followed her and her candle up the creaky wooden steps. "I didn't mean to interrupt anything."

She glanced back at him, her mouth a hard line. "Believe me, it's no trouble."

They emerged into a narrow passage lined with four doors on each side and leading to a large open space at the end. "You can bed down in the loft there or take a room if you want privacy."

"A room, thank you."

She showed him into a slant-ceilinged chamber furnished with a bed, a chair, and a washstand with a pitcher and basin. Firewood lay ready for lighting in a small iron stove.

"I didn't expect the best room," Crane protested.

"Trust me, it's no better, and smaller than the others."

"What do I owe you?" He took out his moneybag.

"The room is two duls a night, but for three, you get the room and three meals. How long will you stay?"

"I'm not sure. Maybe two nights?"

"Then put your purse away. We'll settle up before you leave." She went to the bed and turned down the covers. "Why did you come through the forest? Most travelers use the road." She plumped the pillow.

"I didn't exactly know I was coming *here*." He dropped his knapsack on the floor by the bed. "So I went the long way, did I?"

Ketty laughed. "I'm sure it will be much more exciting to tell about afterward."

"I'm glad I chose it so carefully." Would she find the story exciting? He tried to imagine how to tell her about his journey without coming across as a bumbler.

She rubbed her arms. "It's chilly this evening. I expect you'll want a fire."

"You don't need to bother." He pointed his staff at the stove and whispered the fire spell. In his fatigued state, even this small use of magic left him dizzy, but the staff glowed more brightly for a moment and a cheerful blaze sprang up.

"Oh!" Ketty moved toward the door. "Will there be anything else, sir?" Her voice came out a choked whisper.

"No, I —" Crane broke off at the sight of her pale face and startled eyes. "Are you all right?"

She pointed at the crackling fire. "Was that for my benefit?" Her look of surprise shifted to fierce indignation.

"Oh, the fire? No. Yes. I don't know." How could he have forgotten he didn't want to reveal his magic? "I didn't mean anything by it. It's a little something I can do. I'm sorry I frightened you." He offered a weak smile.

"You didn't *frighten* me. But don't let my father see you do that. Or anyone else in this house."

"That's fair. Your father has a problem with magic?"

"He doesn't think much of wizards."

"Neither do I."

"It's not funny. I could ask you to leave at once."

"Please don't. I promise, I won't do anything suspicious. I just need to rest."

"And to wash," she suggested in a tone of disgust. She lifted the pitcher from the washstand and moved toward the door.

He sank down onto the chair and pulled off his boots, wincing as he released his injured ankle. "If it's not too much trouble, could I get warm water to soak my feet? I've never walked this far before, and they're ..." He paused, reluctant to sound weak or like he was complaining. Ketty didn't seem the pitying type, and she was angry already. "... a little sore." He gasped in pain as he pulled off stockings stuck to blisters and stiff with blood. His swollen right ankle had turned a livid purple.

"*A little sore*? I'm surprised you can walk at all. If you're traveling on foot, you'll be stuck here awhile."

"I'm afraid so. Sorry." He offered a weak smile of apology that turned into a pained grimace.

"Some wizard. Not much of a healer, are you?"

"No, not much."

Ketty limped out of the room as if her own feet ached. Assuming she wouldn't return, Crane lowered his barrier to stray thoughts before it sapped his power. She came back with the full pitcher, and a steaming kettle.

She set the basin on the floor at his feet and poured in cold water from the pitcher, then added hot water from the kettle.

Crane lowered his raw and aching feet into the soothing water. "Aahhh. This is magic enough for me right now." He leaned his head back and closed his eyes.

Ketty was silent so long, he thought she'd left. "Are you looking for someone? Or are you running from something?"

Startled, Crane opened his eyes and met her gaze. "Both. There's a curse —"

"There's no curse on you!" She looked flustered. "Is there?"

"I wish I could be so certain. But, no, it's not on me. It's ... back there. And he's up there ... somewhere." He gestured weakly, then dropped his hands into his lap. "And I can't go another step."

"So you're running from it." Her thoughts shouted, *Coward!*

"I'm seeking the remedy." He was gratified when she looked ashamed. "I don't know what to do, but I might know where to find out. I'm the only ... the only one from Deep River who can do it." He paused. "Maybe I'm the only one who cares."

Ketty stared as if trying to peer through his skull. She moved her gaze to his feet soaking in the basin. "Give me your foot."

"Why?" He raised his left foot out of the water.

"If you can show off, so can I." She held his foot in one hand and pressed the palm of the other hand against the sole. She closed her eyes, her brow furrowed in concentration. The blisters stung under the pressure.

After a moment, a pleasant tingling replaced the sting. Ketty lifted his right foot from the water and scrutinized the swollen ankle. "That looks painful. How long have you been walking on it?"

"Since yesterday afternoon."

"You're tougher than you look." She gave him a hint of a smile. "From the extent of the healing, I would have thought longer."

"I've been using a charm on it. I think it helped."

"It helped a great deal. Maybe you're not such a bad healer."

He snorted in reply. She stroked his ankle gently as they talked, then pressed her palm to the sole as she had with the other foot.

"There. That should feel better." She sat back and looked up at him, her face relaxed now. Wisps of copper hair stuck to her damp forehead. "Sorry I can't do anything for your hand."

"My hand?" Crane glanced at his scarred right hand. He tried not to flaunt it in public, and she hadn't appeared to notice. "What about it?"

Ketty bit her lip. "I'm ... sensitive to trauma. And to magic, I guess. Your scar gives off a whiff of both. How'd you get it?"

"Oh, you know, the usual ... set myself on fire. First magic I ever tried."

She stifled a giggle, which pleased him more than he cared to admit. After five years, he could see the humor and much preferred laughter to fear or pity.

"Anyway, it's not like it hurts anymore. Much better to numb these blisters; I should be able to sleep now. Now I know who to call when they ..." Crane examined one foot, then the other. He stared at Ketty in shock. She hadn't only relieved the pain. Both feet were healed. Not a blister, not a bruise remained. He rotated his ankle without the least twinge.

"How did you do that?" he whispered.

"How did *you* do *that*?" She nodded toward the fire. "I only wish I could take care of your socks as easily." She picked them up gingerly.

"I'm not joking, Ketty. You have an amazing gift. You didn't even say any words! Who taught you? Do you have a mentor?"

"No one taught me."

"You did that with no training? Isn't there someone you could study with, a healer or something? Imagine what you could —"

"Keep your voice down!" she interrupted. "My father would never let me. I've never even talked to him about it. I know what he would say."

"You can't deny your gift."

"Why can't I? No one knows of it." She blushed. "I don't heal other people. Not since the first time, anyway. Only injured animals or small hurts of my own. And if you so much as tell anyone, you desert-dwelling snake, I'll —"

Crane raised his hands. "I'll keep your secret. There's no need to get nasty."

Her face crumpled, and she looked for a moment like a frightened, confused child. Crane longed to comfort her, though he wasn't sure what her trouble was.

"I'm sorry, Crane, I don't know why I'm being so mean to you. I wish I hadn't ... but it's too late now. You can call me a name if you want." She smiled weakly.

"A name? Like what? Forest-dwelling ...?"

"Skunk?"

Crane roared with laughter, recalling his illusion that broke up the council meeting. Elic's favorite trick. "No, not a skunk." Maybe another time, he could tell her about it. When he knew her better. He cocked his head to one side and considered. "No, I'd say you're more like a ... a raven."

"Why a raven?" She touched her red hair.

"Not the color. A raven is harsh, and bold ... and wise. Like you."

"Oh." She looked at the floor. "I'm not sure about wise. But thank you."

"Thank *you*. For my feet, I mean. If I had a gift like yours ..."

"I have work to do, and you should sleep." Ketty got to her feet again. She paused at the door, brow furrowed. "You didn't push Scadi, did you?" He looked away sheepishly, but neither affirmed nor denied it. "Well?"

"I wasn't thinking. I'll be more careful after this."

"You'd better be." She hurried from the room without another word.

Crane undressed and flopped onto the bed. Tired as he was, sleep did not come immediately. He lay awake and considered Ketty. She was abrupt, clearly didn't trust him, and probably didn't like him. Nothing new there. She had met his display of magic, not with the fear to which he had grown accustomed, but with anger, followed by a show of her own power. No wonder he had felt drawn to her from the first. She was nice-looking, though that hardly mattered. He recalled every detail of her freckled, pock-marked face, her determined jaw, her flaming hair and brilliant green eyes, her work-roughened hands, her small form in a simple dress. Over this picture his mind draped her breathtaking gift.

Sounds drifted from downstairs. The clomp of heavy boots, the clatter of crockery, and voices raised in boisterous talk and laughter blended into a familiar and comforting hubbub, a lullaby for one at home with inn life. Sometimes Ketty's voice rose above the others, rousing him from half-sleep. As Crane finally drifted off, someone began playing music. In the darkness, he could see the little bone flute as easily as if he sat downstairs. He could almost see the man playing it. The tune settled into the old wordless ballad Mama used to sing, sweet and sad. Tears filled his eyes as he thought of her and home, so distant though he had been gone only a few days. When he slept, he dreamed he held fire in his hand again — not a burning flame, but Ketty's shining hair.

Chapter 22. The Game

Crane enjoyed a restful sleep and woke refreshed the next day ... at sunset. Once he remembered where he was, and why his feet no longer hurt, he smiled to himself and sprang out of bed. When he stretched, his fingers brushed the slanted ceiling, but he was delighted to move without aching.

For the first time in days, he took out the razor Elic had encouraged him to bring. After a twinge of embarrassment at the vanity of cleaning up for a girl (especially a girl who didn't even like him) he shaved his sparse beard. He put on his only clean shirt and went downstairs, ravenously hungry now that his need for sleep had been met.

The Fogbank sounded and smelled familiar. It was larger than the Blue Heron, with more space for overnight guests and a longer common room. Two long trestle tables, benches crowded with supper guests, ran the length of the space, with a gap between to allow passage across the room. Crane found a place and nodded politely to his neighbors as they moved over to make room for him. Ketty brought a steaming plate of food. He beamed at her. His pleasure at seeing her again exceeded that of filling his empty belly.

"So, you decided to rejoin the living." She filled his cup and smiled in response to his fool's grin, though it was an uneasy smile, and she drew back from him with a barely concealed shudder.

"Thank you." The warmth and joy drained out of him. Perhaps she was more like the girls back home than she had seemed. In spite of all she'd revealed, she was still hiding something.

Crane turned to the man next to him, a youngish fellow with a full brown beard and sparkling blue eyes. "Is it always this busy? These can't all be guests at the inn."

"They're not. Most of the unmarried men in the village, and even a few of the married ones, come here for a good supper and a pint or two of an evening," the man replied. "What brings you here, stranger? I haven't seen you before."

"I arrived last night. I need to rest and re-provision."

"A long journey, then? Where you headed?"

"Oh, here and there. Exploring the mountain country."

Scadi, seated across from Crane, eyed him suspiciously.

"Well, you've come to the right place," Crane's neighbor said. "That little gal is as fine a supper-cook as you'll find in these parts, for all she's barely grown. Not so hard on the eyes, either. Going to try your luck?"

"Uh, no. I saw it last night. Not my kind of game."

"Not a gambling man, eh? Just watch, then. It's a good show, and I'd say it's about to begin."

A fat, black-bearded man slipped up behind Ketty with his arms outstretched, as though to embrace her. While he was a few steps away, she calmly set down the mugs she carried and whipped around, caught his wrist, and twisted his arm behind his back. He cried out in pain, while the crowd roared with laughter.

"I've never seen anyone try more than once," Crane's neighbor commented. "I'm not sure I envy the fellow who finally captures that wildcat."

Crane watched in silence. He was impressed with the number of ways Ketty could foil her opponents. She always knew they were there before they reached her, ready with painful or humiliating ways of thwarting them. It dawned on him this was part of her gift. She was showing off without doing obvious magic, and probably drawing customers to the inn. It galled him she should have to put up with such treatment. For now, it was all good-natured, if ribald, fun, but if even one player were gifted enough to outwit Ketty ... Crane didn't care to finish the thought.

As he tried to devise a way to put a stop to this

disrespectful behavior without making trouble for himself, the door opened. A tall, handsome woman of middle age stood in the doorway, dressed in well-cut riding clothes. She looked around the room with amused disapproval, and the game died down on its own.

She removed her bonnet and patted her salt-and-pepper hair. "Eslo, where are you?" she called in a low, musical voice.

"Nari, is that you?" Ketty's father hurried from the back room. "How wonderful to see you!" They kissed each other on the cheek. The look that passed between them spoke of more than friendship. "Ketty, find Nari a seat, will you?"

Ketty embraced the woman with obvious delight. "Welcome back! Come, there's space for you over here. Crane, will you move down a bit? Nari, this is Crane. He's new to us. Crane, this is Nari, a dear, dear friend of ours."

"Will you be wanting a room?" Eslo asked.

"What do you think, love?" she replied with a smile and a wink. "I'll sleep in my usual place, if you don't mind."

"Not at all!" He grinned as he hurried off.

"So, Crane, you're new to the Fogbank, are you?" Nari asked, her dark brown eyes frankly appraising.

"Yes, ma'am, I got in last night."

"You weren't playing these fellows' awful game. I hope you won't. You look like a better lad than that."

"Thank you, ma'am, I hope I am." Crane wanted to make a good impression on this woman, though he didn't know why. "Um ... who are you again?"

Nari laughed, a warm, comforting sound. "The

closest to a mother our girl has. And perhaps the only one interested in stopping that game."

"Why does she put up with it?"

Nari hooted. "Put up with it? It was Ketty's own idea."

"She likes to be grabbed at?"

"No one touches her, do they? It's the only reason Eslo allows it. She encourages the betting and tells them to invite their friends. She thinks it's harmless. I think she's playing with fire. But does she listen?" She paused and gazed shrewdly at Crane. "What are your intentions?"

"About what?"

Nari laughed. "I see how you're looking at her. What are your intentions?"

"I'm not sure I have any. I mean, she's not even wearing the courtship ring."

Nari started. "The ... what?"

"The earring?" Crane touched his own right earlobe.

Nari grinned. "Now where do you come from that they still practice such a quaint custom? I haven't seen that one in years."

"From Deep River. On the Dry Side."

"Well, I've ridden all over that country. I don't believe I've ever been to Deep River."

"By yourself? Is it safe?"

"Mm." Nari patted a knife belted to her waist. "And another in my boot. No one bothers me. Have you ever seen anything like these?" She took a small deerskin pouch from her pocket. She opened it and poured out a handful of polished, glassy stones in shades of yellow and orange. "I trade for them and sell them to jewelers in the city."

"Agates? Yes, of course, they're all over where I'm from. I've never seen them this smooth and shiny. But look at the color of this one." He reached into his own pocket and produced the deep red stone he had carried with him. "I found this one in the road. And my friend back home has one this big." Crane used his fingers to describe Elic's egg-sized stone.

Nari's eyes lit up. "You don't say? I may have to visit this Deep River of yours."

"Good luck. It can be hard to find."

Nari stayed overnight at the Fogbank, but departed early the next morning, to Eslo's obvious dismay. That night at supper, the game resumed in earnest, and no one came in to stop it. Nari was right about one thing — no one managed to touch Ketty. Crane doubted Ketty still thought it was harmless fun, though. She looked tired, and her forced smile barely concealed growing irritation. As if she had started something she didn't know how to stop.

After watching three attempts, Crane slipped out of his seat. He didn't want to draw attention, but the men around him cheered and pushed him forward. The room was noisy, and Ketty didn't notice. He crept up behind her, and as with the others, she spun and caught his wrist before he could touch her. She froze, her fixed smile replaced with a look of horrified surprise.

Her expression pained him. He was glad he'd blocked

her thoughts. He bent and whispered in her ear. "Remember Scadi? Like this." He added one more word. She frowned; a slow smile spread over her face as she understood.

"Now you won't even have to touch them," Crane murmured as he straightened up. Ketty squeezed his hand once and released him. He bowed gallantly and returned to his place at the table.

"What did you say to her, lad?" his neighbor pressed. "No one has ever gotten so far."

Crane merely smiled, drained his mug, and returned to his room. From downstairs, he heard the cries. "Did you see that? She never touched him!"

Crane laughed, alone in his room. She had more use for the repelling charm than he did. He was glad to help her and did not expect more thanks than her smile. But he did hope for more.

Chapter 23. A Deep Longing

As soon as Crane was rested enough to think clearly, the pull that had drawn him from Deep River reasserted itself. He was sure he must be close to his goal. Because of Ketty and his hope of kindling a friendship — or more — Crane stayed a few more days at the Fogbank. He delayed buying provisions and pretended he was still recovering from his earlier trek. Who wouldn't prefer flirting with a pretty girl to a dangerous quest? When he was with her, the thrill and terror reminded him of the first time he spoke magic words. He didn't know what was happening, but he couldn't stop if he tried.

He contrived to be near her as much as possible. He ate every meal offered in the common room and spent part of each day reading the healer's book there. It was too hot in his room during the day, a good excuse. Although Ketty always greeted him with a wave or a smile, she didn't seem inclined to closer contact. Crane would have been willing to accept Ketty's attitude as businesslike. Like Mama, she was friendly and hospitable to all her guests without showing obvious favor to anyone. Eslo kept a similar cordial distance, with everyone except Nari, who was clearly more like family. Crane suspected Ketty deliberately kept her distance from him for more than business reasons. When he approached her or she had to be near him, she drew back with a pained wince. But he couldn't bring himself to leave.

A couple of days after he'd given her the repelling charm, Crane stayed at the table following lunch and pored over a page of the healing book. He didn't know all the herbs it referred to, nor the conditions, nor even the body parts, but it was written with such reassuring confidence, he devoted himself to each section on the chance of learning anything useful.

"So, you can read, too."

Crane started and looked around at Ketty with undisguised pleasure. "Of course. What do you mean, *too*?"

"Not many people here ever learned to read, but my mother taught me. She had plans to open a school ..." Ketty closed her eyes as she trailed off. "What sort of book is it?"

"Here, see for yourself." He closed the book and handed it to her. "This will mean something to you, so I'm glad you can read. I didn't know what a rare thing it was around here. Where I come from, we all know how to read, thanks to a man of vision."

She glanced at the cover and the first few pages. She beamed. "Healing charms? Medicinal herbs? All in a book?" Greedily, she flipped through the pages.

Crane laughed. "I'm trying to learn something useful. I don't know whether it's working, though that one charm was helpful. Whoever wrote it, I trust her. Well, I assume it's a *her*."

Ketty held the volume out to him, though he could tell she didn't want to. "I have work to do. May I borrow it later?"

"Hold onto it for now," he said. "It's probably more useful to you than to me."

"Thank you! I'll take good care of it." She slipped the book into her pocket, tied on a bonnet, and picked up a large basket. "It's market day."

"Let me come with you. I need provisions for my journey."

As they walked toward the center of the village, Crane stared around him, taking in every detail of Misty Pass. It wasn't as strange now to think of other places, but the fact of being in one still astonished him.

"So, how does Misty Pass compare to Deep River?" Ketty asked.

"It's larger, I think. Not as spread out," he said. "The houses are different, though. Your roofs look steeper. And we have stone houses, mostly. I've never seen such big logs before!"

"When you live in a forest, you build with logs. I'm not sure I can even picture a house built of stones."

A din of voices, laughter, and music announced the market, where booths offered all kinds of goods. Crane had never been in such a crowd, but took a deep breath and plunged in. Yet another new experience.

"I've never seen anything like this!" He gazed over heads at the colorful displays.

"Don't you have markets in Deep River?"

"They're not much. A few local farmers and craftsmen. But this! Look at it all!"

Ketty gazed around at the piles of produce and other goods. "We do get a lot of variety. Everybody passes through here. We get crops from the east, and goods from the west; from the city."

"What city?" Crane asked.

She laughed at him. "Eukard City. The capital!"

"Where is it?"

"West of here, about a day by coach. I'll show you on the map when we get back." She shook her head. "Don't you know anything? This is the main road over the mountains. Don't your young people dream of going away to the city?"

"No. We never talk of other places. Except ... they used to. Not anyone my age."

"We all talk about the day we'll leave this place, even those who never will."

Crane scowled. "Well, here I am, the first person in years to leave Deep River, and I miss the old place so much it hurts. Yet I'm not sure I'll ever go back. I did promise, though." He gave himself a shake. "Never mind."

Ketty smiled uneasily. She walked on with him, though she kept her distance. Here he thought he'd made progress, but she still didn't trust him.

Crane visited every booth, even those with nothing he needed for his journey. Ketty humored him and at least glanced at everything for sale. Her purchases were all practical — cooking staples, new winter blankets, an iron skillet.

He stopped at the back of a crowd of children watching a puppet show. He knew a version of this story about a wizard on a quest to collect magical dragon scales, but he delighted as much as the young ones in the colorful figures and funny voices.

"I've seen it," Ketty said. "Meet me over there."

She wandered away to a nearby booth they hadn't visited yet. Without her there, Crane soon lost interest in the show and followed her.

A pungent fragrance rose from a display of dried leaves, twigs, and bark, set out in jars on a shelf at the front of a booth. Even from a distance, Crane recognized a few as common medicinal herbs, found in most households for treating simple complaints. Aunt Sudi would have grown them in her own garden or gathered them from the countryside; he wasn't sure why anyone would buy them at the market. Most of the display was foreign to him, and apparently to Ketty, too, to judge by her interest. He wished she could buy these things and learn their uses, instead of sneaking around, keeping secrets and wasting her power.

"Do you have any questions?"

Ketty took a step back. A silver-haired man had appeared from the shadowed back of the booth. He wore a patch over one eye. The other gazed down at her from an unnatural height. Crane stepped closer in case she needed help.

"Um ... yes, what is this for?" She pointed to a curled piece of stiff, brown bark.

The herbalist smiled, showing large teeth. He stepped back from the shelf and emerged from the booth. He must have been standing on a box — he wasn't much taller than she was. He lifted a piece of the bark between his thumb and long forefinger. He held it under his equally long nose and sniffed delicately. "You have a healer's eye. This is tana bark, a powerful medicine."

"A powerful medicine for what?"

"Swamp fever. Rare at this elevation, so you're unlikely to ever need tana. Still, I have a loyal customer near here who always keeps a supply on hand. Here, take a whiff."

He broke off a fragment and held it under Ketty's nose. She sniffed and grimaced. "Oh! I can taste it!"

"Powerful medicine. What else can I show you, Miss ...?"

"Ketty. Nothing, thank you, sir. I must go."

"Please, call me Fane. But are you sure? A good healer should be well-stocked for any turn of events."

"I'm sorry, sir ... Fane," she stammered. "You must have me confused with someone else. I'm not —"

"No need to explain. If you wish to buy another time, I'll be back this way in a month."

"I ... I'll think about it."

Ketty turned away from the herbalist's booth and nearly collided with Crane. He couldn't tell whether she was frightened or irritated, but she didn't look pleased to see him.

"Why didn't you buy anything?"

"I can't. Do you have everything you came for?"

"No, I need travel rations. Here, let me carry some of that." Crane held out his hands and she passed him the larger bundles that wouldn't fit into her basket.

"Thanks." She made her way through the crowded market. "Can I ask you something, Crane? You say you keep an inn with your mother. What about your father?"

Crane tensed all over. He forced himself to speak calmly. "My father ... left, the same night I was conceived. Without saying goodbye. What about your mother?"

Ketty didn't answer immediately, but fingered a pockmark on her cheek, just below her left eye. "She died. When I was eight years old, we both got sick. Many people did, even our healer, so there was little help to be had. I ... I got better. Mama didn't. Papa heard a wizard was in town and sent for him. He wouldn't come, the horrible old thing! I hate him, I hate Yrae!"

Ketty spoke with such heat, Crane felt burned. She pinched her lips together and looked at the ground. Crane didn't say anything for a time. "No wonder your father has a low opinion of wizards. Do you think you healed yourself?"

"I don't know. Probably I was lucky. Other people survived, too. Soon after I recovered, I discovered this ... ability. Too late to save her."

"You were only a child! Maybe even Yrae couldn't have saved her."

Ketty didn't answer. She pointed out a booth selling nuts and dried provisions, both fruits and meat. Crane made his purchases. When he joined her again, she seemed calmer, though still edgy. No surprise, if she had to deny and hide her spectacular gift. But now she had openly displayed it to Crane, a stranger, and a wizard. And the herbalist said she had a healer's eye.

"Let's go," she said before Crane could speak. "So, he's alive? Your father?"

"I don't know. My mother thinks so."

"That's good, isn't it?"

Crane stopped in the middle of the road. His chest ached. "You knew your mother. You remember her, and you know what happened to her. You miss her, but at least you know."

"She's still dead." Ketty shivered, though the midday sun beat down. "Isn't alive always better than dead?"

"It should be. I don't know. I never knew my father. I don't know who he is, or what, or where. All I know is, he didn't want me."

"How can you be sure? Did he even know about you?"

Crane shook his head. "I don't know. I guess not. I don't know who he is. Why should he know who I am?" He slashed the air with his hand. "Never mind. It's too pathetic!"

They walked toward the inn, more slowly now that they were burdened with their purchases. Crane appreciated how Ketty didn't try to fill the silence with chatter. He listened to the breeze in the treetops. The soothing whisper calmed him.

"You don't even know his name?" she asked.

"I know a name he used; I even share it. I doubt it was his real name." This wasn't even close to the conversation Crane wanted to have with Ketty, but it was better than nothing. She walked beside him, more than an arm's length away, as if wary of his reaction. "I know what my mother believes about him or wants me to believe. I don't know if any of it is true." He sighed and his shoulders drooped.

"Why don't you try to find him? That's what I would do if I were a wizard. Search for him!"

Crane's anger kindled again. "Why would I want to do that? I already have one quest that will probably be the death of me." He strode on, more quickly now, past the log houses and workshops lining the road. Ketty hurried to keep up.

"Crane." She grasped his sleeve. He turned and glared at her. She gasped but didn't move away. "The day you arrived my feet ached all day. They didn't stop hurting until I'd healed you. When you speak of your father, I feel another ache, an empty place inside you, a deep longing."

He stared at her, then stalked away. This brief conversation had scraped every nerve. It hurt to talk openly about his missing father. It hurt in a different way to be near Ketty, to be for the moment the center of her attention, close enough to hear her breathe. The shock of her outburst about Yrae didn't help.

He arrived at the Fogbank first and shouldered the door open without waiting for Ketty. Once inside, he didn't know where to go. He paused at the door to the stairway. His upstairs room held no appeal in the heat of the day. He wasn't sure he trusted himself in the more public space downstairs.

Ketty followed him inside and opened the door to her own room to set her basket inside. She approached Crane, hesitated, and laid a hand on his shoulder. Her touch tingled all through him, and he drew a sobbing breath.

"I'm sorry," she said. "I presumed. You're angry."

Crane took a moment to control himself. "No. I mean, yes, but not at you. At least, not only at you. Because you're probably right." He turned to give her the parcels he'd carried for her.

He followed as Ketty added them to the pile in her room. "Then, what —?" When she found him blocking the doorway, she took a startled step back.

"Ketty, I do have a deep longing, but it isn't for my father." Crane worked to speak quietly while his feelings shouted. He gripped her shoulders and pressed his lips to hers. He'd never kissed a girl before, so it was rougher than he intended. For a moment, she seemed to be teaching him how to do it better. She broke away.

"How about that?" Ketty's voice was breathless and laughing. "No one's ever taken me by surprise before. That's two points for you."

Already aflame, Crane had no patience with her light tone, which only added fuel. He gripped her tighter and bent to kiss her again. She squirmed and turned her head aside so his lips landed on her ear. He drew back but kept his tight hold on her.

She stared up at him, her eyes wide and her cheeks red. Not scared. Furious. "No. Not like this." She pushed him away and spoke the repelling charm in a sharp voice. Crane gasped as it struck him, a solid punch. He stumbled backward out of the room. Ketty slammed and bolted the door behind him.

Chapter 24. A Common Enemy

Ketty leaned against the door, fully expecting Crane to either batter the door down or offer a chastened apology. She heard instead his heavy tread on the stairs. When his door slammed overhead, she slid to the floor, trembling. Her heart pounded and she could barely catch her breath. She set her jaw and gritted her teeth, fighting back tears. She had resisted or deflected unwanted attention before, but she had never felt this confused and upset afterwards. Perhaps because this time, a man's attention wasn't altogether unwanted.

She rested her cheek against her drawn-up knees. It wasn't only that he was young and attractive, unlike most of the men she rejected without a thought. He was ... like her. That was part of the problem. How could she be with a wizard? But he needed her, foolish as that sounded. His father had hurt him. She wished she could help him somehow. If only it weren't so hard to be near him.

Ketty stayed in her room long enough to calm down. She tried to view the situation with cool logic. *You don't love him, and he doesn't love you. He's another guest at the inn, no better, no worse.* She stood up resolutely, splashed cool water on her hot face, and returned to the day's work.

Busy with cooking, washing, and serving other guests, she hardly had time to think about Crane. He didn't come down for supper, and she was just as glad. *Let him go hungry, for all I care. I'm not his mother.* She had no patience for games of any kind. The few guests who dared try their luck got an unusually vicious response, and everyone else took the warning.

Crane stomped into his room and slammed the door behind him. The air was hot and still, but there was no way he was going back downstairs. He opened the window and flopped onto his bed. He wanted more than anything to leave his room, leave the Fogbank, leave Misty Pass. But Ketty was downstairs. He reached into his bag for the green book. It was downstairs with her.

He was trapped with nothing to do except regret his wrongheaded move.

After a while, he got up and packed his belongings and provisions. He could leave as soon as the inn settled down for the night. He counted out fifteen duls to cover his lodging and meals and left them outside the door. Ketty could believe what she liked about him, but not that he didn't pay what he owed.

Crane lay down to wait, stewing in his anger and guilt. His stomach hurt. Even the smells and sounds of suppertime couldn't whet his appetite. The room stayed stuffy and hot though the window was wide open. He doubted he'd get any sleep this night. He might as well be on his way.

When all the other guests had finally gone home or to bed, Ketty relented and went upstairs to ask if Crane wanted supper. Even through the closed door, a dark storm of anger battered her. She stepped back without knocking.

Something on the floor gleamed in the light of her candle — a neat stack of old silver duls. He'd settled his bill. He planned to leave.

"Good." Ketty scooped up the coins and dropped them into her apron pocket. "About time." She retreated to her own room and bolted the door. If Crane wanted to talk to her, she might listen, but she wouldn't let him surprise her in her sleep.

As it turned out, there wasn't much chance of that.

She lay awake most of the night.

The next thing Crane knew, he was waking in a cold, dark room. He didn't feel rested, but the inn lay hushed. It was time to go. He gathered his things and crept down the stairs, his boots in his hand. With his bill settled, there was no reason to disturb anyone on his way out.

Ketty was already in the kitchen, cooking something that made Crane's mouth water.

"I couldn't let you leave without a decent breakfast," she whispered

"How did you know I was going?"

"You paid your bill."

Crane sat and accepted porridge, bread, and tea. Ketty's behavior and even her words again reminded him of his mother, an unsettling comparison now. "Thank you. I have plenty of food with me."

"I was awake already. And you paid for the meal."

Crane ate in silence. The lack of supper had finally caught up with him, and he didn't know what to say. "I'm sorry" fell far short, but there wasn't anything else. Ketty dished up breakfast for herself and sat across from him.

He sipped tea to moisten his suddenly dry throat. "I'm ... surprised you want to be in the same room with me."

She sucked in a breath. "I trust you."

"You shouldn't. If I knew the right spell, I'd erase yesterday."

"Don't wish that. We had a good time for most of it."

"Until I ruined everything. But I'm not like that."

"Aren't you?"

Exactly the question he'd been asking himself. "You're the first girl I've ever really gotten to know. Certainly, the first I ever kissed! At home, they're all afraid of me or ashamed of me or ... I don't know what. It was new for me, talking to you, maybe being friends ..." He trailed off with a sigh. "I didn't mean to spoil everything. I can't tell you how sorry I am."

"You don't have to tell me. I know. Next time you kiss a girl, don't do it that way. Ask first."

Crane tried to smile. "Then you don't hate me anymore?"

"When did I ever hate you? I just couldn't stand to be close to you."

He frowned again. "Oh, so I merely disgust you."

"You don't understand, and I don't think I can explain. Please don't be angry with me."

"I'm not!" he said. "I thought *you* were angry with *me.*"

"I was. Maybe I should be, but ... I don't know. You have enough anger for both of us. And there's little I couldn't forgive, except leaving without saying goodbye. Especially on my birthday."

"Is it today?" Crane asked. "I'm sorry if I ruined it."

"You haven't yet," she said. "You were going to sneak off, weren't you?"

"Yes," Crane admitted. "I guess I'm just like my father."

"How? Lonely and scared?"

Crane answered Ketty with a scowl. It was disconcerting, how she knew what he was feeling almost before he did.

She rolled her eyes at him. "What's wrong? The big man can't admit he's afraid?"

"*Lonely and scared* describes me well. Maybe my father was, too. I don't suppose I'll ever know. To think I would try to take advantage of a defenseless girl, and then leave without even apologizing."

Ketty snorted. "I'm hardly defenseless, Crane. Thanks to you, I'm better armed than ever."

"Let me say it anyway. I'm sorry. You deserve better. I hate to see them treat you that way, like a game piece. They don't even know what you're capable of. And I showed myself to be just as bad! Hah!"

"You're the first who was ever sorry."

Crane shook his head. Her assurance didn't help much. "What do they hope to get if they win?"

"What did you hope to get?" Ketty looked straight at him, but Crane was too ashamed to hold her gaze. "Don't worry about me, Crane. Anything anyone gets from me will be freely given, or not at all. Their kind will never catch me."

"How do you do it, though? Is it ... magic?"

She smiled. "You're the wizard — you tell me!" He shrugged, and she went on. "You know how they say a dog can smell fear?"

"You *smell* them?"

"Some of them." She grinned. "I *know* they're there, before they're nearly close enough to even touch me. I sense their feelings, their nervousness, their embarrassment, excitement. I focus on the players, and I always know right where they are. None of them have a chance of sneaking up on me."

"You ... feel what they feel? That must be hard to live with."

She laughed. "You have no idea!"

"Maybe I do. When people are stirred up, I sometimes hear their thoughts."

"Really?" Ketty's voice rose in pitch, and her cheeks went pink.

"Don't worry, not yours. Before I left home, I figured out how to block them, and I've been practicing here. With this many people, I wouldn't be able to hear my own thoughts."

Ketty drooped with relief. "I wish I could do that with emotions. Ordinary, everyday feelings aren't so bad. If someone is, as you say, *stirred up*, I have to leave the room. That's usually enough. But with ..." She looked away, no longer so self-possessed.

"With me?" Crane guessed, with a resigned sigh. "Leaving the room doesn't help. Why not?"

"Have you ever felt, even when you're surrounded by other people, you're alone in the world?" Ketty asked.

It didn't answer his question, but he let it go. "Most of my life. I'd never met another person like me, until I came here. Until I met you."

"We're the same in that. The night you walked in, it was like a window blew open inside me, and I don't know how to close it. I can't hide my gift from you, and I can't shut you out."

"Ah. That settles it. I should leave."

"You don't have to go on my account. I'm ... managing."

"Do you want me to stay, then?" Crane leaned forward, unable to hide his eagerness.

Ketty sighed. "No. But if you're not ready to go yet…"

She was giving him an out. He could pretend he needed more rest and preparation, and maybe she'd warm to him. "Thanks, I'd better go today. This quest won't finish itself."

"This quest of yours … what is it?"

"You haven't guessed by now? I'm seeking Yrae."

Ketty flinched. "What have you to do with that old villain?"

"It's the curse I was telling you about. He put a spell on my village before I was born. I'm going to find out why, and force him to lift it, if I can."

"You're going to fight him?"

"Everybody asks that! No, I hope not. What chance would I have?"

"I know where he is."

"Where?" Crane dropped his spoon in his sudden excitement. "Is it far? How do you know?"

"Well, not exactly where. He's up the mountain, somewhere over Sunset Ridge. He comes into the village for supplies. He disguises himself, but I can see through it. I guess I can't block him out, either."

"He comes here, to the inn?"

Ketty frowned. "After what he did to us, he wouldn't dare."

"We have a common enemy, then."

"If you're leaving, I need to return this." Ketty reached into her apron pocket and pulled out the book of healing charms. "It seems so long ago you let me borrow it, but it was only yesterday." She held it out to him across the wide tabletop.

The decision made itself. "Keep it for me. You'll

probably get more out of it than I could. But be careful. That book's borrowed, and I'll have to return it … someday." Although Crane hadn't been away long, it was hard to imagine returning to Deep River.

"You'll return here, on your way back?" Ketty asked, eyebrows raised.

"Do you want me to?"

"I think so." She blushed and a shy smile lit her face. It was an uncharacteristic look for her, but appealing.

"If I survive this quest, I will come back, if only to get my book." Crane tried to cover his fear with a nervous joke.

"That isn't funny. But do come back." She rose from the bench and took their empty bowls to the dishpan. "Wait a moment and I'll show you the trailhead."

"You don't need to — I can find it."

"It's my birthday and I want to."

Crane gathered his things and stepped out of the inn into the misty darkness. It was so chilly, he could hardly believe it was still summer, and he was grateful for his warm cloak. Ketty joined him, wrapped in a cloak of dark green. They walked side by side a little beyond the village limits. Crane stopped before Ketty did. They stood at the edge of the forest.

"How did you know?" she asked. "This is the spot."

"I've been following a pull all the way from Deep River. It's stronger than ever now."

"Maybe he's calling you."

Crane shuddered. "Then he knows I'm coming. Who else uses this path?"

"Hunters and berry pickers, but they don't go far. And there's a hot spring people claim is good for their health." She pressed his hand between hers. "Be careful. Don't die."

The warmth of Ketty's hands lingered after she released him and hurried away. His heart soared. Under the circumstances, *Don't die* from her was almost *I love you.*

Chapter 25. The Journey Continues

The Forest

Crane entered the dark forest physically ready to hike all day, though haunted by a touch of his old dread. At the end of this trail lurked a powerful evil, waiting for him. That grim thought dissipated as he climbed the narrow switchback trail through the dripping forest. It was cool and pleasant under the trees as the sunlight slanted through the branches, drying up the mist and Crane's fear with it.

It was a relief to get back on his quest. No more distractions. He no longer feared the trees would fall and crush him. He whistled as he hiked, answering the tweets and trills of the birds in the trees. A doe leaped across his path, then froze, watching him. In the dappled shade, twin fawns waited, almost invisible in their spotted coats. Crane smiled and hurried on so they could follow their mother without fear.

The sun had climbed high in the sky by the time Crane reached the top of the ridge. He shed his heavy cloak and stuffed it into his pack. He stretched and looked down and ahead. Not far below, a green meadow spread before him. He continued down the trail and was soon in the meadow, crossing a trickle of a stream on a narrow plank bridge.

Crane had not seen another person since he left Misty Pass, but Ketty had said people used the trail. A bridge meant some of them came at least this far. It wasn't as wild a place as he had imagined. Unless this was Yrae's private bridge. Crane shuddered at the thought. When no magic tried to turn him back, he finished his crossing and hiked onward.

All along the trail grew a tall plant with graceful, nodding plumes of bright purple flowers. Crane smiled at the sight. Fireweed. He had never seen this flower before but remembered Soorhi teaching it, with a sly smile especially for Crane. Bees buzzed in the blossoms. Several bumped Crane as they flew, too busy to sting. Each time a bee touched him, he knew in a flash where the honey was hidden. *They're lucky I'm not a bear*. The knowledge vanished with the insect, but a new confidence in his power remained.

Soon after he came under trees again, a tiny rill crossed his path, too narrow to need a bridge. Its streambed was lined with orange mud, and sulfurous steam rose from the water, flowing from a pool a few steps off the trail. Someone had built a stone basin around the spring. Ketty hadn't said whether people drank the water or soaked in it. Crane didn't know how anything that smelled so bad could be healthful. He was more curious about what heated the water in the first place.

Beyond the stink of the spring, he stopped to rest and eat in the shade. Gazing out from the cool, shady woods at the lush, sunlit meadow, Crane wished for someone to share it with; not out of loneliness, but because the scene was too perfect to keep to himself. *If only Ketty could see this.*

Crane laughed at his earlier dread. What evil could possibly lurk in this idyllic spot? The delight and eagerness reminded him of the first day of this journey, when he hiked with Elic. *I'll see you soon, my friend,* he thought with a rush of confidence. *The danger was all in our heads.*

Misty Pass

In the dawning light of the new day, Ketty returned to the Fogbank and her daily chores. Crane was gone. Life could return to normal now. But her thoughts continually strayed to the strange young man who, from the day they first met, had known her better than her own father did.

She didn't have to wonder where Crane was. As soon as she'd had the thought, she knew, and with a certainty that shocked her. She saw him striding through the forest as clearly as if she hiked at his side.

Is there more to my gift than healing? How will I ever find out if I can't tell anyone?

She had lived all her life at the Fogbank, happily, proud of her contributions to the family business. Today, the heavy log walls closed in on her, and she wanted more than anything to be somewhere else, doing something else. Her heart raced with excitement and restlessness. Her hands trembled as she set out breakfast for the inn guests. Thankful she wasn't handling knives, she worked with extra care so no one would notice.

The first guests were at the table when the door opened to admit Trilmi, the midwife.

"Morning, Ketty."

"Good morning, Trilmi. What can I get you?"

"I wouldn't say no to a bite of breakfast." Trilmi took a seat with a weary laugh. "I've been up all night, delivering a baby in the backwoods. All the way back to town this morning, I was imagining Mountain Folk behind every stump. When I can't trust my own eyes, I'd rather not try to cook."

Ketty served the midwife. "You were all alone? I thought you had an assistant."

"I did, but she got married last month. Up and moved to Silver Falls."

"That's too bad."

Trilmi cackled. "For me, it is! Say, you know why your hands shake like that? Means you've got a secret."

"It ... it does?" Ketty clasped her hands behind her back.

"Girls your age are made of secrets!" Trilmi winked and turned her attention to her breakfast.

As the midwife was leaving, Ketty's father came in with an armload of firewood and a bleeding hand. "I can't believe what a clumsy fool I am." He dumped his load into the wood box. "Cut my hand on the ax." He held out his hand to show Ketty a long, shallow cut across the palm. "That young fellow's gone, is he?"

Ketty nodded; she didn't trust her voice. She glanced toward the door where Trilmi had exited, then turned her attention to her father's wound.

"Seemed a good sort," he continued as she washed his hand. "I wouldn't have minded if he'd stayed on longer."

"He said he might come back."

"Well, I expect you're pleased." Eslo nudged her gently with his elbow.

Ketty drew a deep, tremulous breath. "Papa, there's something I have to tell you."

"About him?"

"No." She drew one finger over his oozing cut. It sealed and vanished. "About me."

Chapter 26. The Secret Valley

The Forest

After lunch, Crane rose with a contented sigh and continued hiking. The trail was steeper here, a challenge rather than an ordeal. By midafternoon, he was among the tall, slender trees. He climbed higher until he left the forest altogether. A rocky meadow covered the steep slope all the way to the top of the ridge. The trees here grew in scattered groups of two and three. Brightly colored wildflowers dotted the sunny expanse, some familiar from the dry lands around Deep River.

Here and there, low-growing bushes heavy with

green and bluish berries tempted Crane. He plucked one and popped it into his mouth. It crunched between his teeth. He shuddered and spat out the sour, unripe fruit. Instead of a berry feast, he ate some of the provisions he carried and continued his hike. Judging by the strength of the pull, he must be near his goal — another day at most. Probably less than that.

The trail ascended in switchbacks across the face of the meadow toward the top of the high ridge. Beyond, the great mountain seemed close enough to touch. The breeze off its snowfields cooled Crane's face as he settled his cloak over his shoulders

Crane reached the top of the ridge and peered down into a secluded valley on the other side. The setting sun shone bright on the meadow and up the mountain, but the valley lay in shadow. A glassy green lake reflected the gleaming peak. Crane considered making camp on its shore.

Crane peered farther up the valley. In the fading light, he saw his journey was at an end. The landmarks were just as they had appeared in his dream, including the house surrounded by gleaming threads of magic. It was not the fortress he had expected, but a humble cabin.

Cautiously, he continued down the narrow trail into the twilit valley. About halfway down, the trail ended abruptly, cut through by a rushing waterfall. Across the stream, the trail continued. There was no bridge. Crane didn't want to risk jumping across the wide gap, especially in the dark. Except it wasn't as dark as it should have been. Where it crossed the trail, the waterfall gave off a faint bluish glow, almost hidden by the foaming water. There was something familiar about that light — the magical radiance he could see around his own staff. Smiling, he reached out with the staff. It tapped on a solid surface. A stone bridge appeared. So Yrae did have his own private bridge. Crane hurried across.

Close to his goal, he fought the urge to turn back. His hands shook, his heart pounded, and his throat was so dry, he thought he might never speak again. Where had his earlier overconfidence gone? He took a calming breath. The memory of the jewel-bright meadow and the sunlit mountain steadied his resolve.

I may die tonight. It doesn't matter. I'm where I need to be.

Before he could change his mind, Crane marched up to the cabin, lifted his staff and rapped it against the door.

"Who's there?" a deep, clear voice called from within.

"I seek Yrae," Crane replied as firmly as he could, though his knees shook.

"Yrae sees no one."

"I am ... an apprentice seeking a mentor."

After a moment of silence, the door flew open, and a figure almost as tall as Crane stood silhouetted in the doorway. "How did you find this house?"

Crane gulped. "By looking for it."

"How did you cross the waterfall?"

"By the stone bridge." Crane's confidence returned.

"You may be wizardly, indeed," the voice said, with a note of humor. "Come in and let me have a look at you."

The mysterious figure stepped aside, and Crane entered the cabin. The door banged shut behind him. As his eyes grew accustomed to the firelight, he studied his host. A shaggy black beard and wild hair surrounded intense blue eyes that peered out of a dark face. The black hair was streaked with white, and the face was lined, but not so wizened and ancient as Crane had expected from Mama's Yrae stories. The back of Crane's neck prickled. Something about the shape of the man's nose and the slant of his eyebrows seemed strangely familiar. As with Ketty, he sensed hiddenness, though not the thing hidden. Crane pulled back his hood.

"You resemble someone I used to know," Yrae said. "Have we met before?"

"No," Crane said abruptly, before his voice could quaver. How could such a simple question sound like a test?

"You say you seek a mentor, yet you already carry a staff. May I?"

Crane extended the staff to be examined. Yrae stroked the smooth wood and studied the staff from every angle. "Finely wrought, indeed. Who crafted it for you?"

Crane flushed with pride. "I made it myself."

"Did you? Not the usual way, but it took great skill and patience. Perhaps I will teach you, after all. What is your name, my boy?"

"Crane, sir."

Yrae flinched. "Odd name," he said after a moment's pause. "Where do you come from?"

"Deep River. Perhaps you've heard of it."

Yrae stiffened. "I have." He jerked the staff out of Crane's hand and dropped it to the floor. Before Crane could react, Yrae pointed his finger and spoke one sharp word. Crane fell to the floor next to his staff, bound so tightly by invisible cords, he couldn't move even a finger. "First lesson: never give another wizard your staff. When you've gotten out of that, we'll talk about your real reason for seeking me."

Crane heart hammered and his thoughts raced. He had been defeated easily, without any fight at all. Ketty would be appalled if she knew. Ketty. He felt again the warmth of her hands and her parting words: *Don't die.*

He struggled against his bonds, to no avail. The relief that he hadn't been killed outright was small comfort. He gazed with despair at his staff, only a hand's breadth away but useless if he couldn't grasp it. *Is this how it ends?*

Only when his strength was exhausted did he think about what Yrae had said: *When you've gotten out of that* ... Perhaps it was less a trap than a test. He closed his eyes and tried to recall the unbinding spell. He remembered studying it, could even remember in which book and its position on the page. *If only I had that book.* He could remember bits of the spell, which was worse than remembering nothing. This frustration sapped Crane's remaining energy. He sagged against the dusty floorboards. *Well, I don't care. He can kill me now, if he'll only let me rest.* Crane allowed himself to relax and doze. He dreamed he was back home, in the Village Hall, and Jelf was in his library, asking, "What will it be today?"

Crane stood in the doorway to Jelf's library in the Village Hall. Daylight was fading. Jelf hunched over a book, writing steadily.

"Jelf?" Crane's voice didn't want to work, but he managed a faint whisper.

"Crane? Have you come back?"

"I need your help, Jelf. Get me that book — Magical Combat — the big black one, there."

Jelf got up and pulled the heavy volume from the shelf. He laid it on the table. Crane reached for it, but the pages turned by themselves to the right page. Crane traced a line of text on the page with his finger, whispering the words to himself.

A muttering voice woke Crane. His own voice. He opened his eyes and stretched. He was unbound! He grabbed his staff and jumped to his feet.

Yrae turned calmly from his fire. "Out of it so quickly?" He nodded his approval. "Have you eaten?" Crane shook his head. The snack in the meadow seemed long ago. "Come, share my meal."

The wizard dished up stew and bread. He set them on the table in the middle of the small room, while Crane took off his cloak and hung it on a peg by the door.

"How does such a young man come to have such an old cloak?" Yrae stared past Crane at the ragged garment.

"Old family relic," Crane explained with a nervous smile. He crossed warily to the table and sat down. He watched Yrae in silent puzzlement. He saw no further sign of malice, no madness or evil in the man. On the contrary, Yrae spoke softly, and appeared incapable of doing harm. All during the meal, the only magic Crane observed was when Yrae gave the fire a stern glance to calm it when it popped.

"How's the stew?" Yrae asked.

"Good, though I'd eat it even if it weren't." Crane sucked a small bone. "Is it rabbit?"

"Hare. He had designs on my garden, but walked into my snare, instead."

"Snare? What about magic?"

Yrae chuckled. "That's hardly sporting. I let them nibble around the edges of my cabbage patch, and in exchange, they give me meat to eat, and fur to trade down in the village."

"You trade for your supplies? In Misty Pass?" Ketty had said as much, but Crane hadn't believed her. It was not at all how he had imagined the life of an infamous wizard. "Aren't the people afraid of you?"

"They don't exactly see me. I can disguise myself." He passed a hand over his face, and it changed instantly from thin and dark to round and red, and back again. "But, yes, I trade for what I need. I may be a villain, but I'm an honest villain."

Crane turned his attention to the warm, firelit room. There wasn't much to see: another cloak hung next to his own, and a staff leaned against the wall near it. Shelves of old books filled one wall. A long, low pallet bed filled the space between the fireplace and that wall. There were only two small windows, one near the door and another next to the fireplace.

"What were you really seeking?" Yrae drew Crane's attention back with his quiet question.

Only the truth would do. Even if Yrae couldn't read his thoughts, he would know a lie when he heard it. "An enemy." Crane was surprised at how calm his voice sounded.

The older man raised one eyebrow. "And did you find one?"

"I'm ... not sure."

The back of Crane's neck prickled again as he considered what or who he might have found instead. Whatever Yrae was, he behaved in a quiet and thoughtful manner, which was not what Crane had expected. He certainly hadn't looked for hospitality here. Yrae refrained from the casual flinging of spells that was a part of his legend. Crane shuddered to remember what had happened at the door.

"Well, whatever you're looking for, you can't go any farther tonight. I suppose we can make a bed for you here by the fire. Have you got your own blanket? Yes, I think you'll be quite comfortable." Yrae puttered around, preparing for the night.

"Why —?"

"No questions tonight. Sleep now. Tomorrow, we'll talk."

Sleep. Not much chance of that. Crane removed his boots before lying down. He left his clothes on. His fear returned as he lay in the warm glow from the low fire, listening to the soft snore from Yrae's bed. *I'm spending the night in Yrae's house! If I sleep, he's likely to kill me where I lie. Not that I could stop him even if I were awake.*

Before long, warmth and weariness took over from anxious thoughts, and against his better judgment, Crane drifted, dozed, and slept.

Chapter 27. The Sleeping Mountain

A golden-haired child stood on the summit, tiny, yet at the same time monumental. Weeping, shining like the sun while her tears fell like rain. The flood of tears melted ice and snow. An angry roar filled the valley.

Crane snapped awake, his heart racing. The roar had

ceased. The night was quiet. The spring gurgled behind the cabin. Branches sighed in a gentle breeze. In the moonlight that filled the cabin, Yrae sat up in bed, alert.

"What's happening?" Crane whispered.

"It's all right," Yrae replied. "There will be work in the morning. Go back to sleep."

Crane doubted he could sleep again, but the next thing he knew, someone was shaking him awake in cold darkness. Why would Mama wake him before sunrise? "Let me sleep," he mumbled. He turned onto his side and pulled the blanket over his head. "It's the middle of the night."

"Where we're going, it is already morning," a deep, clear voice replied. "Wrap up and come."

Crane remembered where he was and with whom. Too groggy for fear, he rolled out of bed, shoved feet into boots, and slipped his cloak from its peg. He stumbled after his host, out of the cabin into the chill gray dawn.

"So, you're going to dispose of me outdoors?" Crane's voice was hoarse with sleep and returning fear.

Yrae glanced back at him and laughed. "You didn't find an enemy, remember?"

"I said I didn't know what I found."

They hiked in silence through the dark fringe of trees behind the cabin, emerging above the timberline. Both had long legs, but Yrae set a challenging pace, and Crane panted for breath as he struggled to keep up.

Yrae paused once for Crane to catch up. "You're not used to the thinner air, but we're almost there." He set off again before Crane had a chance to rest.

Yrae's idea of almost there was very different from Crane's. They kept on at the same steady pace over a long level stretch, cut across the face of a rock-strewn slope. From there, they descended into a draw where they crossed a narrow snowfield with a trickle of water running out of it. On the other side, they climbed a steep, rocky slope like a giant's staircase. At the top, the trail broadened into a flat plateau at the base of a basalt outcropping. Before them, the land dropped abruptly away. Yrae stopped near the brink of the precipice to gaze out over the canyon below. Above, the snow-capped peak glowed in the sunrise.

"Why are we here?" Crane shivered and kept well away from the edge. He pulled his cloak more tightly around him and stamped his feet against the solid rock underfoot.

Yrae turned toward him. "You'll soon see. Meanwhile, sit, and we can talk. Last night, you were going to ask me something that sounded urgent."

Crane took a deep breath of icy air to clear his head and sank down to sit next to Yrae on the cold stone. He had so many questions but chose only one.

"They know of you in Misty Pass. Years ago, the innkeeper there asked for your help when his wife was ill. You refused. The woman died, and their daughter grew up with no mother. Why didn't you go with him? It would have required so little."

"Little, you think?" Yrae stared at him for a moment. "She wasn't the only one ill. Should I have spent my power healing everyone in town, and hiked home in the dark?"

"He didn't ask you to heal the whole town."

"Maybe if he had brought her to me ..." Yrae sighed. "But I don't enter other people's houses. Not anymore.

Bad luck."

"Bad luck for ...?" Crane asked.

"Everyone." Yrae turned from Crane and gazed up at the looming mountain.

Crane glared at Yrae's back, unable to believe what he was hearing. "So, you hide up here by yourself, not using your power when you could do so much good?" Too late, his good sense caught up with him. What was he thinking, chiding a legendary villain? Yrae hadn't moved, but Crane edged toward the trail without getting up. How far could he flee before a curse caught him?

The rock beneath him shuddered. He toppled over, then leaped to his feet. "What is it? An earthquake?"

Yrae smiled. "This mountain? She's alive. Alive, and fretful."

He got to his feet, more calmly than Crane had, and walked over to the exposed rock face. He pressed his hands gently against the gray rock and crooned words Crane couldn't understand, in the tone of a mother soothing a restless infant with a lullaby. The trembling lessened, then ceased altogether.

Yrae looked at Crane again. "Never trust a sleeping mountain. Do you see now what I do with my power?"

Crane swallowed hard, trying to find his voice again. "Could I learn to do that?"

"You have power. If you have the right kind of ability, and patience, and training, you could learn this work. Would you want to? It is a lonely life."

"And a dangerous one. I'm not very good at danger."

"There are many kinds of danger." Yrae eyed Crane keenly.

"Isn't it risky, living so near such a mountain?" Crane

asked. "A ... what do they call it?"

Yrae chuckled. "A volcano? Yes, if she were to really blow, my little valley would be a very bad place to be. That would be a powerful blast, enough to knock me, and my cabin, and the whole forest flat. So, you see why I'm interested in keeping her quiet. Then again, I wouldn't want to live down any of these river valleys if she worked up a big eruption. Even a small one could do serious damage."

"I don't understand." Crane forgot his fear as he grew interested in this subject about which he knew nothing. "What would happen to a river valley?"

Yrae smiled and stroked his beard. "Let me tell you a story."

The ground was solid and still now, but Crane sank unsteadily to sit again, dizzy with hearing his mother's words from this man's mouth. "I ... I'd like that."

"This is the Legend of Aku's Tears."

"I don't know that one. I thought I'd heard them all by now."

Yrae stared down at Crane for an uncomfortably long time. "You have much to learn. Hear now the Legend of Aku's Tears."

Crane made himself as comfortable as possible. Even if he hadn't heard this particular story before, he knew how stories went. Or he thought he did, until Yrae stretched to his full height, closed his eyes, lifted his head, and sang. The wizard's voice was a little raspy, but deep and rich. There was something familiar about the song or chant, though Crane didn't understand a word of it. As he listened to the consonants and rhythm of it, a picture of giant Chamokat rose in his mind.

Crane almost forgot to breathe until Yrae finished his song and sat beside him. "It's not quite the same in translation, but it goes something like this: Great Mother Aku, Source of All That Is, had many children. They loved their Mother, but as they grew up, they formed their own clans and families. They had their own lives and did not always remember to spend time with Mother Aku, who was usually sleeping, in any case. In those days, she woke and found herself all alone. She waited for her children. She wanted them around her, Aku in the center. But they had forgotten her, and Aku grew lonely, and in her loneliness, angry. In her anger, she roared, and her roaring knocked the forest flat. She flung handfuls of dust into the air, and the dust darkened the sky. She cried boiling tears that mixed with the dust and cascaded down her face in rivers of scalding mud. Her rushing tears moved boulders and great tree trunks. They scoured away camps as if they had never been. Many of Aku's children were swept away or buried. The survivors hid until Mother Aku wore herself out and fell asleep again. Then they decided what must be done. They sent one of their number to stay with her, to comfort and reassure her when she woke up frightened and lonely. And so it is to this day."

"So Aku is ... the Mountain?" Crane saw again the golden-haired child, weeping on the summit. "I think I dreamed about that — the tears and the flood and everything. Did it all happen?"

Yrae looked at Crane with new interest. "Aku spoke to your dreams? That's a good sign."

"Mountains speak?"

"Everything has a voice, if you know how to listen."

Crane thought about the trees and the beaver. Those were questions for another time. "But did that flood in the story happen?"

Yrae nodded. "Many times, or so I understand. I've never seen it myself. It makes sense, though. Look at Aku's peak, at all the snow and ice. Hard to believe it's hot inside. But if it gets too hot, all that ice could melt and flood the rivers. Combine that with a landslide or ash blown out, and you have a fast-moving river of mud roaring down the mountain. It would scour the valley of anything in its path."

Crane gulped as he imagined a muddy torrent leaping over a dam, grinding and tearing toward a tiny village, sweeping it away. Before he could speak, Yrae continued. "I don't think we need to worry. Aku and I get on well. We have an understanding."

"How can you have an understanding with a mountain?"

"I told you — pressure builds up inside. I help her let it off gently. See there?" Yrae pointed at a puff of steam curling away from the summit. "Like burping a baby."

It was a reasonable explanation. Yet once again, Crane had a sense of something concealed. "Why did you choose this life, if it's so lonely?"

The older man sighed and closed his eyes. He opened them and looked straight at Crane with his intense, disconcerting blue gaze. "Did I choose it, or did it choose me? It's a strange gift we have, you and I; a strange gift that makes us strange. If we were like other people, we wouldn't be wizards. But before I was a wizard, I was a lonely boy. You know what I mean.

"When I began my wizard's training, I dreamed of

being a hero. I was strong in magic, but no less lonely than I had been before. I craved ... adoration. My mentor instilled in me that those with magical power have a responsibility to those who lack it. We should use our magic to help them. Never to take advantage or dominate. I vowed to use my power only for good. To earn my staff, I developed a way to combine a finding spell with a fever charm. With enough power behind it, the combined spell could clear some kinds of infection, curing them completely."

"Like the illness you refused to treat in Misty Pass?" Crane asked.

"I might have cured a handful of patients, and I wouldn't have been good for anything for days afterward," Yrae said. "But when I was young and didn't know better, I might have tried it. I really did want to help people. I traveled from village to village, aiding whoever needed help. Crowds gathered around me, and I developed a reputation for goodness. I was proud of my reputation, but the crowds would always disperse, and I would move on, alone."

Crane shifted on the hard rock. For this story he was willing to endure discomfort. As the sun climbed into the sky, he sat and listened.

"I controlled storms and the sea, I defeated wild beasts," Yrae continued. "I healed illness and injury that should have resulted in death. I had control of nature, of life and death, of everything ... except myself.

"I was not much older than you are, when I made a terrible mistake and hurt the one person I should have done anything to protect. I was so ashamed, and so angry, and so afraid — yes, afraid! — I made a new vow.

To leave human society behind. I ran away, found a place where I could do some good, and I have stayed here." He stared off over the lower peaks and valleys, now touched with brilliant sunlight.

Crane studied Yrae and struggled to find the right words. When he did speak, he couldn't bear to look at the other man. He gazed at his boots stretched out in front of him.

"I am the mistake you made."

Chapter 28. Yrae's Story

"What do you mean?" Yrae asked, his voice tightly controlled.

"Father ..." Crane croaked, the word foreign on his tongue. "I am your son." He stared at the rocky soil under his feet and kicked a shower of gravel that rattled down the steep slope.

Yrae cleared his throat, and Crane risked a glance at him out of the corner of his eye. "I am nobody's father." Yrae's scowl was the very expression Elic had often faulted in Crane.

"Am I nobody, then?" Crane's voice came out tinged

with more bitterness than he'd intended. He raised his face to look his companion in the eye.

Yrae's expression softened. "You are perhaps more *somebody* than you know. But I have been a poor excuse for a father."

Crane couldn't argue with that opinion. "Did you know?"

"Did I know! How could I not know? How many times have I transformed myself into an eagle to fly down and watch you from a distance?"

"An eagle? I think I saw you."

"I wanted you to. I perched on the roof and heard your first cries. I have watched you struggle to learn your craft."

"Why didn't you help me?"

"I almost did, many times. I was waiting. I wanted *you* to come to *me*. I called you, yes, but I wanted it to be your own choice. When I saw a traveler approaching my home, I wondered: could it be you at last?"

"Didn't you recognize me when I stood at your door?"

"I didn't want to recognize you." Yrae peered into Crane's face. "I had been waiting all these years, and yet, it felt too soon. I wasn't ready. But how could I miss it?"

"That I look like you?"

"No, that you have Stell's eyes. Such beautiful, trusting eyes she had." He sighed and stared off into the distance again.

"Has," Crane corrected him. "She hasn't forgotten you."

"Nor forgiven me."

"She forgave you for leaving long ago. She loves you."

"Love!" Yrae snorted. He blinked rapidly, and his

voice shook.

"Oh, I see!" Crane leaped to his feet. "You didn't even care. You went from town to town, the great hero wizard, taking advantage of innocent girls. You probably left wizard children all over the place."

"No!" Yrae sprang up to face him. "It wasn't like that at all." They stood face to face, equal in height and temper, if not in age and strength.

"Then what was it like?" Crane demanded.

"I ...don't know." Yrae slumped down wearily. Crane crouched nearby, sullen but attentive. "I mean, yes, I do know, but ... as I said, I was a little older than you are, but less experienced with people. I knew magic, nothing else. I had never learned friendship. Imagine, twenty years old, and I had never been alone with a woman before!"

Crane allowed a grudging twinge of compassion. "I can imagine it."

Yrae gave him a half smile and went on with his story. "When I came to Deep River that time, I was as low as I thought I could be. Even in crowds, I was always alone. I wanted a new life, and in looking for it, I came to the Blue Heron."

Crane had a feeling Yrae was leaving out details already. Perhaps another time, he would tell what he sought in Deep River.

"When I stopped at the inn that night, I had a sense before I even opened the door, if I didn't leave immediately, I would die in that house. But I was weary, and lonely, and the food smelled better than anything. So I went in, and there she was, a fountain in the desert." He sighed at the memory. "I planned to rest and eat and go on my way the same night. Until I heard her telling stories. I thought I could risk stopping there for one night. I lingered, and after everyone else had gone to bed, she fed me and talked with me.

"I was used to being adored, but she didn't worship me. I gave her no reason to. I may have been a famous wizard somewhere. Not in those parts. She didn't know me from the woodpile." He chuckled softly.

Crane had to smile at the rustic expression. It sounded like something Jelf would say, or Soorhi. "You told Mama you had seen a wizard cure an entire family of fever and put out a barn fire with magic. Did you witness those things, or did you do them?"

"I showed her no magic and didn't let on I was a wizard. But I wanted to impress her, so I told about the places I'd visited. And fibbed about seeing magic rather than working it. I'm not much of a talker. It was all I could add to the conversation."

"You succeeded in impressing her. She still remembers everything you said."

"Stell impressed me more," Yrae said. "She offered simple kindness and dignity without my having to earn them. She sat and talked with me, like a ... like a friend. In my loneliness, that touched my soul. I wanted to drink and drink at that fountain. I drank too deeply." He rubbed at his cheeks, which looked drawn and tired already, though it was the beginning of the day. Crane thought the story had ended, but Yrae continued.

"She showed me to a room, probably the best she had to offer, certainly better than I could afford. Better than I deserved. She insisted, and I would have done anything she asked. She tried to say good night, but I didn't want her to leave me. Because I couldn't bear to be alone again. And she didn't leave. She took my hand, and that touch was ... it changed me. I don't know how else to say it. When she hugged me, I held her close, and then she kissed ... I mean, I kissed her. And kept going, small step by small step. It was all as new to me as it was to her, but we ... I mean, I sent my mind somewhere else and let my body figure things out." His voice faltered.

Crane looked away, sharing his father's embarrassment. Did he need to know all this? "Did you ... did you put a spell on her? In order to ...?"

"No! At least I remembered that much of my mentor's rule. Not that it makes much difference. I failed in my responsibility to someone I was supposed to help." Yrae shook his head. "Wizards have no business forming personal relationships with regular people."

"What if she wanted you there?" Crane asked. "Are you sure she was unwilling?"

Yrae sighed. "She didn't say, and I never bothered to ask. I did what I did when I should not have. And ... here you are." He forced a smile. "My vision at the door came back to me. Was this why I would die in that house? Because of this kind, beautiful storyteller? She had mentioned her father. Were there other relatives, or a jealous suitor? I didn't want to fight anyone. I didn't want to die. I didn't want her to see me killed. Oh, did I panic! So after it was too late, I did use magic. I put her into an enchanted sleep and returned her to her own room. I sensed what had begun, but I didn't know the magic to end it. So I ran."

"Why didn't you come back in daylight?" Crane couldn't imagine anyone attacking a visitor to the inn, especially if they didn't know what he had done.

"And do what? Marry her? As if she would want to. Even if she did, what kind of life is that for a woman, traipsing about the countryside with an itinerant wizard? Or constantly waiting for him to return?" Yrae picked up a pebble and flung it into the valley below.

"I don't know." But Crane thought, *She* is *waiting.* "Why didn't you at least wait to hear what she thought of you?"

"I was a coward."

"What, because you didn't want to die?" Crane asked. "She would have kept you safe."

Yrae shook his head and turned away. Crane wasn't yet ready to excuse his father's past actions, but he'd heard his mother's side of this same story, as well as Yrae's own hesitations and amendments. Which story was true?

"I called you a coward once, before I knew you were my father. Why did you curse Deep River?"

"What curse?" Yrae's expression looked genuinely surprised. "Oh, that? It's not a curse, I assure you. Call it an enchantment, a protection. Never a curse. But I had to do something, didn't I? Even if it wasn't the right thing." He paused and gazed thoughtfully off into the distance. "What was I thinking?"

"I don't know, but I wish you'd tell me." Crane spoke more sharply than he intended.

His father gave him a startled look and smiled. "I guess I was thinking several things. At first, I only planned to protect myself from any sort of search. I laid down a mild, general charm to keep people from wondering too much about the father of Stell's child, prevent them from planning a search for me, divert their thoughts, keep them at home. Then I thought I'd better protect her, too. Her father wasn't going to live much longer, considering the condition of his heart. I gave him another four or five years, at most, so I added a layer to keep travelers away."

This curse or enchantment, which Crane had already judged peculiar, now appeared both ridiculous and pointless. Who could possibly be interested enough to go searching for the father of Stell's child, and why would it matter if they did? A powerful wizard like Yrae could protect himself from attack. If anyone really cared. According to Mama's version of the story, he hadn't committed a crime, after all. He had enjoyed a night of passion with a fellow lonely stranger. The worst act was leaving without saying goodbye.

"Didn't it occur to you travelers might be her livelihood?" Crane asked.

Yrae shrugged. "What do I know about business? Strangers in the place all night seemed more dangerous than friendly locals coming for supper. It's still a living, isn't it?"

"Barely."

"Almost as an afterthought, I decided to protect the child."

"How considerate," Crane grumbled. "From what?"

Yrae went on as if he hadn't heard. "I added a special discouragement to wizards who might identify the child's magical ability, if there were any, so if he did know about his magic, he might not find training."

Crane sputtered a nervous laugh. "Why didn't you just kill me? It would have been less complicated."

"I thought about it," Yrae admitted, and grinned as Crane edged away. "For a moment, I thought about it. I wished I could erase my mistake, but that wasn't the way."

"Why didn't you want me to be trained as a wizard?"

Yrae sighed. "I hoped you might have a normal life. Or if you wanted training and couldn't find it at home, you might be driven to find me."

"But how —?" Crane stopped himself and answered his own question. "The dreams. The pull. You were calling me, all along."

Yrae smiled and stood. "I'm hungry. Let's go make breakfast before the morning is gone."

Crane followed Yrae back down the trail toward the cabin. The hike felt shorter now. He no longer feared the man as an enemy but found him even more puzzling and disturbing as a father.

"They call you 'the Mad Wizard'. Everyone thinks you're evil and horrible. You're something I can't quite figure out, but not evil."

Yrae glanced back. "Thank you. I hope not. I took a new name and started a few rumors so folks would leave me alone. It isn't difficult to develop a bad reputation, as long as there are gossips about."

"The rumors reached Deep River, even though no travelers pass through. How did you manage it?" He paused as a chilling thought struck him. "Did you come in disguise, and spread them yourself?"

Yrae snorted. "I wasn't that brave. I used to fly over, or lurk nearby, scattering rumors and sowing nightmares to grow in whatever mind received them."

"Mama turned her nightmares into stories."

"Were they good stories?"

"The best," Crane replied, remembering the delicious chill of hearing these tales when he was supposed to be asleep. "I thought she was making them up, but everyone else believed they were true."

"I hope I sent her a few dreams that weren't nightmares. As for mad, perhaps I am, a bit. I have been alone for as long as you have been alive."

"Are you sorry I'm alive?"

"Not anymore. Are you sorry you found me? Do you still want me to teach you?"

"That was just a ruse to get inside!" Crane laughed as he remembered his words the night before, standing outside a closed door. "Will you, though? More than anything, I've longed for a mentor to teach me, perhaps even more than a father."

"Then I will try to be both." They had reached the cabin, and Yrae opened the door for Crane.

"But first, will you lift the curse on Deep River? That's what I came for."

"Enchantment," Yrae corrected him. "I don't need to." He put water on to boil and opened the porridge bin. "It will lift on its own, on your eighteenth birthday."

"Why that day?"

"For once I was planning ahead." Yrae's laugh held no mirth. "I guessed by then, either you would have found me, or another teacher, or another way of your own. It seemed a good time to stop interfering with your life." He smiled broadly. "I guessed pretty close, didn't I?"

"You can't lift it sooner?"

"I would have to go there, in my own form." Yrae winced. "Even then, the spell would be complicated to unravel, especially after all this time. I don't remember every detail. I invented it as I cast it, in layers all worked together. It's kind of my specialty, like what I did to earn my staff. Spells intertwined that way take on their own character. Trying to undo it, I could easily make things worse. Better to let it lift on its own schedule. Your birthday is when, about three months from now?"

"That's right," Crane said. "I told Mama I would be home by then."

"Good. You need to be there for it to happen. You can see the spell break and take credit for it."

"I have to be there?" Crane asked in alarm. "What if I'm not?"

"The enchantment remains. As you've seen, it doesn't hurt anything. I'll wager no one else even notices it."

Crane stared. "So, if I had stayed home a few more months, the curse — sorry, the *enchantment* — would have lifted on its own, but by leaving, I may have endangered even that? Will I never do anything right?"

"No, you had to leave," Yrae said. "That's one of the conditions."

"Conditions?"

"Yes, the enchantment will lift on your eighteenth birthday if four conditions are met. First, you must leave the enchantment's range, demonstrating courage and a strong will."

"So the enchantment made me come here?" Crane asked.

"You could have gone anywhere outside the enchantment's range," Yrae said. "I hoped you would come here, though. So that's the first condition, already met. Second, you must return to Deep River, demonstrating your love and loyalty. Third, you must be present in Deep River on your eighteenth birthday. And at some time prior, you must do a necessary thing."

"What necessary thing?" Crane asked.

"I have no idea," Yrae said. "It's possible you've already done it. Only the magic will know for sure."

"How does magic know things?" Crane asked.

"Big, complicated spells develop their own logic, their own rules," Yrae said. "They also know people. The enchantment on Deep River recognizes me as its caster. And it also knows you."

"You put a spell on me?"

"No, not on you. But it's *about* you."

Crane considered the deceptively simple conditions. He had completed one already without knowing it. Returning home and staying at least until his birthday were also under his control. But what was the necessary thing? If even Yrae didn't know, it was hidden, in a way. Would Crane sense it in time? "I don't suppose coming here counts as necessary," he said.

"Let's assume it doesn't," Yrae replied. "But maybe you will do it here. We can begin your training tomorrow, if you like. Today, catch your breath."

Yrae's reassurance calmed Crane, and he allowed a new hope to kindle. "Then we can go to Deep River together."

Yrae did not answer.

Chapter 29. Magic Lessons

Yrae woke before sunrise. What had disturbed his sleep? Both mountain and weather were quiet, yet a forgotten worry nagged at him. The fire crackled and popped. Yrae smiled and closed his eyes again, comforted by the familiar noise. What could worry him?

Fire? Yrae sat up, all his senses alert. A young man who looked like him knelt before the fire, stirring something in a pot. He shook his head. Of course, it was Crane. Stell's son. His son.

Crane turned and nodded at him. "I woke up early,

so I took the liberty of making breakfast. It's nearly ready."

"So I see. You are used to being the host, not the guest."

Crane grinned. "I don't want to be a burden, sir."

Yrae's neck prickled at this polite, formal address. He wasn't used to being addressed at all. He shook himself.

The boy dished up two bowls of porridge and set them on the table. "How do we begin my training?"

Yrae tried to appear stern, but he couldn't help smiling. He'd had that eagerness, once. "Before I can teach you, I must know what you have already learned. I've seen you use an unbinding spell. What else can you do?"

"Fire." Crane closed his right hand as if to hide some small, secret thing. "Illusions. Moving small objects. A repelling charm."

"That isn't much for someone your age. Anything else?" Yrae asked.

"Well, the illusions are convincing. And Aunt Sudi says I have … a sense for hidden things."

"Aunt Sudi?"

"My friend's mother. She's a midwife."

"A midwife, you say." Yrae nodded. "What about healing?"

Crane shook his head. "I know some. I don't have much talent for it."

Yrae snorted impatiently. "And who taught you this vast store of skills?"

Crane's jaw tightened, though he answered in a calm voice. "No one. I had books to study, but no one to explain how to use the spells."

Yrae stared. There must be some mistake. How could any son of his be such a failure? Yet somehow, the boy had found him. "How many years did you waste, trying to learn magic from books?"

"Five, ever since I discovered my gift."

"Five years?!" Yrae flung down his spoon. It bounced off the tabletop and clanked onto the floor. "Five years, and that is all you've learned? By the time I was your age, I was a fully trained wizard!"

"Maybe if someone hadn't cursed my village, I could have had a proper teacher!" Crane jumped to his feet. "If I'd had a *father*, maybe he would have recognized my gift and trained me sooner. Maybe if you hadn't run away ..." He sank back into his chair, shaking. He rubbed his eyes roughly with the heels of his hands.

The blood drained out of Yrae's face, and the warmth from his body. He stared across the table. "You're right." He forced himself to speak calmly. "I should be glad you've learned anything at all. And you did make your own staff, which required power and patience. Most wizards receive their staff after their first quest, not before, and crafted by a mentor. So you have been your own mentor up till now. Perhaps there's hope for you yet. Shall we begin again?"

"All right," Crane said, though he didn't sound certain. "What do you want me to do?"

"We could use fresh air. Come outside. Show me what you can do."

Crane started his demonstration with illusions. Although confident in those skills, his heart pounded with fear. What if he angered Yrae with his ignorance? By the time he'd moved from illusions of stationary objects to moving animals and fragrant flowers, most of his nervousness had burned away.

"Good, you at least know the basics," Yrae said. "What about concealment?"

Crane searched his memory. "I didn't find that in any of the books. Maybe those pages were missing."

"Illusion and concealment go together! Everyone knows that." Yrae hissed impatiently and strode up and down the lakeshore. "Never mind. Levitate that rock."

Nervous again, Crane raised the stone and held it aloft a moment before letting it drop. At least Yrae had asked for something he knew how to do.

"Again! Hold it this time and add another."

Crane followed these instructions, adding more stones and the occasional stick at Yrae's request until seven rocks and four sticks floated in the air. He trembled and sweated with the effort of holding them.

"Arrange them in a circle."

Crane had never done that before. It sounded familiar enough that he must have read it at least once. After several fruitless attempts, he got the objects into a lopsided loop.

"Close enough. Spin it."

That was new, too, but not too different from calling or repelling objects. Crane made a stirring motion with his staff. The circle lurched, stopped, lurched again, and then spun. One rock hurtled away and plopped into the lake.

"Set the rest down, one at a time."

Crane's arms shook as he directed the objects to the ground. Two sticks came down together, but the rest followed his orders. He blew out a breath when the last rock reached the ground.

"Room for improvement. Read my thoughts."

Crane swallowed. He had never tried to read thoughts. They spilled out of people, and he picked them up. Thoughts were the most hidden of hidden things, though. He closed his eyes and reached out tentatively. His magical senses hit a solid wall. It dissolved as he was about to give up the effort.

Is this a good idea? He has talent. Neither of us knows what we're doing.

"You're not sure this is a good idea," Crane said.

The wall returned. "Good enough. Take a break."

Crane flopped to the ground, his strength spent, almost as helpless as he'd been in the clutches of the binding spell, though without the paralyzing fear.

"What you do, you do with skill," Yrae admitted. "You know more than you realize."

Crane smiled at the compliment, though he was too exhausted to move or even open his eyes all the way. "I haven't wasted five years of my life? That's a relief."

"There is one thing I don't understand. You know a great deal, more than you showed me, and have the power to use what you know. Yet you either can't or don't." Yrae crouched next to Crane. "Why are you so afraid?"

At this direct question, Crane rose halfway. He leaned on his elbows and looked down at his hands, one clenched into a fist, the other loosely closed. He took a deep breath, looked up at his father, and slowly held out his right hand, opening the fingers to reveal the stiff, shiny scar. Yrae touched the scar and winced at that shadow of pain.

"It's old." Crane withdrew his hand self-consciously. He couldn't joke about it the way he had with Ketty. "It was … an accident. I didn't know what I was doing."

Yrae shook his head slowly. "This was your introduction to magic? It's my fault."

Crane let this go as he went on with his story. "When they brought me home, afterward … I don't remember much. I wasn't in my right mind. But I do remember Mama saying, 'If only your father would come.' I didn't understand why it mattered. Now I do. She believed you could heal me, like you'd healed her father."

"Maybe I could have. When did this happen?"

"When I was twelve."

Yrae's eyes widened. He stood and walked away a few paces, then returned. "I … I heard her wish. I was there, afterward. Maybe not the day it happened, but soon after. I didn't believe I had the right to walk in and heal you, after …" He turned and gazed out over the lake. Dragonflies and swallows darted after insects, and the still, dark water reflected an inverted scene of trees and mountain peak. "I wish I had been there, before. Perhaps it wouldn't have happened at all."

"Could you … can you … is there anything you can do about it now?" Hope charged Crane's whole body.

"Not for your hand, no. I'm sorry. But a scar can be a useful reminder." His voice trailed off. "What can I do about it now? What I *am* doing: helping you get over your fear. We are well matched. You've never had a mentor, and I've never had an apprentice!" Yrae laughed, which put Crane more at ease. "I must plan how to go about this. But I have a job you can work on until I am ready to start your lessons. Come back inside."

Crane rinsed the dust from his hands in the lake. The water was so cold, his bones ached. He withdrew his hands after one dip and dried them on his shirt. They were warming up again by the time he reached the cabin.

He hoped for a practical lesson, but Yrae led him to the bookshelves. More book work? He swallowed his complaint. He would gain nothing by being uncooperative, and he didn't want to risk angering his unpredictable host. Crane had already lost his temper twice since finding Yrae, who had thus far responded with surprising control. Crane didn't want to trust luck in the matter and resolved to keep his retorts to himself.

"How ... how did you get so many books to such a remote spot?" Crane asked.

"One at a time. Booksellers sometimes come to the market in Misty Pass, and I know an herbalist who keeps his eyes open for anything ... interesting. His eye, I should say. A few of the smaller things I brought in my pockets when I first came here. Like this one."

Yrae carefully extracted a document, not even a book, but a sheaf of loose pages in a cracked leather case. They were yellowed with age and covered with faint writing. "These pages of ancient lore were handed down to me by my own master," Yrae said. "They were damaged when the roof leaked during a rainstorm."

"Your roof leaks?" Crane interrupted in disbelief. *It's not polite to interrupt*, he reminded himself, and bit his lip.

Yrae smiled slightly. "I built it and conceal it with magic, but it's a real roof on a real house. Magic is only so useful for repairs. I fixed the roof. I haven't had a chance to copy the pages. How's your handwriting?"

"Not bad."

"Good. Here are pen and ink, and plenty of paper. Sit here and copy the text. You'll be helping me tremendously, and you may learn something from the material."

Chapter 30. The Ballad of the Birds

Yrae watched Crane with secret wonder as he carefully recopied the old work in a clear, strong hand. This young stranger was so like himself, yet so different, with those eyes that haunted Yrae's dreams. The boy started out writing with his left hand. When that hand tired, he switched the pen to his right. His scarred right hand held the pen clumsily, but the writing continued clear and steady.

"You can write with either hand," Yrae commented, breaking the silence in the cabin. "Even an injury can bring a gift."

Crane glanced up with a half-smile. Yrae returned an uneasy smile of his own and walked out of the cabin. He hurried back to the lake. The day had turned hot enough, the icy water looked appealing. He stripped off his clothes and waded in. The mud squished pleasantly underfoot, though the water numbed his legs almost immediately. He dived forward and swam to a fallen tree that lay with its top beneath the lake's surface. He pulled himself up onto the log and sat cross-legged, letting the sun dry and warm him. He gazed out over the glassy water, communing with the reflected image of the mountain.

A strange boy, this Crane. He pictured his son's face, angry and scowling one minute, and then, that smile, startling in its warmth and joy. *Did I ever have such a smile? Or is that from her, too?* He studied his own reflection and tried out a smile. Ripples distorted the image before he could see how it looked.

The boy had suffered the pain of loneliness and rejection, that much Yrae knew. *And yet, he spoke of a friend. He grew up with a mother's love. Stell's love,* Yrae thought with a twinge of envy. And there were those gentle eyes, alert and curious and playful. They revealed a tender heart. *Too tender for what I'll be teaching him? Can he bear it when he is already so full of fear? Yet ... he had the courage to come here, by himself, expecting who-knows-what kind of horrible monster. And he has the power ...*

Indeed, Yrae had already glimpsed depths of power

in Crane that Crane himself did not yet suspect. *Dare I teach him?* He shuddered. *Dare I not?*

Resigned to book work, Crane began recopying the pages, wrinkling his nose at the musty smell. He expected arcane wisdom or strange old spells, but found the material homely, though interesting enough in its own way. It wasn't one thing, but a collection of shorter pieces: fables such as his mother told, poetry, even something that looked like a recipe, though Crane didn't recognize the ingredients.

Crane pretended not to notice Yrae watching him. Being observed, even at so simple a task, didn't help his nervousness around the wizard. More surprising was Yrae's sudden departure from the cabin. When he didn't return immediately, Crane went to the window and peered out. He couldn't find the wizard at first, but eventually spotted him as he emerged from the lake onto a log. Crane had never been in water deep enough for swimming. He was impressed Yrae was willing to immerse his whole body in that frigid water. Crane watched to see what he might do next.

Which wasn't much. He sat for a long time, his head bent toward the water. Maybe that was his favorite thinking spot, though it seemed strange someone who lived alone would need such a spot. Had Crane driven the man from his own house? Then again, Yrae wasn't the type to do anything against his will. Mystified, Crane returned to his task.

For a long time, the only sound in the cabin was the scratching of his pen. Yrae came back inside without speaking and padded to the shelves in stocking feet, quiet as a cat — whether to avoid disturbing him, or to avoid his notice, Crane wasn't sure. He sat across from Crane with several books open in front of him.

With care, Crane turned a tattered, yellowing page and began to copy a set of verses. They were set out like poetry but had an unusual meter and didn't rhyme. The meaning was clear, though with awkward phrasing, as if they were translated from an even older work. It was the most interesting piece he had copied so far.

As Crane worked, he hummed the song without words his mother used to sing. The words he copied fit the tune perfectly. At first, he was delighted to discover words for the lovely, haunting melody.

Crane's song cut off mid-phrase. He dropped his pen and sat back as if stung as his delight turned to horror. The ballad unfolded into tragedy with eerie parallels to Crane's own life.

"What ails you, boy?" Yrae asked.

"Father ..." Crane said. Yrae grimaced and looked away. Crane slumped in his seat. It didn't matter how hard he tried to be helpful and polite. Without meaning to, he kept finding small ways to offend or irritate Yrae. Crane reminded himself to be patient, as his mother would have been. "Now what?"

"Please don't call me that." Although the wizard spoke in soft tones, his voice had a strangled quality.

"But you are —"

"I know," Yrae snapped. "Don't you think I know? What I don't know is how to *be* a father, to you or anyone. Don't remind me of my moment of weakness."

I can't help it. Here I am, your moment of weakness, in the flesh. Crane swallowed the lump in his throat and willed himself to speak politely. "What shall I call you instead?"

"Anything. Anything but that."

Crane couldn't speak for a moment. He had hoped to call this man "Papa," but the label didn't suit the reality, and would probably aggravate Yrae even more than "Father." That left his name. Crane wasn't about to use the name that had for so long been associated with cruelty and evil.

"Listen." Crane drew a full breath and sang the ballad he had been copying.

Bluebird, bluebird
have you seen my love?
For I am great with his child.
"He passed me on the dusty road,
his face set toward the mountain."
Oh bird, will he return this way?
"Oh no, tra la, oh no.
He has gone from you."

Blackbird, blackbird,
have you seen my love?
For I have borne him a son.
"He passed me in the cattail swamp,
wading toward the mountain."
Oh bird, will he return this way?
"Oh no, tra la, oh no.
He has lost his way."

Heron, heron,
have you seen my love?
For his boy asks for his papa.
"He skirted 'round my fishing pond,
headed for the mountain."
Oh bird, will he return this way?
"Oh no, tra la, oh no.
He lives as a wanderer."

Raven, raven,
have you seen my love?
For my son has gone to seek him.
"He hiked through my forest,
hiking toward the mountain."
Oh bird, will he return this way?
"Oh no, tra la, oh no.
He shuns humanity."

Eagle, eagle,
have you seen my love?
For my son returned with bloodied hands.
"He climbed past my aerie,
climbing up the mountain."
Oh bird, will he return this way?
"Oh no, tra la, oh no.
He lies dead, stabbed through the heart."

Tell me, tell me,
did he remember me?
For now I'm all alone.
"He looked in his son's face,

and saw the mother's eyes.
He smiled, spoke your name,
and died."

Yrae watched him while he sang, eyes widening as a smile spread slowly across his face. "How do you know this song?"

"I learned the tune from Mama. We thought the words had been lost long ago."

"And I wondered what the tune was."

"I always guessed it must be a sad song." Crane picked up his pen again. "I never thought—"

"—it could have been written for us?"

"You don't need to worry. Surely, I'm not strong enough to kill you."

Yrae didn't join in Crane's laughter at the ridiculous idea. He betrayed so little emotion, Crane couldn't tell whether the ballad unnerved him. For Crane's part, this story haunted him — a son killing his father, by accident or in anger. And could not the tale as easily have gone the other way? That thought quelled any desire to sing.

Chapter 31. The Rules of Magic

On their third morning together, Yrae cooked breakfast. Sitting at the table with him, Crane could almost relax, though Yrae watched him without comment. At least they weren't tripping over each other in a house that was small for two. Crane was already tired of excusing himself every time he got in his father's way. Yrae assured him over and over he was not imposing, though his smile seemed forced. Crane continued to fear an angry outburst. He couldn't forget Yrae's reputation any more than he could the haunting ballad.

When Crane finished eating, he cleared the dishes for

washing. Yrae motioned him back to his seat.

"Let them soak for now. Yesterday, you showed impressive abilities. Today, we'll begin your formal training."

Crane remembered the surge of confidence as he worked increasingly complicated magic in the open air. He was sure he would feel less awkward and underfoot once he had something specific to do. "I'd love to learn transformation."

Yrae chuckled and shook his head. "That's much too advanced. Based on what you've told and shown me, your magical education has been ... spotty."

Crane squirmed at the superior tone but remembered his resolution to cooperate. He nodded politely and kept listening.

"Incomplete and broken," Yrae continued. "You don't understand the theory or how one thing relates to another. I've thought it over, and the only remedy is to start over from the beginning."

Crane's jaw dropped. The beginning? As if he were a boy of ten, newly discovering his abilities? "But that's–"

Yrae held up a hand to cut him off. before he could say *unfair*. "I know. No one likes to go back and relearn something he thought he knew." He smiled benevolently, an expression Crane already called his patient-and-tolerant mask. "These books you studied — how did you get them?"

"They belonged to a wizard named Lok."

Yrae's eyes widened. "Lok, you say? I never met him, but I know the name. He figured as a colorful character in a number of stories."

"Mama never told a story with Lok in it."

"These were stories wizards told among themselves. What was Lok doing in Deep River?"

Crane shrugged. "I was told he retired there for the dry climate."

Yrae chuckled. "More likely he was hiding from enemies."

"Enemies?" Crane sat up straighter. Maybe Deep River wasn't such an uninteresting backwater, after all.

"Or rivals. According to the stories, Lok was always ready to duel. That's a good way to make enemies."

"So he was evil?" Crane tried to make sense of it. "Or was he good?"

"Neither." Yrae grinned. "He was a talented hothead. I suspect many wizards who said they dueled with him never even met him. My own uncle claimed he began to lose his eyesight after an encounter with Lok, though he wasn't even a wizard."

"How do wizards duel?" Crane asked. "Did you ever …?"

Yrae shook his head. "I learned the techniques, but I never had to use them. A duel usually started with basic magic — repelling charms to push each other around, levitation to fling objects. If things got serious, they might manipulate fire or water, or even the weather. As a last resort, there's a spell to drain an opponent's power, but I've never seen it used."

"I didn't know Lok was such a legend," Crane said. "I guess I should feel proud to have studied his books."

"I don't know about that." Yrae wore the tolerant mask again. "He lived long enough to amass an *interesting* collection, but …"

"But what?"

"Perhaps they weren't entirely … appropriate for a

beginner."

Yrae launched into a lecture on elementary magical theory. Crane tried to pay attention, but his mind wandered. Although he hadn't approached the subject from this direction before, it was basic enough that he understood immediately, as if Yrae were merely reminding him of something he already knew.

His real question was what his mother could have seen in this wizard. The reverse was easy to imagine. Of course Yrae had fallen in love with her. She was pretty, friendly, a good cook, and an enchanting storyteller. She had a talent for making any guest feel cared for, though she never singled one out. Why had she singled out this man, this pompous know-it-all with no thought for anyone except himself? Had he been so different when he was young? What had won her heart?

Yrae hadn't intended the first lesson to turn into a dry lecture. He could tell Crane was bored even as he plodded ahead. Crane's education had been so haphazard, Yrae didn't know how to correct it. Lok's books were an unforeseen complication. Crane had managed to learn a surprising amount from them. It was an odd mix of basic knowledge and advanced magic. Yrae didn't relish untangling that mess. He had no experience teaching, though he was confident he could have handled a genuine novice. In this case, he could only try to reproduce his own master's systematic method.

But was Ordahn this dull? He remembered hanging on his master's every word. *Still, I was only ten and knew almost nothing. It was all new to me.*

"That's enough for today," he said.

Crane jerked back to alertness. Yrae pretended not to notice. He went to the bookshelf and selected a small volume, roughly bound in heavy cloth. He hadn't opened this book in decades, though in some ways he prized it above all the others. He had saved it as a memento, and as an heirloom to pass on to his own favorite student, if he had one. Or to his son. The story was too sentimental to share with Crane. But perhaps he would get some good out of the book, all the same.

"I expect you're more comfortable reading than listening." He passed the book to Crane.

"A book. How nice." Crane opened it and perused at the first page, though without the enthusiasm Yrae hoped for.

"It will probably seem terribly basic to you after Lok's books. Go ahead and study it now. Tomorrow, we'll have a practical lesson."

Crane sighed and settled down to study. As soon as his gaze was directed elsewhere, Yrae slipped out the door. Outside, he could breathe again. He had always preferred the outdoors. He had never before known the need to escape his own house. It was cramped with two tall men living in it. There was more to the problem than space.

"This is a terrible idea," he muttered to himself. "I can't teach him! What was I thinking, luring him here?"

It wasn't the boy's fault, Yrae knew. Crane might have had another, better teacher, if the enchantment hadn't kept magic folk away from him. Yrae had wanted to teach his son himself, little knowing what would happen when they were together every day. Living alone, cut off from society, Yrae had managed to shut away his guilt and heartache over what he had done to Stell, and by extension, to Crane. With Crane here, that box was open, spilling its contents everywhere. Yrae felt crowded and accused, though Crane said nothing.

"There's nothing I can do about it." He trudged a short way along the path to the lake and sank down on a stump beside the path. "I can't fix it or make it better. All I can do is teach him the right way to do magic."

Crane could hardly believe it. *More* book work? That was the last thing he needed, and he thought Yrae knew it. He'd been Yrae's apprentice for only two days. Already he questioned the value of the experience. What was the point of having a teacher who wouldn't teach him anything new?

"Patience, Crane," he told himself. "He must have a plan."

Having nothing better to do, he examined the odd little book Yrae had given him. It was no larger than the healer's book he had left with Ketty. Unlike that book and the others he'd studied, which were bound in decorated leather, this book was covered in rough, sturdy cloth, unadorned. It lacked the ancient look of those books, though the worn pages and stained cover implied it had been around many years.

The door opened and closed. Crane looked up to find Yrae gone. He had a disconcerting habit of ducking out without a word. Mama had taught Crane always to announce when he was leaving, even if he didn't know where he was going or when he would return. She showed him the same courtesy. But Yrae probably didn't mean to be rude. He didn't usually have anyone to tell. Crane supposed he was going for his daily swim. Or else he was so frustrated with Crane as a pupil, he had to step outside to vent his anger.

Crane pushed that thought away and opened the book to peruse the first few pages. These contained ordinary text, not spells, written in large, clear letters. On the first page were listed rules:

Magic is a gift. Use it for good.
Magic is a tool, not a toy. Use it wisely.
Respect all forms and users of magic, no
    matter how small.
Do not look down upon those without magic.
    Treat them kindly.

And so on, many rules Crane was sure Yrae had not always followed. He flipped further on and found much of the theory Yrae had lectured on, followed by some basic spells. Many of these included illustrations with captions in different, less tidy handwriting. The style of the drawings reminded him of something he had seen before. The crane on his wall at home.

Home. His gaze strayed to his knapsack, standing open against the wall next to his folded bedding. Did he have to stay? He had made no promises. When Yrae offered training, Crane had been excited about learning to use his power, before he knew it would be this tedious and frustrating. But he had what he came for, the key to breaking Yrae's Curse. Yes, he'd also found his father, but the man had no claim on him. If he left right away, he could be back in Misty Pass before dark, and on the road to Deep River in the morning.

Crane glanced at the door. He half expected Yrae to walk in and force him to stay. The door remained closed. Crane left his seat and gathered his scattered belongings and stuffed them into the knapsack.

"Thank you for offering to teach me, but I've changed my mind," he muttered, rehearsing an explanation for Yrae. "No, that sounds like I blame him, and I don't want to make him angry." He rolled his bedding into a neat roll and strapped it to the sack. "I was glad to have met you, but I'm needed at home ... no ... Thank you for your hospitality, but I don't wish to waste any more of your time ..."

There was no polite, truthful way to say it. He would have to sneak away, without saying anything. With the knapsack on his back and his staff in hand, he crept to the window and peeped out. He hoped Yrae was swimming now, which would allow a clean escape. He wouldn't even leave a note. Just go. It was best that way.

Then he saw Yrae. He hadn't gone as far as the lake this time. He sat on a stump near the cabin. So much for getting away unseen. But his attention was not on the cabin. Perhaps there was a chance to sneak by. Yrae appeared to be talking to himself, Crane could only guess what about. Or who. He didn't want to imagine what it would be like to have Yrae angry with him. The most frightening aspect of the Yrae stories was the Mad Wizard's unpredictable temper. All the more reason to leave now, while they were on cordial terms.

Crane couldn't hear Yrae's words. Nothing obvious happened. It must not have been a spell. He didn't even look particularly angry. In fact, he didn't look angry at all.

As Crane watched in secret, Yrae dropped his face into his hands. Crane slipped his knapsack from his shoulders and let his staff tip against the wall. He wouldn't have believed it if someone else had told him. Could it be? The Mad Wizard ... in tears?

Yrae dried his eyes and stood up from the stump. The bout of emotion had overwhelmed him just as he had determined the proper course. It had been a long time since he had wept for his wrongs. At least it hadn't happened in the cabin, where Crane would have seen. He didn't want the boy to fear him, but it wouldn't do to appear weak. And he wouldn't have been able to explain. Why should his son's presence cause such grief when Yrae had longed to see him?

He returned to the cabin, pleased to find Crane immersed in the book.

"You're farther along than I would have expected."

Crane looked up. "I skipped ahead."

"Never skip anything!" Yrae bit back his temper and forced a smile onto his face. "I grant you, it's basic. But you ... might miss something important."

"Where did this book come from?"

"My master Ordahn and I made it when I was a boy, as a way of reviewing our early lessons. I've carried it ever since."

"Who did the drawings? They're excellent."

"I did." Yrae swelled with pride in his youthful work. "I loved to draw when I was a boy."

"Not anymore?"

"I do magic instead." Before Crane could respond, he continued. "We'll do the practical lessons outdoors, weather permitting. I think better in the open air."

"Thank you. So do I."

Chapter 32. The Healer's Touch

Misty Pass

Ketty finished her morning chores as quickly as she could and hurried out the door. She hugged herself for warmth as she jogged to Trilmi's house. The sunny fall day was still cool, though not cold enough for Ketty's heavy cloak. It would turn warm by the time she came home.

Ketty had permission to visit Trilmi twice a week to learn midwifery and herbal remedies. Papa had reluctantly agreed after Ketty demonstrated her healing ability. "How could I deny a birthday girl her wish?" he'd said, his voice choked with emotions she could feel even as he tried to hide them. Fear. Worry. Pride. He hadn't granted all her wishes, though, forbidding her from apprenticing with Healer Kruff or speaking to Fane, the traveling herbalist.

Ketty kept any complaints to herself. In the month since she'd entered this arrangement, she had learned practical skills that might benefit from magic but didn't require it. The midwife also provided care in situations other than pregnancy and childbirth. She had taught Ketty how to properly wrap a sprain, clean a wound, treat a burn. Herbs were often good for pain, bleeding, nausea, sleeplessness, and other maladies. Magic might help them work more quickly, but they were usually effective on their own.

Ketty was willing to use magic without making a spectacle of it, if it would help. She frowned. Why not use it openly? Hiding and secrecy had become her habit. She didn't need to show off, but who would care if she added a touch of magic to help someone heal? It wasn't like she would become Yrae.

The thought of one wizard turned her mind to another. Thinking of Crane revealed him on the mountain, well beyond Sunset Ridge. She couldn't see him the way she had when he was on the trail. She sensed his presence. He had been in the same place for weeks. Had he found Yrae there? If that were so, wouldn't he have completed his quest and returned by now? Ketty shuddered. What if he couldn't leave? What if he …?

No. Ketty was sure she would know if any harm came to him. But maybe not if Yrae had taken him prisoner or put him under a spell.

She set these thoughts aside when she arrived at Trilmi's. Crane was a wizard. He could take care of himself. And if he couldn't, there wasn't much Ketty could do for him. She might be able to help someone else.

As Ketty opened the gate, Trilmi came out the door. "Good, you're here. Come along, we need to visit Marna and her children."

"She's not near her time, is she?" Ketty asked. "I thought it was at least two months more."

"That's not why she asked us to stop by," Trilmi said. "Mardo, the five-year-old, was playing chase with his friends and ran smack into a tree. Hurt his head, poor little one."

When they arrived at the house, they found the other children playing outside, building little cabins with sticks.

"Kennan wants to run. I told him no." Docna, a girl of seven, kept a close eye on her three-year-old brother.

"Running is all right," Trilmi said. "Just not into tree trunks like Mardo. Tell Kennan to watch where he's going."

Marna met them at the door. She was visibly pregnant but moved easily. Trilmi had explained to Ketty that this part of pregnancy was comparatively easy.

"He says his head hurts and the light bothers his eyes," Marna said. "I don't know how you're going to examine him in the dark."

"It's good he's talking and making sense," Trilmi said. "I'll cover his eyes, so the room doesn't have to be dark."

She wrapped a bandage over the child's eyes before lighting a lamp. He had a few bruises, but no serious injuries. With permission, Ketty laid her hand lightly on Mardo's head. He had a big bump. The real injury was inside — not too bad, but he'd be recovering for a week or so. She sensed it the same way she'd sensed Lalik's pregnancy.

"Will he take medicine?" Trilmi asked.

"He's had trouble keeping anything down," Marna said. "That's why I sent for you."

"I could try a pain charm," Ketty offered. "Then he might be able to eat and drink."

She had memorized it but hadn't had a chance to use it yet. It was much less tiring than using her power alone to relieve pain. And it was effective enough that the child was willing to sit up and drink the sweetened herbal remedy Trilmi offered.

After she'd given Marna instructions for care, they headed back, only to meet another neighbor with an urgent need.

"The baby is coming now!" the young man said.

"A little early, though not overly," Trilmi said. "But it's Pallin's first, so having two of us will be a help. Run back and tell her we're on our way."

Although Trilmi's legs were even shorter than Ketty's, she set a brisk pace. Ketty saved her breath for the walk. Pallin lived at the west end of town, as it happened not far from the trail to Sunset Ridge. Her husband was waiting outside when Trilmi and Ketty arrived.

"Her mama's with her," he said. "They think it's

close."

"I'll let you know if they're right," Trilmi said.

Ketty followed the midwife into the snug little house. The laboring mother lay on her side, curled around her belly. Her mother rubbed her back as she whimpered and moaned.

"Here we are," Trilmi announced. "I've brought a helper along. Do you know Ketty?"

Trilmi asked Pallin questions between pains, then washed her hands to examine her directly. She explained to Ketty what she was feeling and pronounced the labor well advanced.

"Next time, I'll let you do it," Trilmi said. "I'm not sure there's time now. Baby's coming soon."

In next to no time — though it probably felt long to Pallin — the child slithered into Trilmi's hands.

"Looks like you've got a fine little girl," the midwife announced. "A few more pushes and you're done."

Ketty cleaned the squalling baby's face, dried her off, and laid her on her mother's chest while Trilmi delivered the afterbirth. She showed Ketty how to cut the cord. The baby was alert and eager to nurse, with help from Pallin's mother with positioning.

Trilmi spoke quietly to Ketty about what they would do next. "There's some bleeding — perfectly normal, especially with a first baby." She explained what she was doing to stop it. It wasn't stopping. "All right, I'm going to put pressure here. Ketty, run and get Kruff."

"Right now?" Ketty asked. "Where?"

"Right this moment! Across the road, green door. Go!"

Ketty ran out of the house. Across the road and back

in the forest stood a small log house with a green door. She'd never gone there before. She wasn't supposed to have any dealings with the old healer. But this wasn't her own dealings. She was speaking on Trilmi's behalf. She pounded on the door.

Kruff opened it and peered out. "What?"

"Trilmi needs your help. We delivered a baby and there's too much blood."

"She knows I don't deal with women's issues," he said.

"Tell me what to do," Ketty said. She wasn't allowed to study with him. What about one set of instructions, though?

Kruff sighed. "No, that would take too long. I'm coming."

Ketty turned and ran back, the healer following at a slower pace. At least they didn't have far to go. She burst through the door and held it for him.

"I don't usually ..." The volume of blood silenced him. He grabbed Ketty's hands and placed them on Pallin's abdomen. "Repeat after me."

It was a powerful spell to stop bleeding. She'd seen it in Crane's book but hadn't had occasion to use it before. Her power rose from her core and rushed into her hands, into Pallin, mingling with Kruff's power. His felt weaker, maybe because it wasn't hers.

"Thank you, Kruff. It's working," Trilmi said.

They kept at it until Trilmi was sure the bleeding was under control. Kruff cleaned his hands and left without a word.

All this time, Pallin's mother and husband had been helping her support the baby, which slept on her breast.

Pallin was ashen and trembling but conscious.

Trilmi smiled at her. "Well, you gave us a scare. You'll be all right now. I'll brew something that'll perk you back up."

She unpacked herbs and showed Ketty how to brew a drink to restore the new mother's strength and help replace some of the blood she'd lost. The scent of it alone was enlivening. They helped the family change the bed and put the blood-soaked bedding in a washtub of cold water. The new grandmother was already preparing a meal when Trilmi and Ketty left.

"Kruff told me he doesn't deal in women's issues," Ketty said. "But then he did."

Trilmi laughed. "That one's full of objections. He always comes through. I call on him only as a last resort, but when I need magic, I really need it."

"You can use mine whenever you need it," Ketty said. "I don't know how to use it like he does, but I'm learning."

"That was a good lesson today. Think you'll remember it?"

Ketty still felt the tingle of power in her fingers. "I doubt I'll ever forget."

Chapter 33. Something New

Yrae's Valley

"The next spell you'll learn is the Eavesdropper's Charm."

A chilly breeze off the lake ruffled Crane's hair and brought him to brief alertness. He knew this charm from his own study, though he'd never managed to work it. He suspected he could do it now without further explanation. A month with Yrae had taught him his instructor didn't appreciate interruptions. At least this was a practical lesson — always more engaging than a lecture.

A long hike would have made better use of the sunny day just past Fall Balance. After a month in the valley, Crane's boots were broken in and comfortable, allowing him to pay attention to more than his feet. The bright light gave extra fire to a few vine-maple leaves that had already turned color. With the change of season, Crane grew restless for something different.

"It allows a wizard to overhear words spoken at a distance, as long as the speaker is in view. The technique is almost exactly the same as Far Voice, so it should be no problem for you. If you're ready, I'll tell you the spell. Repeat after me."

"No." Crane hadn't intended to voice his rebellious feelings. Too late to take it back.

Yrae turned his attention to Crane with the apparent speed — and power — of a glacier. "What did you say?"

Crane swallowed. Defiance went against his nature, and his promise to himself to cooperate with Yrae's instruction. Yrae's frown was almost enough to persuade him to back down. But he couldn't keep quiet any longer. He took a deep breath.

"Teach me something new. You can choose. Give me something I can't do already."

Crane had adjusted with alarming quickness from thinking he had to fight Yrae, to learning from him. With Yrae's practical training, magic that had been difficult and awkward to learn from books began to make sense. Crane worked hard all day at lessons and chores and slept peacefully at night. In the satisfaction of this new life, he could almost forget Deep River. He didn't even remember most of his dreams. The only one that lingered was a brief, troubling image of Elic, sitting alone and still in a dim, dusty room. But he could do nothing for Elic from here, and after all, it was only a dream.

On dry days, he spent hours outdoors beyond his lesson time, acquainting himself with the mountain. His powers of observation sharpened with the strengthening of his magical skills. Hidden things continued to reveal themselves to him. Also small, visible things he previously might have overlooked. On misty mornings, the mountain and forest veiled behind luminous fog, he encountered brilliant green moss, grotesque fungus, crimson paintbrush. When the fog burned away, he could explore and observe. He met his first bear, a surprise encounter over a berry bush. He was frightened at first; in stories, Mama depicted bears as monsters, but the bear was fat and happy, and ignored Crane as long as he stayed away from its patch. Like Yrae, its intimidating appearance hid a less fearsome disposition.

On rainy days, or even the occasional snowy one — rare, though not unheard of at this altitude in late summer and early fall — the wizards sat indoors, reading by the fire. Yrae assigned books to Crane, material related to what they were practicing, while Yrae himself read ahead, his lips moving silently as he pored over the pages. On one of these days, he taught Crane to make ink from wood ash, and how to enchant ordinary ink for writing spells. Crane welcomed these quiet, cozy days, though the confinement of the cabin sometimes led to short tempers. Books were familiar friends, and study was no longer as frustrating, now that he could ask questions and get answers. He was even willing to overlook sarcasm if it increased his understanding.

Above all, Crane's heart swelled at having a father at last, a presence he hadn't known he missed until he unexpectedly found it. Although Yrae resisted the fatherly role, Crane watched him every minute they were together, learning to be a wizard; learning to be a man.

Crane learned quickly and was always eager for the next lesson, but Yrae demanded perfection before he would teach something new. Perfection required endless repetition, even when Crane thought he'd mastered the subject. The next lesson built on the previous, so it wasn't really new. Crane saw the value in learning the theory and relationships behind different spells and charms. He worked as hard to be patient as to perform his lessons perfectly. It was difficult to control his frustration when he had to do the same things over and over.

"Give me something I can't do already." He expected to be sent home for his defiance, but there was no taking it back.

"You want a challenge?" Yrae's eyes narrowed. "All right. You asked for it."

Crane could hardly believe his ears. He attended to everything his father said. They set to work on a lesson requiring both power and finesse, a concealing spell that could be used to hide any size or shape of object. Performed correctly, the concealment would last until a wizard released it. This was the spell that hid the cabin from non-magical eyes, and unlike anything Crane had yet attempted. But hadn't Yrae said illusions and concealment were related? Maybe this would be easy.

"I can see right through it." Crane gazed at the cabin,

screened behind a glittering blue and red network. "What does it look like to a normal person?"

Yrae laughed. "Like nothing. Like an empty valley. Although once, someone tried to get too close, and I had to add the illusion of a charging bear. I won't ask you to do that today."

Even without any extra illusions, it wasn't as easy as Crane had hoped. He tried again and again to hide a small fir tree. Birds fluttered around in confusion as a flickering blue net swirled around the tree, hiding it one moment, revealing it the next.

"No, not like that!" Yrae raged. "You've got to ... no, you're doing it wrong! Do I have to show you again?"

"No, you don't have to show me again!" Crane flung down his staff. Yrae huffed and stalked back into the cabin. Crane dropped onto the ground. For a moment he forgot about all the good things he had learned and wondered only whether it was too late in the day to set out for Misty Pass. "No. I won't give up. I'll show him yet."

As the spell faded, the birds settled onto the branches. Crane watched them, breathing deeply. He let his anger evaporate and picked up his staff, his jaw set. He shouted to startle the birds, then put his full concentration into working the spell. It required him to speak the words in conjunction with special movements of the staff. Crane recalled Yrae's demonstration, which he had tried and failed to imitate. The words weren't a problem. The motions, which had seemed authoritative and dignified in his father, felt stiff and awkward to him. He shifted his staff to his left hand and spoke as before, modifying the motions to be more fluid and graceful, almost a dance.

In the middle of this performance, Yrae emerged from the cabin. Crane ignored him and kept his concentration on the task. Yrae moved as if to speak, but halted, silent, just outside the door. He watched until Crane finished and lowered his staff. The spell held, obscuring the tree from the eyes of the twittering birds.

"And that, lad, is how to do that." Crane started and flushed but smiled with pleasure at the compliment. "It wasn't how I would have done it. Your way worked as well. Perhaps even better."

Crane gaped at Yrae's grudging admission that there might be more than one way to do things. Yrae put an arm around Crane's shoulders in a rough hug, an even greater surprise than the compliment. Together, they admired the glowing blue network that veiled the tree.

"How do I reveal it again?"

"Later. It's much easier. I'm interested to know how long this holds, aren't you? Let's take a break and go visit Aku."

Crane hid his amusement at the wording. Wasn't Aku right there all the time? He almost argued against going, though he'd been dreaming of a hike most of the morning. He'd mastered something difficult, and he wanted more. But a morning of magic always took its toll. He wouldn't be good for much more, anyway.

They provisioned themselves with nuts and dried berries from Crane's travel rations, purchased in Misty Pass but barely needed before he arrived in the valley. They hiked through the band of trees behind the cabin. Above the timberline, the narrow trail stretched level across a rocky talus slope. The cleared stones formed a sturdy wall that kept the rest of the slope from sliding down. Who had done all that work? Ahead of him, Yrae pointed his staff at a rock in the path. It leaped obediently into its place, and Crane had to smile. The man had everything under control.

Chapter 34. Aku's Keeper

Crane followed Yrae along the trail to the cliff they had visited on Crane's first morning. He lay back on the sun-warmed stone. He remembered the fear of that visit, but the memory belonged to someone else — the boy he'd been, not the wizard he was becoming. In a way, he missed the simple fear of the old days. Now he had to face more complicated troubles.

Yrae touched the cliff face and hummed the melody that calmed the volcano, then sat nearby. Crane shielded his eyes and watched the cloudless blue sky before he rolled over and peered at his father, who sat gazing in another direction.

"What's on your mind, lad?" the older man said without looking back.

Crane lay back again and gathered his thoughts. "Why is it so hard?" Although he hadn't meant to complain, he couldn't hide the slight anguished note in his voice.

"What, living with me?"

Crane had a thousand things to say on the subject, and no words yet for any of them. After a long silence, he tried again. "It requires so much effort to learn anything at all. It's easier now, working with you. Once I finally learn something, I can do it, but it's so much work to get there."

"So it is for most of us, my boy." Yrae turned and met his gaze at last. "Magic is a raw talent. It's rarely any use without training and practice."

Crane sighed. "Then it's like everything else. I thought it was supposed to be special."

"It is special. Did you think it would be easy?"

"You say *for most of us*." Crane sat up and turned slightly toward his father. "I know ... a person with the most remarkable gift for healing, who has had no training at all. Who, without saying a word, heals injuries as if they had never been."

Yrae chuckled. "You sound a bit envious. I have heard of such instinctive talent. Rare, but it happens. A woman, is it?"

The blood rose from Crane's neck to the tips of his ears.

"Healers often are," Yrae continued. "Pretty?"

Crane avoided the question. "Well, can she ... should such a one be trained?"

"Certainly, she *can* be. Knowing the words can reduce the effort required to heal. I'm sure she works as hard as you do, in her own way."

Crane recalled Ketty's red and perspiring face after she healed his feet.

"There may be even greater talent there, waiting to be unlocked. I would certainly encourage her to seek training, if she wished it. If she is doing no harm, it isn't required. Perhaps I will meet her someday?"

Crane wasn't ready to share Ketty with anyone. He stared off over the treetops in the valley below. Scattered over the slopes were bright spots of color where vine maple and huckleberry had turned scarlet and orange, autumn's fire licking up the mountain. He hugged his knees and rested his chin on them as he gazed far away.

"You have more on your mind than your healer friend."

"The aspens will be turning soon, by Deep River," Crane said, in what he hoped was a casual tone.

"Are you ... homesick?"

Crane glanced at him sidelong. "This is my home." His own words surprised him as he spoke them. He could only shake his head when he thought how quickly his enemy's stronghold had become his own home, the place he had sought his whole life. And yet ...

"Perhaps it is possible to have two homes," Yrae said with a smile.

"Or three." Misty Pass rose in Crane's imagination. "Never mind. I'm just confused."

His father didn't say anything but appeared to wait for more. Crane struggled to put words to what he wanted to express. He was confused about more than this question of home.

"How can you love a person and hate them at the same time?" His voice came out strained and hoarse. His words sounded foolish as soon as he'd said them. He couldn't explain it any better. Here he was, with the father he had never expected to know, let alone admire. Love, even. He'd hated the father he'd never met, for what he'd done or not done. It had been easy to hate him. Even now, the feeling sometimes came roaring back when Crane remembered his mother, left in the middle of the night with no explanation. And then there was the father he now knew: the wise and powerful wizard he revered; the exacting taskmaster he loathed; the self-exiled man he pitied.

"Perhaps it's the nature of the thing." At least Yrae took the comment seriously. "Why would you bother to hate someone you didn't care about? If you love someone, you're bound to clash, aren't you? I don't know; I've never been any good with people. Are you speaking of someone we know?"

Crane hadn't planned to get that specific. He hadn't planned to blurt out his question at all. There was nothing to do except plunge ahead. "When Mama finally told me about you, her story made me so angry. I thought she should have hated you."

"She had every right to."

"But she loved you, even though she was ... disappointed."

"Is that what you call it?" A question heavy with bitter regret.

Crane doubted Yrae wanted an answer. He went on with his own thought. "I didn't understand how one person could inspire such mixed feelings. Until now."

"It's all right, my boy." Yrae squeezed Crane's shoulder. "You wouldn't be the first to hate me, though you may be the first to love me; the first since ..."

"Since my mother?"

"She didn't know me."

At first, Crane couldn't imagine who else he meant. But it didn't have to be a woman, or that kind of love. "Did you fight with your father?" He had vague memories of Grandpa Stoli, but no idea who his other grandfather was.

"I wish I had. All I have of his are my eyes." Yrae pressed the heels of his hands to those dark blue eyes. "He died when I was a small boy, along with my mother. I barely knew either of them. Damned swamp fever!"

Startled at the sudden vehemence, Crane turned and searched his father's face. "Where are you from?"

Yrae gave him a sidelong look. "Didn't I tell you? I was born in the swamps east of Deep River." Crane was too surprised to say anything before Yrae went on. "After my father and mother died, I lived with my Uncle Soorhi, until I was ten and he apprenticed me to Ordahn, an itinerant wizard passing through. Soorhi was swamp people, too, my father's brother, but a more learned man I dare you to find. He got away somehow. He came back to care for us ... for me."

Crane listened with growing wonder and sympathy. He hadn't expected the name of his beloved old teacher.

"I used to draw pictures of the cranes and herons in the swamp, and when my legs grew long, he said I would turn into one. So I took 'The Crane' as my name." Yrae laughed at this memory. "Those birds were the only beautiful things in the swamp."

"I knew him," Crane said.

"Uncle Soorhi? Is he still alive?" Yrae's eyes brightened with eagerness.

"No, he died about a year ago. He was so old, we thought he would live forever."

"He must have been over ninety. That counts."

"He was our teacher for a long time, at least since Mama was little. He started a school because he had a vision that one of us would need to know how to read, so why not teach all? He would have been teaching in Deep River ... when you were there last."

Yrae's face crumpled. He swallowed hard before speaking. "I went there to find him." Crane leaned closer to hear his whispered words. "I tried to go home, to start over. I went to the house in the swamp. When I found it not only deserted, but collapsed, I assumed he was dead. It hadn't occurred to me to look for him in the village. He never went into town when I was with him. I ended up there myself only when I needed a place to spend the night, out of the rain." He shook his head. "Who knew where that would lead? If I had known Soorhi was living ... but he would have been an old man even then."

"And you hadn't seen him since you were ten?" Crane asked. Yrae shook his head. "I can't imagine leaving home so young. Especially with someone I didn't even know."

Yrae shrugged. "It's the way things were done. Maybe still are, I don't know. If a wizard found a likely candidate, he took him along. For me, it was a way out of the swamp." He sighed. "Wizard Ordahn was a good man. Not warm, but not unkind. Neither of us had a settled home. I lived the traveling life eight years with him, and a few more on my own. It should have been the right life for me. I must have been living it wrong because it was an empty life. I couldn't fill it. So I came to the mountain and found a home at last. I'm settled here, all right." His face wore a shadowed look Crane could almost read.

"You saved me from that. Is that why your spell kept wizards out?"

"I didn't want her to lose you so young, not after her other losses."

Crane smiled. "You did love her." Yrae flinched but didn't deny it. Crane returned to the previous topic. "Soorhi was my uncle, too, and I never knew it. He gave me a drawing of a crane once. I'd never seen one. One of yours, maybe?"

Yrae chuckled. "Probably. The man never threw anything away."

"He must have suspected you were my father, with my looks and my name. He must have known, but he never said anything. Still, he was kinder to me than almost anyone."

"He wouldn't have known by your looks."

"What do you mean? If I had a beard, we'd be nearly identical." Crane looked his father in the eye now, and it was like gazing into a magic mirror that aged the reflection.

"That may be. But Soorhi never saw you, and barely saw me. He was blind. He lost the last of his vision when I was a small boy."

Crane stared, speechless. "I never knew. How could that be?"

"He hid it skillfully. It was as if he *could* see, in some other way. I often suspected he had wizardry in him."

Crane unfolded his hand and stared at his scarred fingers, remembering Soorhi's leap over the desk to extinguish the flames. He remembered something else. "It was you!"

"What was me?"

"An old census listed three, then four, and finally two people living in the swamp. The two must have been Soorhi and you. The other numbers — were they ...?"

Yrae looked down at his own hands, lying in his lap. He spoke softly. "My father, my mother, and me: that's three. Soorhi came to nurse them in their illness: four. And then ... two."

"Why would anyone want to live in a swamp?"

Yrae glanced at Crane out of the corner of his eye. "I'm not sure my parents *wanted* to. Maybe they were hiding, or maybe it was the best they could find. Swamp people don't have much, in terms of money or possessions. They don't always live in swamps, but it's a convenient term for the sort of folks who dwell around the margins. They'll set up camp wherever they think they won't be bothered — swamps, middens, graveyards — and try to get work to sustain them until they get restless and move on. They have a reputation as thieves. Most want to be left alone."

Crane considered this. He had never been aware of such migrants around Deep River. Yrae's Curse had probably kept them away during his lifetime.

"I wish I remembered more," Yrae continued. "I remember people I called Mamam and Dadad. I can't remember their names. Soorhi claimed my mother was descended from Mountain Folk. Perhaps that was why they hid."

Crane remembered the sneering references to swamp people and Mountain Folk he'd heard in Misty Pass, and his anger rose. "Why are people so hateful about nothing? I got some of that growing up, and I couldn't understand what I'd done wrong. But with a whole people ..."

His father sighed. "Doesn't seem fair, does it? There are no swamp people around Deep River now, thanks to me. Nor any swamp, thanks to the dam." He smiled grimly and rose from his rocky seat.

Father and son were both silent on the walk down to the cabin, each alone with his own thoughts. The sun was high now and warmed their faces, though the air held an autumnal crispness. A chorus of marmots whistled all down the valley. A hawk circled overhead, then suddenly stooped after some small prey. Chipmunks popped onto the trail and sprang off rocks and tree trunks as they continued on their brisk way. It was a perfect day to be out walking, Crane thought, especially after the hard work and talk of the morning. He was grateful not to think or talk for a while.

Rounding a bend in the trail, they surprised a big mountain cat padding uphill. The dusty-brown animal backed against the rock face. It hissed and bared long, yellow fangs.

"What should we do?" Crane gasped.

"Don't run. Do what I do." Yrae grabbed the edges of his cloak and flapped his arms and shouted. After a moment, Crane did the same. The cat crouched, watching them, then turned and bolted away on silent paws. They continued to shout and flap until it bounded up a slope far from their current path.

"That was an odd spell," Crane commented as they continued walking.

Yrae laughed. "What spell? That's how you deal with mountain cats — look big and make noise. And don't run."

"Really?"

"Really. She didn't want to fight anything as big as you! We surprised each other, that's all."

"I guess I don't know much about wild animals."

"You see? I can teach you plenty besides magic. You're disappointed?"

"No. Well, maybe a little. I thought you could command the beasts."

Yrae snorted a laugh. "Trick them, maybe. Fight them, if necessary. Command them? Not likely. Sometimes you can speak to them. The wild ones don't listen very well. An animal that's used to people, a dog or a horse, they'll listen sometimes. Not cats, though. You can't tell cats anything." He laughed again. "Well, if you want to learn to talk to animals, I'll try to teach you."

As they neared the cabin, Yrae threw open his cloak and lifted his arms toward the sun. "Ah, it's finally warming up! I can have a swim before lunch." Crane shivered at the idea, and Yrae laughed. "You don't swim, do you?"

"There was nowhere to swim where I came from, remember?" Crane scowled, then chuckled at himself.

"Ah, yes. Sorry."

"So you *did* block our river! I thought it must have happened naturally. Why would you do such a thing?"

Yrae gazed at him for a moment. "I dried up that pestilential swamp. For my mother. For revenge."

"Quite the memorial. But what about the people who were using the water? Did you even stop to consider them? And what about the cranes and other birds? They're all gone."

"People adapt, and birds can fly. Cranes can find a new home. Now for my swim. It's fine exercise, but you wouldn't want to learn here. This icy lake takes even my breath away." He walked down to the lakeshore and stripped, folding his clothes into a neat pile. He ran into the frigid water with a shout and plunged in to swim, his economical strokes barely disturbing the glassy surface.

Crane lay down next to the folded clothes and closed his eyes. It wasn't long before Yrae came splashing out of the lake and flopped down next to him to dry in the sun.

"Hoo! That's invigorating, all right! And probably the last swim of the season. I'm not as young as I used to be."

"How did you find this place?" Crane asked drowsily, his eyes only half open. "It's so beautiful."

"I didn't find it. I was ... brought here."

"Who brought you?"

"When I ran away, I didn't run to the mountains by accident. Certainly, it's easy enough to lose yourself in all these valleys and forests. I wanted to find someone ... some people."

He left it at that, and Crane pondered for a moment. "Mountain Folk?"

"Yes." Yrae sat up and pulled on his shirt. "They call themselves *Aklaka*. Soorhi had spent time with them when he was young and taught me a few words of their language. They have power and wisdom different from ours, and I had always wanted to learn it. After all, if my mother was of them, I was, too. So when I was ready for a change ..."

"Where are they? I haven't seen anyone around here but you." Although Crane's one encounter with Mountain Folk had been friendly, he sat up and looked around uneasily.

"No, you don't see them unless they want to be seen. They don't come to this place much, not since they found me to stay with Aku for them. I have one friend who visits once or twice a year, but he's the only one. They needed someone here, I needed a place to hide. It seemed a fair bargain at the time. They introduced us, tested my strength, and when they were satisfied, left us to our honeymoon."

His embittered tone surprised Crane. "Honeymoon?"

Yrae glanced up with affection and irritation at the peak above them. "And they said it wouldn't last! Well, I'm hungry. Let's go in."

He got up and moved off toward the cabin, leaving Crane, as usual, with more questions than answers.

Chapter 35. Leaving Aku

Crane and Yrae still argued from time to time, but anger was now tempered by understanding and growing affection. In the warmth of this budding friendship, Crane enjoyed learning magic in the magnificent setting. He continued to count the days, but as summerlike weather stretched into fall, he didn't always trust his own sense of time passing. Had he been there months, or only days?

He woke one morning to find winter had arrived overnight. Snow dusted the trees, and the mountain glistened in the cold light.

"You should probably think about going home soon,"

Yrae said as he served the breakfast porridge. "You're welcome to spend the winter here if you've lost interest in lifting the enchantment, but I thought that was important to you."

"The trip should take only four or five days. My birthday is still weeks off, isn't it?" A stab of panic killed Crane's appetite. His count said he had been with Yrae just over two months. He doubted he had done the necessary thing yet, but there should still have been time.

"Yes, but winter comes earlier here than down in Deep River, and I can't hold off the heavy snows forever. The sooner you go, the easier your travel will be."

Crane nodded agreement. "I'll leave tomorrow." Was that a good idea? He had left Deep River on equally short notice, with no real plan, which had put him in peril. He was more experienced now, and at least it was better than sneaking out in the middle of the night.

It wouldn't take long to pack his clothes and other belongings. He would have to beg a few supplies from Yrae. If there wasn't too much snow on the trail, he could reach Misty Pass in one day, and re-provision there. Depending on Ketty's welcome, he'd spend a night or two, then get directions for the shorter route to Deep River. He'd be home in no time.

"I'll be sorry to see you go," Yrae admitted. He hardly seemed the same man as the intimidating figure who had stood in the doorway on a long-ago summer night.

"Come with me, in case I don't get home in time to break the spell."

"I couldn't leave my Aku. Who would calm her?"

"You wouldn't have to stay away. Come and see the

enchantment end. Make peace with Mama."

"I can't leave." Yrae turned away.

Crane stared at Yrae's back, startled at his sharp reply. Until now, he had appeared the freest of men, his own master, living alone in the wilderness. Yrae had not said the word, but Crane's mind echoed with it: *trapped.*

After supper that night, Crane packed his knapsack. He had so few belongings, he should have been finished in almost no time. He folded and refolded his clothes, unpacked and rearranged items several times, delaying the moment when he could say, "There. I'm ready to leave."

Yrae sat in silence at the table. He had a book open in front of him. Crane suspected he wasn't even looking at it. He never turned a page, and his lips were still. He finally closed the book and watched Crane load his pack for the third time. He got up quietly, returned the book to the shelf and took down another. He went to the crate where he kept his clothes and blankets. He pulled out a heavy flannel shirt, a fur-lined tunic, woolen underwear, and lined trousers. For one hopeful moment, Crane thought he was about to fill his own knapsack and come along.

"They don't fit me anymore, and you'll need warmer clothes for this trip." Yrae handed the clothes to Crane. "And I want you to have this now." He laid the book he'd made with his own mentor on top of the clothes.

"Thanks." Crane gazed at these gifts, a lump of

disappointment in his throat. He let gratitude melt it and looked up at his father. "You can turn into an eagle. I wish you'd taught me that. It would make my trip much easier." He smiled to lighten the mood.

Yrae shook his head. "You're carrying too much, and you're not ready. Someday, but not yet." He turned away, threw on his cloak, and went outside without another word.

Crane removed his own clothing and put on the warm underwear, which would be cozy for sleeping. He packed his things and laid out the winter clothes for the morning, moving his little agate to the pocket of the warm trousers so it wouldn't be lost. He was about to pack the two pots of ink but didn't want to risk ruining his clothes if one of them spilled. There was a small pocket in his cloak that would hold them. Others were the right size to hold the book and his water flask.

After everything was packed and ready for the morning, Crane tried to wait up for Yrae to return, but he couldn't keep his eyes open. It wouldn't do to travel if he was exhausted. He went to bed and fell asleep almost as soon as he lay down. Nothing disturbed him all night.

The next morning was cold and gray; foggy, with none of the dazzling golden light of summer. Crane didn't know when Yrae had come back. He was making breakfast by the time Crane woke. Now fed, Crane stood in the doorway, staff in hand and ready to go, but hesitant.

"Not a very nice day." Yrae looked out over Crane's shoulder. "Sure you want to leave today?"

"I don't know. Is it likely to improve much, this time of year?"

"No. Not without my help."

Crane turned to his father and smiled. "You've done enough. So ... goodbye. Thank you." It seemed too little for such a moment, and yet, there was nothing more to say.

Yrae laid his arm across Crane's shoulders. "My dear boy." It wasn't much — a touch and three words — but from Yrae, it was lavish.

Yrae walked with Crane a short distance along the path, his hand resting on Crane's shoulder as if he couldn't let go. At the bridge, he reluctantly withdrew his hand. "Well."

Crane turned and clasped his father's hand in both of his. "I'll come back," he promised, just as he had promised his mother when he left Deep River. "May I take a message to Mama?"

Yrae took a deep breath but didn't reply immediately. As he gazed into Crane's eyes, he burst out, "Wait right there!" He hurried back to the cabin. Crane stood, puzzled and curious. When Yrae finally reappeared, he was dressed for travel. "I'm coming with you. To see the enchantment end, like you said. Not to stay."

Crane had to suppress a smile. Yrae's beard was neatly trimmed, his wild hair brushed back and tied behind his head.

"What are you staring at?" Yrae asked. "You shaved, didn't you?"

"Yes, for a girl I know. Who did you tidy up for?

"Now, you wouldn't want me frightening the populace, would you? And you'll be famous as the man who tamed the Mad Wizard."

"I don't care about fame. I'm glad to have you along." Crane thought he might burst with happiness. Though Yrae had told him he wouldn't stay in Deep River, Crane couldn't help imagining, if only for a moment, his family united at last.

Yrae didn't share his happiness. He kept looking back nervously as they hiked out of the valley, glancing up at the fog-shrouded mountain, his lips moving in soundless words. Crane worried he might turn and bolt back to the cabin. He grew calmer as they reached the top of the ridge and descended across the great meadow.

The flowers were gone. Patches of snow covered part of the dead, pale brown grass that lay wet and limp against the contour of the slope. Wisps of mist clung to trees and flowed over the ground. Here and there, berry bushes showed crimson and orange, brighter for not having to compete with the sun.

"Lovely day for a journey, isn't it?" Crane was in high spirits despite the weather, and eager to reach Misty Pass, with its promise of warm shelter and friendly faces. The thought of one particular friendly face hurried him forward, but Yrae lagged. Without warning, he stumbled, prevented from falling only by his staff and Crane's quick arm.

Crane gazed with concern at his father's haggard face. "Are you all right? Should we go back?"

"Go back? And climb that again?" Yrae looked back the way they had come. "No, I'm fine. I'm only tired."

"Did you sleep at all last night? I never heard you

come in."

"I spent the night with Aku. If all goes according to plan, she should sleep until I get back."

"You *were* planning to come with me."

"I changed my mind twenty or thirty times during the night. Now I'm committed, so let's get moving!"

For Yrae's sake, Crane was glad they wouldn't have to climb until after lunch. Even hiking downhill made for a strenuous morning. The trail was slick with mud and slush. By the time they reached the timberline, Crane's knees ached, and his thighs and calves protested at the effort not to run or slide. At noon, the weary travelers dropped to the ground near the hot spring and ate a simple meal.

Yrae smiled at the steaming spring. "Warmed by Aku's own heart," he murmured.

Crane longed to take an extended rest break, even to let his father sleep for a few hours. With the hot spring and the lower elevation, it was warmer than in Yrae's valley, but Crane did not want to spend a night outside if he could avoid it. They had a long way to go, and darkness came early now. Before either of them wanted to, they continued the downward journey.

They soon reached the flat meadow with its bridge and narrow stream. The dead grass here was not yet weighed down by snow. The travelers walked more easily, though the wet grass slapped their legs from either side of the narrow trail. After only a few steps, their trouser legs were soaked, and water dribbled into their boots.

Crane paused a moment to study the tall fireweed's seedheads, like puffs of fog caught there. The sight through the screen of fluff took his mind off his complaining muscles and soaked legs. A pair of half-grown bear cubs wrestled and played off to the right of the trail. He was about to point them out to his father when Yrae touched his shoulder.

"Look," he said. "A bear. Late for them. Thought they'd be in the den by now."

"Yes, I —" Crane froze. His father looked not to the right, but to the left. A huge, shaggy brown bear raised its head and turned toward them, snuffling the air. Yrae watched the bear, as if dazed or unconcerned. Crane grabbed his arm and whispered, "Do something!"

"What do you suggest?"

The bear rose on its hind legs and huffed.

Crane looked from Yrae to the bear, his mind a blank. *It's up to me?* He tried to think. He remembered the episode with the mountain cat. Something told him trying to look big and intimidating was the wrong idea. What else had Yrae said? Trick them? Fight them? It would be better to disappear.

The big bear dropped onto all fours and charged, cutting the distance between itself and the wizards at a speed that seemed impossible for such a massive beast.

Crane began to intone the concealing spell. He had never tried using it on himself, but he didn't have any better ideas. Without warning, Yrae staggered against him and grabbed at Crane's arm as he slid to the ground. Crane lost his grip on his staff. He swore through clenched teeth and flailed for it. It fell to the ground. He dropped to his knees next to his father and wrapped an arm around Yrae's shoulders.

"Don't move," Crane whispered. He lunged and

grabbed up his staff. *In the wrong hand. This had better work.* In a low voice, he started the spell again, saying the words as rapidly as he could and wielding his staff with the tiniest motions he could manage. When he finished, they were wrapped in the shimmering strands of the spell. Crane held his breath and waited.

The bear kept charging. Even if she couldn't see them, she would run right over them if he couldn't turn her aside. His mind running as fast as the bear now, Crane remembered his father's offhand comment about an illusion of a charging bear.

This time, it's the bear that's real. He almost laughed aloud at what he had in mind. He added what he hoped was a convincing illusion of a skunk, complete with smell. It waddled toward the bear, turned, and raised its tail.

The bear veered to one side so suddenly, it nearly fell over. Grumbling, it crossed the trail in front of Crane and Yrae and galloped across the meadow to join the cubs. As soon as the bear family had disappeared into the trees, Crane spoke the revealing spell and fell over against his father.

Yrae leaned against him, and they held each other up, both spent. Yrae touched Crane's shoulder. "Well done."

Crane barely heard the compliment. He found himself staring into blue eyes glassy with fever, shining out of a flushed face. "You're not well. Fly home, I can go on by myself."

His father shook his head. "Not strong enough for that, but I can still walk. Let's go." He climbed stiffly to his feet, and Crane did the same. He was torn between making camp so Yrae could rest, and hurrying on to shelter. An icy drizzle and the memory of the bears decided the issue.

Crane observed his father closely as they hiked. Though Yrae protested he was not ill, his steps wove dizzily. By turns, he would throw open his cloak and complain he was too warm, then clutch it tightly around him, shaking with chill. It reminded Crane of the one time he'd been really sick as a boy, when he was nine or ten. Mama called it the winter wobbles and made him stay in bed for a week. Even after the fever broke, he'd coughed and felt wobbly for days, but recovered with no permanent damage. Whatever afflicted Yrae was probably something much worse.

"As soon as we get to Misty Pass, I'll find a healer for you," Crane said.

"I do not need any village healer." Yrae's jaw clenched to keep his teeth from chattering. "I can take care of myself."

"At least let me help you," Crane said. "I'm not a great healer, but I'm sure I could manage a fever charm."

"There's no need. Let's keep moving."

"Fine, have it your way." *He doesn't trust anyone, not even me.*

Chapter 36. Yrae's Illness

Misty Pass

Darkness had fallen by the time Crane and Yrae trudged into Misty Pass, a darkness deepened by the cold, persistent mist that always marked the coming of night there. Yrae hesitated at the edge of the village.

"I don't show my face here."

"Show a different one," Crane said.

A rounder, clean-shaven visage appeared for a moment over Yrae's real face, not hiding it. The illusion flickered away.

"I can't." Yrae pulled his hood farther forward.

Crane took his arm to urge him on and once again followed his nose to the welcoming Fogbank. When they reached the inn, Yrae hesitated again.

"Bad luck," he muttered.

"Worse luck to stay out here when you're sick. You need a warm room and a good bed even more than I do." Crane put his arm around his father and guided him inside.

It was crowded and noisy around the supper tables. Crane spotted Ketty in the kitchen, her back to them. He was about to call out to her when Eslo came over to greet them.

"Welcome, travelers! What can we get you? Why, Crane, welcome back, young fellow!"

"It's good to be back, Eslo." When Crane spoke, Ketty's head jerked up, but she didn't turn enough that he could catch her eye. "And this is —"

"Yubi," his father finished for him. He shook Eslo's hand.

"My ... *Yubi* needs rest." Crane tried to act as if he knew this name. "He hasn't been well today."

"In that case, perhaps bed now and supper after." Eslo took the sick man's arm and led the way to the stairs. "I'll send Ketty up later with a tray."

"I'll bring it up myself." Crane hurried to the kitchen.

Ketty glanced up and smiled. "Hello, Crane." Her voice was quiet, almost shy, which seemed out of character for her. "I knew you were coming, since this morning. I ... I thought you might be ill."

"No, he's ill, I'm not, I mean ..." Crane burst into a foolish grin. "I'm so glad to see you, I can't even talk. I've never felt better."

"That's good." She peered at him. "You look well, but ... I don't know. Older. Different somehow."

"Two months closer to eighteen. And you look like you have a secret that won't keep."

"I can't keep anything from you!" Her eyes shone in the lamplight. "After you left, I couldn't stand pretending anymore. I told Papa I wanted to study healing. Can you believe it, I'm apprenticed! Sit down, I'll tell you all about it as soon as I get a moment." She steered him to the nearest seat and hurried away to deliver supper to another guest.

It was comforting to be back in the warm, lighted room. Crane found it especially warming to watch Ketty. He could still feel her touch on his shoulder. Her smile glowed as brightly as her hair, and he hoped he was the cause of at least part of her excitement.

"You're apprenticed to a healer?" Crane asked when she returned. "I thought your father —"

"No, Papa wouldn't go that far. He suspected my gift for a long time. I guess he hoped it would go away if he ignored it and didn't encourage me to use it."

"How did you change his mind, if he was so set against it?"

"He didn't take it well when I first told him my plan." She broke off abruptly. "Here I stand, talking and talking. Are you hungry?"

"Famished," Crane said. "And damp, but I think I'll eat before I change."

"So, have you had enough rain yet?"

"Yes, but this time of year, it rains at home, too."

Ketty laughed as she returned to the kitchen. How he had missed that sound! "Eat up, there's plenty." She set a full plate in front of him and placed a second dish on a tray. "For your companion."

"Mm, this is exactly what I need." Crane eagerly dug into the fragrant, hearty stew.

"As I was saying, Papa tried to talk me out of my training idea, reminding me about Yrae and my mother."

Blood rushed to Crane's face at her mention of his father's name. He ducked his head to hide his reaction.

"But then I had him. I told him I wanted to learn to use my magic so I could help people, to make up for wizards like Yrae. He wasn't happy about it but settled for a compromise. I'm with Trilmi, the midwife. She has no magical gift herself. She sometimes consults with Healer Kruff. I'm learning from both of them, but don't mention it. Papa doesn't know." She swept off to fill a mug and remove an empty plate, then returned. "Your book was such a help! I wish I could keep it. I'll get it for you after supper."

"A midwife. That's good. I'm glad you're using your gift for something worthwhile."

"I'm glad, too. It's a relief not to hide anymore."

He was quiet a moment, smiling at a memory. "Our midwife back home was like a second mother to me."

"I'd like to meet her. Who knows, maybe I will. Once I'm trained, I could go anywhere!"

He looked at her in surprise and alarm. "You'd leave here? What about the inn?"

"You think I want to keep an inn all my life? No, I want to see the world, maybe do some good for people."

"I never knew a girl who went far from home. I never knew anyone who did." For a fleeting moment, Crane thought of his mother, with her knapsack and water flask. Had she ever dreamed of leaving Deep River?

"See? You're not the only one with an urge to visit other places." With an apologetic smile, Ketty hurried to the other side of the room to serve another guest. Someone tried to grab her, but she muttered a word only Crane understood, and the man hit the wall with a satisfying thump. Crane suppressed a laugh and concentrated on his supper until she returned.

"I helped with a difficult birth awhile back. What about you?" She looked uneasily toward the stairs. "Who's that man you're with?"

"He's my ... my new mentor. I'm learning to use my magic, too."

"Oh, that's a relief. I had a funny feeling when he walked in. At first, I thought he might be —"

"You thought right." Crane gazed at his plate rather than meet Ketty's eyes. She was giving him the benefit of the doubt, but there was no lying to her. "He's Yrae." He looked up timidly. The color drained out of her face.

"I see. You must be tired. Let me show you your room." She snatched up his empty plate, dumped it in the kitchen, and walked to the stairway door without looking back.

Crane juggled the supper tray, his staff, and his knapsack and followed obediently as she led the way upstairs.

Without a word, Ketty opened a door. With a gesture of elaborate politeness, she showed Crane into a larger room than the last time. She remained in the passageway, her eyes boring into Yrae's back as he stood by one of the two beds, rummaging through his knapsack. He started and turned, but she had already spun on her heel and left. Crane's attention was divided between the two of them. His father seemed better already. He was wearing dry clothes, at least, and looked steadier on his feet.

"So, you're Yubi now?" Crane set down the tray and closed the door. "The Crane, Yrae, Yubi ... Just how many names do you have?"

"As many as I need. Do you think these folks would want me in their house if they knew who I really am?"

"What if one of them does know?"

"Ha! Not likely."

Crane chose not to press the issue. "You could have warned me."

"I didn't think about it until that moment. I'm telling you now: for the remainder of this journey, my public name will be Yubi."

"How do you feel now?" Crane changed the subject as he unpacked his own belongings. "If you're hungry, I can vouch for the stew."

"I'm fine. No appetite to speak of, but I'll be better when I've had my medicine. Now where did I put it?" He dumped his knapsack out on the bed and searched the contents with increasing agitation. He looked up at Crane with fear in his glittering eyes. "I forgot to pack my medicine."

"Medicine? What kind? I'll go out right now. Maybe the village healer has what you need."

His father shook his head. "You won't find what I need around here. There's only one merchant who sells it in these parts — that herbalist I told you about. He comes through once a month, and we've missed him."

He sighed. "Never mind. What I need most right now is rest." He cleared off his bed, lay down, and was soon snoring peacefully.

Crane gazed at Yrae with worried affection. Pointless to worry about someone so self-sufficient. He couldn't help it. He longed to do something for him but couldn't think of anything he was capable of that Yrae would allow. He spread a blanket over the slumbering form.

Crane peeled off his damp clothes and pulled on a dry shirt. He extinguished the lamp with a word and stretched out on the other bed. Too exhausted to sleep, he lay for a long time listening to the friendly noises from downstairs.

I wish I hadn't told Ketty. But she already suspected, and she hasn't asked us to leave. Yet. Slight encouragement on which to pin his hopes of continued friendship. At least he and his father had shelter from the cold and rain.

Crane was drifting between sleep and waking when a voice broke the quiet. He sat up in the dark and listened. It was Yrae's voice, whispering, raving, laughing, and crying by turns. Crane sprang from his bed, spoke the lamp into life again, and hurried to his father's bedside. He laid his left hand on the sick man's forehead but jerked it back with a small cry. He burned with fever and talked deliriously in his sleep.

Crane took a deep breath and carefully laid one hand on his father's forehead, the other on his chest. He tried to remember the fever charm he'd read in the healing book. He spoke what he recalled in a soft, uncertain voice. It had no effect, as far as he could tell. He reluctantly withdrew and sat on his bed, dejected and defeated. In the midst of his low spirits, a little flame of anger kindled.

"I faced a charging bear, endured soaking, icy rain, and had the most miserable day of my life to get you to shelter. Are you going to die, and in this house, of all places? Not if I have anything to say about it!"

Filled with new determination, Crane lacked the one thing he needed: healing ability. And who had that? Ketty, the one person he was afraid to ask.

You faced a charging bear, but you're afraid of a girl? he asked himself, and had to answer, *Yes. But I must help him somehow.* Crane scraped together what little courage he had left, pulled on dry trousers, and went downstairs.

A few guests lingered while Ketty cleaned up. She leaned on her broom, her back to Crane as she chatted with a young man who lounged, arms folded, against the wall by the front door. A stab of jealousy startled Crane. He shook it off. Something else was happening. Another fellow sneaked up behind Ketty while the first man distracted her.

Before Crane could shout a warning, Ketty turned and glanced at her would-be assailant. She neither spoke nor moved more than an eyebrow. He sat down hard on the floor, as if she'd shoved him with all her might. The first fellow looked on in surprise, then burst out laughing. Soon, the man on the floor joined in. His friend helped him up. Behind them, Ketty rolled her eyes and blew out a breath. The two men brushed past Crane on their way upstairs, still chuckling.

When she saw him there, Ketty turned away.

"Ketty ..."

She continued to ignore him. She wouldn't look at him or even acknowledge his presence. In frustration, he lunged to grab her arm. She snapped it out of reach and whirled to land a stinging slap on his cheek. "There, now you have my attention. What do you want?"

He touched his burning cheek. She hadn't held back and didn't look any less angry. He couldn't let that deter him. "I need your help. My ... teacher is ill, and I'm no healer."

"Why should I help him? He wouldn't help my mother. How dare you even ask! How dare you bring him here!"

"Please. It might be necessary. For me?"

"Hm!" She turned away. "I wish I'd never met you!"

That hurt more than the slap. "Then do it for her! Do it for your mother. Do it ... for my mother."

Ketty turned. "What's that supposed to mean?"

"He's family. I have to take care of him." It was a dirty trick, throwing her own words back at her. Crane swallowed hard and went on, barely above a whisper. "He's my father. I'm taking him to her. Bringing him home."

She stared for a moment. "Your father?" Her anger flared again. "Your father?! Oh, I know how good he was to you. He can cure himself, or you can do it."

"I can't."

"Fine, you can stay here until he's on his feet, or dead, and then, out!"

Ketty turned away. Speechless, Crane trudged back upstairs.

Chapter 37. Healing a Stubborn Wizard

Ketty kept her back turned until she heard the door close and Crane's footsteps on the stairs. That would teach him to bring an enemy under her roof. The moment of triumph drowned in her disappointment. She had so looked forward to Crane's return, but Yrae spoiled her happiness. Again. Yet for all her anger at Crane for bringing the wizard back into her life, she had almost granted his request.

She rearranged pans in the kitchen, an excuse to bang things. "His fault." Bang! "Why'd he have to bring him here?" Bang! "Of all the men in the world, why is it my enemy's son I care for?" Bang!

What kind of healer are you, if you won't help a sick man? a voice inside her asked. *He hurt me*, she argued. *Did he mean to? How should I know? Aren't you better than that?*

Ketty stopped clattering pots. "I *am* better than that."

She stomped to her room. She'd been practicing with medicinal herbs and had a basket of the most commonly useful varieties, plus a few more specialized things. She didn't know what was wrong with Crane's father, but something in there should help. It would be a good chance to try out the pain and fever charms she'd learned from Crane's book, too.

She returned to the kitchen for the teakettle, steaming away on the stove. Ketty could relate — boiling inside, trying to be useful. She climbed the stairs to Crane's room. The door stood slightly ajar. Crane's voice stumbled through part of the fever charm. He claimed he was no healer, but he was trying. Trying and failing. He might as well try to heal a log for all the good the mangled charm would do. It was up to Ketty.

She shouldered the door open, harder than she intended. It banged off the wall. She glared at Crane and kicked the door shut behind her.

She set the kettle on the stove.

"You came!" Crane exclaimed. "What changed your mind?"

"Unlike some people, I can't ignore a fellow creature in need. And I told you to look for him, didn't I?"

"That was before either of us knew who he was," Crane said. "I'm glad you're here."

Ketty approached the man on the bed, her anger ready to burst out again. She took a deep breath and laid her hands on his forehead and chest. He burned with a high fever. *Swamp fever,* a voice within Ketty said. She didn't question how she knew. She was learning to trust the magic.

"Ah, you poor man," Ketty murmured as grudging pity replaced hostility. "No one should be so ill, not even you. Crane, build up the fire. I'm going to need to make a special tea."

While he laid firewood on the glowing embers in the stove, Ketty spoke the beginning of the fever charm. Although unconscious and weakened, Yrae raised a shield against the magic, keeping it out. Ketty broke off with a frustrated squawk. "I don't believe this — he's resisting!" She needed more power to break through. She remembered working the bleeding charm with Kruff. "Crane, get over here and help me."

"How?" He stood across the bed from her.

"If we say the charm together and combine our strength, maybe we can get through his shield."

Crane laid his hands hesitantly over hers and listened as she recited the charm. After a couple of rounds, he joined in, haltingly at first as he struggled with the words. Ketty spoke out strongly and pushed more power into the effort. Crane's confidence grew as he said it with her. His power, weaker than Ketty's but steady, combined with hers in a thrilling tingle. Together, they overcame Yrae's resistance.

Ketty chanted more loudly, almost singing the charm. It took hold at last, and the fever lessened. She stopped chanting. Crane continued for a couple of words after her voice ceased, a weak echo. Ketty withdrew her hands, breathing hard. Crane sank onto his bed.

Ketty stared at Yrae's face, relaxed now in sleep. He perspired heavily as the fever broke but breathed more easily. Ketty tore her gaze away and searched her basket. She pulled out a piece of stiff bark and pressed it into Crane's hand. "Break this up into the hot water, and let it boil for a bit." Her gaze wandered back to the sleeping wizard. "Then bring me a cup of the brew."

Crane stumbled to the stove and did as she had instructed. He returned with a cup, averting his face from the steam that rose from the hot liquid. Ketty stared at Yrae.

"Wherever did he pick up swamp fever?" she asked.

"Is that what it is?" Crane asked. "I thought it might be winter wobbles. I had that once, and I was never so sick in my life."

"Winter wobbles is unpleasant, but not usually dangerous if you're healthy otherwise. Swamp fever, on the other hand ... I've never seen it up here in the mountains. I read about it in that book you lent me."

"He was born in a swamp," Crane said. "He left when he was ten years old, but swamp fever took his parents."

"Both of them?" Ketty caressed the sick man's forehead. "He must have had it then, too, and maybe more than once before he left. The book says even if you recover, you're never free of it. It can come back as a mild fever. If you're sick with something else or exhausted, it gets dangerous."

"He didn't sleep last night."

"And then hiked all day, even though he probably already felt the fever coming on. Men!"

"This one, anyway," Crane said. "Before he went to bed, he said something about forgetting to pack his medicine."

"Of course, he's been treating himself." Ketty said. "Probably thinks he's the only one who knows what to take for it."

Yrae's eyelids fluttered and opened. He fumbled for Ketty's hand and gently kissed the palm. "Thank you," he whispered. In her mind, she heard more: *I'm sorry.* His strong feelings of regret backed up the words.

She smiled and blinked back tears. "Crane, help him sit up. Here, my friend, drink this." She held the cup to his lips, and he took a swallow.

His face wrinkled with disgust. "That stuff never gets any better. It tastes like it should kill you. How do you happen to have such a thing? It's not exactly common around here."

"I bought it from Fane when he came to our market a couple of weeks ago. He had all kinds of unusual things. I passed over most of it. This bark seemed like something I should have."

"Healer's intuition. I'm glad you listened to it." Yrae lay back down. "It may have saved my life." He closed his eyes and was soon snoring.

Ketty watched the sleeping man, but there was nothing more for her to do. She turned to go. She stumbled and fell against Crane. He caught her as she sagged toward the floor.

"Are you all right?" he asked.

She sensed his alarm. "Yes, but ... oh, I can barely stand." Her teeth chattered. "I need to sit a moment."

He helped her to a chair by the stove. She sank down

and leaned forward, resting her face in her hands.

"Here." He knelt beside her and held out a cup. "Drink some water. It might help."

She took the cup from him. Her hand trembled so badly, the water splashed and slopped onto her dress. "I can't stop shaking."

He took the cup back and held it for her, carefully tipping a little into her mouth. "Something I learned up there. This is how it is when you use a lot of power all at once. Sorry I wasn't more help."

"You were ... as much help ... as you could be." She clenched her jaw against the shaking that ran all through her. "I ... he ... oh!" Sudden tears streamed down her face as she sobbed.

Crane knelt at her side. "I'm ... I'm sorry. It was too much to ask. We never should have come here."

"No, it's all right." She reached out and laid her hand gently on his cheek. "I'm sorry I hit you. You didn't deserve it."

"Not even for what I just put you through?"

"Perhaps." She managed a smile and looked over at the slumbering wizard. "I'm glad you told me who he is. All of it. He's not a madman, is he? Or evil?"

"Not really, no." Crane shifted around to sit on the floor. "He's strange, but that might come from being alone for so long. Or maybe he was always like that, and that's why he's been alone."

"I wish I understood."

Crane sighed. "You mean, why didn't he help your mother? Why not ask him when he wakes up?"

"I don't know. Maybe when he's better. I know he feels terrible about it, but he's been so ill ..."

"You truly are a healer." Crane smiled. "I'll try to explain as best I can. I'm not sure he understands, either. I suspect it had more to do with my mother than with yours. With his greatest mistake."

"What mistake?" Ketty asked.

Crane pointed his thumb at his own chest. "You're looking at it. Or the result of it. I don't think he *meant* to hurt anyone. He was trying to protect himself."

"Protect himself from what? He's supposed to be the most powerful wizard living."

"He had a vision that he would die in Mama's house. He didn't want that, so he doesn't go into other people's houses at all. Bad luck, he says." Crane shook his head. "I suspect there's more to it. When he was young and proud of his heroic reputation, he would have healed everyone he could. He developed a special technique of his own to cure dangerous illnesses. But Yrae the Mad Wizard cultivated ill opinion, planting false rumors to keep people at a distance. All to protect himself from ..." He broke off, a puzzled frown changing to a smile.

"From what?" Ketty repeated.

"Love," Crane said. "After my mother, he wouldn't risk caring for someone or having them care about him. It didn't matter to him if he hurt a person he didn't know."

"Does he have any idea how much trouble he's caused, thinking only of himself?" Ketty asked.

"He's beginning to," Crane said. "But he hasn't caused only trouble. If it weren't for his foolish spell on Deep River, I never would have met you."

"If it weren't for his *greatest mistake*, you wouldn't exist at all."

Crane smiled and took her cold hands between his. He rubbed the warmth back into them. "Do you still wish we hadn't come?"

"I'm glad you came back." Ketty wished he could go on warming her hands all night. She hid her disappointment when he released them. "And what do you mean, you're no healer? I couldn't have done it without your help."

"You felt it, too? I never got the knack of it before, but when we worked together, I was beginning to understand. Maybe I do have some healing ability, down deep inside."

"Oh, you do, and a good thing. That stubborn man is used to doing everything himself, and even delirious with fever, he didn't want anyone to try to help him. He couldn't fight the two of us."

Crane laughed. "I'll tell you one thing, it wasn't like studying from a book!"

"Book!" Ketty cried. "It's down in my room. I'll give it back tomorrow, I promise. Don't let me forget."

Crane opened his mouth to speak, before a huge yawn took over.

Ketty laughed and stood up, her strength restored. "Go to bed now. You've had a long day, too. We can talk more in the morning." She turned in the doorway and looked back at him, smiling. "It is so good to see you again."

Chapter 38. Back to Deep River

The Forest

Besides Ketty's smile, the only reward Crane received for his day of discomfort and worry was a night of untroubled rest — a treasure he spent in full. He woke refreshed hours past sunrise. Worry for his father flared but died down again as soon as he looked at Yrae's face. He, too, slept late. He appeared peaceful and well.

Yrae opened his eyes. "Now that we've rested, we'd best be on our way. I've no patience for this lolling about, and the sooner we reach Deep River, the sooner I can return to Aku."

Despite this brave show, when he got out of bed, his legs trembled so much he could barely stand. He dropped back into bed with a groan.

Crane fed a log into the stove. "You may be a powerful wizard, but you've been a very sick man. You need to regain your strength."

"I hate being weak. I want to be doing."

"I know. I do, too. One of Ketty's breakfasts will do you a world of good."

A knock on the door announced both the girl and the breakfast. Crane let her in and helped with the tray laden with bowls of porridge, a teapot, and three mugs.

"You tried to get up, didn't you?" she accused Yrae. "I don't care who you are. Right now you're my guest and my patient, and I order you to stay in bed today."

"Yes, ma'am."

Crane couldn't help laughing at the mighty wizard, ordered about by a girl who didn't quite come up to his shoulder.

When Yrae held out a hand to Ketty, she smiled and grasped it. Though he hadn't spoken aloud, she whispered, "I know who you are. It's all right." She met Crane's gaze. "It's all right with me. I can't speak for my father. It's probably best if we don't reveal his identity outside the three of us." She turned back to Yrae. "Downstairs, you're Yubi."

Ketty gave him another dose of the bitter medicine before serving breakfast. She poured three mugs of tea and gave them each a bowl of steaming porridge with sugar and cream. "Things are quiet downstairs. I'll stay a bit, if you don't mind." She sat in the chair.

Crane settled onto his bed with the warm bowl in his hand and his tea on the floor close by. He looked around the little group, and for no reason he could name, laughter bubbled up again. He didn't realize he was also crying, until he saw tears on Ketty's cheeks. "I'm sorry. I forgot you feel what I feel."

"I'm all right. But what is it?"

"Not sure I can explain." He couldn't control the grin on his face. "I told you I can sense hidden things. Hidden objects, secrets ... I can tell when something is hidden, and unless it is skillfully concealed, I can tell what it is. Just now, I looked around at the three of us, and we're not hiding anything from each other. It's such a relief."

"Keeping secrets is hard work," Ketty said. "And we're not done with it yet."

His father needed to rest, so after breakfast, Crane volunteered to chop wood for Ketty while she washed the breakfast dishes. It was a brisk, clear day after the previous day's rain, and it felt good to get back outside again. He made this his routine over the next several days while Yrae recovered his strength — helping Ketty with whatever chores needed doing and taking long walks around Misty Pass. Sometimes Ketty joined him, but she had responsibilities she couldn't shirk, and he was used to walking alone.

She spent more time with Yrae than with Crane. Although Crane was glad his father had such an excellent nurse, he didn't like sharing either of them. Ketty was always quiet after these meetings and looked at Crane oddly. He couldn't bring himself to ask what they said.

The meetings came to an end when Yrae was ready to travel. Crane stood with his father in front of the Fogbank early in the morning, eager for home, reluctant to say goodbye to Misty Pass. Yrae's mountain cabin seemed long ago and far away. Deep River called. But if that was home, what was he leaving? Crane sighed and listened as Ketty gave them directions. She pointed down the road, toward the rising sun.

"Stay on this road. Probably about a long day's journey, with your stride. Or maybe two days, since you've been ill. You'll pass through Sweetwater and Oxbow. They're little places, but you'll be able to get water and a meal. Somewhere past Oxbow, you'll reach the road to Deep River. There should be a signpost. I expect you'll know, anyway, men like you. Then it's only a few more hours, and you're home." She sighed and stared at the ground.

Yrae was the first to break the silence. "Thank you, my dear. For everything." He held out his hand. She embraced him in a fervent hug that obviously surprised him. He probably hadn't received many hugs in his life.

Crane wanted to be happy Ketty had forgiven Yrae. He would have been, had she given him a hug like that, too. She wouldn't even look at him while he shook her hand and muttered, "Goodbye." She ran into the inn and closed the door behind her.

Crane turned and set off walking down the road. "We could be there tonight, if we push ourselves," he said. He would not let his father know how much the unequal farewells stung.

Yrae caught up and walked beside Crane. "What's the hurry? Let's go through the forest."

"That's a three-day journey, even in summer! And you've been sick."

"I am well now. There are things I need to show you, and a project I want to check on."

Baffled, Crane shook his head and reluctantly agreed. "If we have enough supplies, there's no reason not to go the long way. You were the one who was so impatient."

"Impatient to leave here, not to get there."

Yrae left the road for the forest trail. Crane plodded behind. Branches dripped with collected moisture. Crane inhaled the damp air, pungent with bark and needles, earthy with moss and duff. It was all so familiar now, he couldn't believe it had ever seemed strange. It wouldn't hurt to spend more time in the forest before he returned to the treeless open spaces of Deep River.

They hiked in silence, up through the forest to the barren ridge top from which Crane had first spied Misty Pass.

"That Ketty is an interesting girl." Yrae's voice startled Crane after the quiet of the dense woods.

"Yes, she is." Crane gazed back the way they'd come and fought down an urge to run to her and declare his love.

"She has tremendous power — more than you do, I suspect, and that's saying something. She could probably use my technique for clearing infections. I might offer to train her myself when I come back. If you'll let me."

That snapped Crane out of his daydream. "If *I'll* let you? Why should my opinion matter?"

"I thought I sensed jealousy. What is your relationship, then?"

"We're ... friends." Crane wished it were more. He knew even wizards didn't always get their wishes. "We've shared secrets. Including the one about her father's disapproval of wizards in general, and one in particular. I don't think Eslo would take your offer of training kindly."

"A good, if unfortunate, point. And she may do fine without my help."

The going was easier than Crane had feared. There was snow in places, but not deep yet, and after they got over the first steep ridge, most of the hiking was downhill and gentler. Yrae pointed out landmarks that could guide them to the Aklaka winter camp, though it was too far out of the way to visit on this trip. Maybe another time, after the enchantment was lifted from Deep River. Crane was eager for home, but he could imagine other journeys.

The pair made good time. They were both well and rested, and Crane was in much better condition than he had been in the summer. His main concern was the cold. They hiked in shadow long before sundown.

Late in the day, they reached the river and camped near the beaver pond. As soon as they stopped moving, the icy chill closed in. The campfire helped, but Crane shivered at the mere idea of sleeping in the open.

"Here's something you should know." Yrae answered Crane's unasked question and showed him how to cast a spell tent. This invisible shelter held in the heat of a small fire while letting the smoke out and clean air in. Like the concealing spell, it could be made in any shape or size. It was a long-lasting spell, though it needed to be refreshed to be effective for more than one night. The two spells could even be combined to provide both shelter and concealment, though Yrae seemed to have lost his desire to hide.

When they continued their journey in the morning, Crane took comfort in being reunited with his old guide, the river. As they hiked, Yrae taught Crane more about forest plants and animals. Crane could almost believe he was back in Soorhi's classroom.

"When do they fall?" He indicated one of the many logs on the ground. "I've never seen it happen, but there are so many of them."

"During winter storms." Yrae grinned at Crane's wide-eyed expression. "You needn't worry. It's early yet, and I'm holding the weather calm until we get out of the forest."

Yrae could control the weather for days at a time? Of course he could. Crane laughed. "Is there anything you don't meddle with?"

His father smiled sheepishly. "Habits are hard to break. Besides, I intend to get you safely home."

"I appreciate that," Crane said. "At least let me help. It must be tiring."

"It is, a little. But you haven't done weatherworking yet."

"Aren't you my teacher?"

"Am I, still?"

Crane wasn't sure how to answer, or whether an answer was even expected. They stood watching each other, until Yrae said, "I'll try."

"Tell me what to do." Crane was eager to learn something new, though apprehensive about handling something as powerful and elusive as the weather.

For all his doubts, Yrae fell easily back into the role of mentor. Crane carefully followed his instructions. At first, he doubted he was having any effect, that the weather was naturally calm and there was nothing for him to do. As he was about to give up the effort, he felt something. It was hard to describe, but as he explored, he found he could sense the air like fine threads between the fingers of his mind's hand, and he could pull this or that thread to change the wind.

"Ah!" Crane exclaimed in delight. "I'm doing it!"

His father looked startled. "Well, that was fast. You wouldn't have gotten it so quickly from a book!"

As Crane played — carefully — with the weather, he also perceived the technique for changing his own form. It wasn't exactly the same as weatherworking. He was sure it was similar, though; an intuitive understanding of himself and what he wished to become. His father had said they were carrying too much to transform now, but Crane was eager to surprise Yrae after they reached Deep River.

His father had said something about a book ...

Crane smacked his forehead with his palm. "Ketty has my book!"

"Good excuse to see her again, I'd say." Yrae grinned.

"It isn't mine, and I said I'd bring it back with me. I suppose Jelf will be glad to have me back, regardless, but still ... he trusted me."

"This was one of Lok's books?"

Crane nodded. "They belong to the village now."

"Not to you?"

"They're mine when I want them. *If* I want them."

On the third day out of Misty Pass, Crane shaved before breaking camp. He would hug his mother in a few hours. Rough whiskers wouldn't do.

"Hurry it up!" his father called. He already had his pack on his back.

"Coming." Crane dropped the razor into a pocket in his cloak and shouldered his own knapsack.

Later that morning, they entered pine woods. Crane grew giddy with anticipation of home. It was a clear autumn day. He wasn't sure who to thank, nature or his father, but the sun shone out of a polished blue sky, light streaming through the pine boughs onto dark red scrub-oak leaves. Just before sundown, the flaming yellow and orange of aspens appeared ahead of them, and the travelers arrived at the dam.

"Here's the project I needed to check," Yrae said. "It's been a few years since I gave it a close look, but it's holding up well." He smiled proudly, examining as much of the dam as he could see. "I should come back to strengthen it while I'm here. See how there are multiple layers of branches? That makes it durable, but it might not hold against a flood."

"You're so pleased with your work, yet this is part of the curse," Crane said. "Why not let it go? I'm sure Deep River would appreciate having its water back."

"Need I remind you, it wasn't a curse, and anyway, I told you, I did this for my mother, to dry up that swamp. Separate from the other enchantment. Speaking of, what day is it?"

"My birthday is more than a week away. We're in time." Nine more days for Crane to do something necessary, if he hadn't already. He was tired of magical logic.

"Let's go, then." Yrae hiked off through the pine woods along the dry river course.

Ahead of Crane, the familiar reddish glow marked his father's strange enchantment. The spell's shimmer blended into the sunset colors that filled the sky. Crane could almost believe it wasn't there. He hesitated a moment as Yrae passed into the enchanted region. Nothing happened, so Crane took a deep breath and followed.

"Oof!" The long-forgotten pressure of the spell fell onto his shoulders like a vast heap of pillows. He stumbled and nearly fell, hunched under the invisible load. How had he lived so many years under this weight, and rarely noticed it?

His father looked around, eyebrows raised. "What's your trouble?"

Crane struggled to stand straight. He rolled his eyes toward the net of enchantment over their heads. "Doesn't it affect you?"

"Affect me? Of course not! And I expect it weighs

lighter on you than on the others. I wanted you to wonder, question, seek ... and escape."

Crane stared after his father as he walked on into the gathering twilight. He was right — the enchantment hadn't been able to keep Crane in, once he chose to leave. But it also didn't keep Yrae out. The one wizard who could have chosen to walk through the barrier at any time was the one wizard who had chosen to stay away.

Crane held himself erect, pushing angrily against the spell's pressure, and strode after his father. Resentment boiled up inside him and threatened to spoil the longed-for homecoming.

He chose to come back now. The past is over. He's coming back now.

Chapter 39. Homecoming

Deep River

Yrae led the way at first. As the light faded, he dropped behind, content to follow. He watched with secret pride as Crane straightened under the pressure of the enchantment. The boy had a feel for the land, even in the dark, and a knack for avoiding obstacles. A sense for hidden things.

A glimmer of light in the distance marked the village of Deep River. Though he had flown over it many times, Yrae had not visited the place on foot, in his own form, since that one fateful night. He had dreamed of returning but lacked the courage to risk it. Even now, he wasn't sure it was a good idea. He returned as he'd left, sneaking in the night.

After a day of bright chill, the night was clear and cold. The rising full moon shed light over their path, revealing patches of snow here and there.

"Snow already!" Crane exclaimed. "We've had snow this early only once or twice that I remember."

"Are you sure she'll want to see me?" Yrae couldn't contain the question.

"She's been longing to see you again for over eighteen years. But we won't know until we get there."

"Perhaps she wants to chastise me. It's all I deserve."

"Let's leave that to her."

As they neared the village, a sudden chill ran through Yrae that had nothing to do with night air. Nervousness over seeing Stell again? The thought of her usually warmed him. No, the trouble lay behind, not ahead. Aku stirred.

Yrae stopped and turned to face the way they'd come. *Go to sleep,* he thought desperately. *It's all right. Go to sleep.*

Crane hurried back to him. "What's wrong?"

"Nothing." Yrae tore his thoughts away from the mountain.

"Then let's go. We're almost home."

Crane stood with his father in darkness outside the Blue Heron. "She might be sleeping," Yrae whispered.

"We should wait until morning."

"She's still up. See, there's a light."

Yrae had been jumpy and hesitant all the way from Misty Pass, especially on the last stretch from the dam. Was he going to back out now? Crane pushed the door open and stepped inside, leaving his father outside to consider his own next move. Mama jumped up from her seat by the fire.

"Hello, Mama. I told you I'd come back." Crane shrugged out of his cloak and pack and strode across the room and into her loving embrace. "I brought you something."

"Crane! Oh, it's good to see you again." She squeezed him tightly as he kissed her cheek. "It's silly, but for a moment I thought you were —"

"Who did you think he was?" Yrae stepped into the circle of lamplight.

Mama sat down hard in her chair. "Can it be?" They gazed at each other, a strange light in their eyes. Crane might as well have been invisible.

"How is it, even now ...?" Yrae whispered in a voice filled with longing. He slid his knapsack from his shoulders and let it fall to the floor. He turned suddenly, staring at something unseen beyond the walls. "No," he whispered, pleading. "Can't you wait? Please, not now."

Crane moved toward the stairs. "I'll ... go get a room ready. While you two ... while you get ... reacquainted."

"No," Yrae said. "I should not have come here. I must leave. Now."

"What? We just got here. We've been hiking all day. It's the middle of the night."

"It wouldn't be the first time I've left in the middle of

the night." Yrae scowled as he gathered his cloak about him and moved toward the door.

Crane glanced at Mama. She didn't speak, too stunned yet to understand what was happening. They'd come so far. Was Yrae going to run right back to the mountain now, back to being alone? As his father pulled the door open, Crane used the repelling charm to slam it and hold it closed. He stepped between Yrae and the door, blocking his way.

Crane gripped Yrae's shoulder. "I can't let you leave yet." Crane's heart pounded like a blacksmith's hammer. Who was he to challenge a more experienced wizard?

"Please, Crane. You don't understand."

"Try me."

"There isn't time! She's going to —" Yrae squeezed his eyes shut and pressed his hand to his head. "You must let me pass." He forced the words through clenched jaws.

"Will you come back?" Crane asked.

"I don't know! I can't ... it may be too late already." Yrae shook off Crane's hand.

Crane reached for Yrae's thoughts. The impenetrable shield had slipped, but they were too disordered for Crane to make sense of. Thoughts of Mama vied with images of Aku and the dam, shifting with overwhelming speed.

The shield slammed back into place before Crane could sort the thoughts he'd read. He stood his ground, prepared to fight if it came to that. A fight he was bound to lose. Crane had never won a fight in his life, but what choice did he have? This was no duel for bragging rights. Crane was fighting for his mother. For his family.

He used the repelling charm to shove Yrae farther into the room. Before he could follow it up, Yrae delivered his own magical shove. Crane dodged the full blow. It caught him in the side and spun him to face Mama. She pressed her hands to her mouth, her eyes wide and scared.

Crane ducked on instinct. Magic tingled over his scalp, but whatever the spell was passed without harm. Crane pivoted toward Yrae and unleashed a binding spell. It wouldn't stop him but might slow him down long enough for Crane to reason with him.

Yrae deflected the spell and sent it back at Crane. No longer a full binding, it wrapped around his knees. Crane hobbled back against the door, whispering the unbinding spell as he raised his staff for a new attack. He wouldn't use fire inside the house, or fling Mama's belongings around, but maybe he could surprise Yrae with a second binding.

Before Crane could finish his spell, Yrae lifted his own staff. A glowing blue stream shot out and surrounded Crane. He felt no pain, but his strength drained away, physical and magical together. His staff slid from his grasp and clattered to the floor.

"Stop it, please stop it," Crane whispered as he fell. The falling sensation continued after he hit the floor. A woman's screams penetrated his fading consciousness, as if from a distance. *This time he really is going to kill me.*

Yrae's face bent near his own, muttering words Crane thought he could understand if only they would slow down. A healing charm? A deathblow? And the words, "Help him." Maybe they were only in his mind. With the words, he had a brief vision of Ketty's face. A good last face to see, if only it were real.

The voice cut off. The floor beneath Crane lurched and shuddered. He sank into darkness.

Chapter 40. Rescue

Misty Pass

Help him.

Ketty froze. She knew that voice. It had spoken in her mind before. And *him?* She knew who that had to be, too. What could have befallen Crane that Yrae couldn't fix? Typical of Yrae, he provided no details. A question for another time. If Ketty could help, she would.

A muffled boom shook the house. Ketty gripped the head of her bed to keep from falling. It was late. She'd been preparing for bed but dressed again as soon as she was sure the ground was done moving. She'd have to borrow a few things. Nari's saddlebags. And her saddle. And her horse. It was lucky she was visiting tonight.

Ketty grabbed the saddlebags from the back porch where Nari had set them, out of the way. Nari had already removed her things, and it didn't take Ketty long to stuff them with a few clothes and all the bandages and medicinal herbs that would fit. She added some bread and a bottle of water. She left a brief note pinned to Papa's door: "Gone to Deep River. Borrowed Smoke." He couldn't read it, but Nari could.

Ketty didn't question how she knew to go to Deep River. She just did, the way she'd known where Crane was when he hiked away from Misty Pass. She had a similar link to Yrae since healing him. It had strengthened as he taught her about the many uses of her power. Simple, strong interactions bound all three of them together.

Ketty threw on her cloak and slipped out to the stable. It felt like one of the adventure stories she enjoyed. The heroes were always jumping onto horses and riding off into the night. Except this wasn't a story, and the horse wasn't waiting for her, saddled and ready to go. Ketty went into Smoke's stall and bridled the dapple-gray mare. Smoke knew Ketty and cooperated. Ketty had once healed an infected sore on the horse's foot, and they had been friends ever since.

Ketty had ridden Smoke many times, but she had never saddled the horse without help. She smoothed a blanket over Smoke's back, then hefted the saddle. It was heavier than it looked, but not so bad once she'd adjusted her grip. She lifted it toward Smoke's back.

"When did you get so tall?" Ketty muttered. She

gathered her strength and heaved the saddle onto Smoke's back.

"I was going to offer to help, but I guess you don't need it." It was Dorgan, the new stable hand. He worked for the coach company but also cared for the animals belonging to guests at the inn.

Ketty cinched the girth around Smoke's body. "Could you check this? I've never done it by myself."

Dorgan slid his fingers between the strap and the horse and tightened it. "That'll be more secure."

Ketty felt for herself and nodded. "Thanks, I'll remember."

"This is Nari's horse," Dorgan said.

"I know. She lets me borrow Smoke sometimes. I'm a healer."

All true, if not exactly relevant to the situation. Ketty swung herself into the saddle.

"Nari's taller. Let's shorten the stirrups for you."

Ketty waited while Dorgan made those final adjustments. She thanked him again and galloped out of Misty Pass before anyone else could ask questions or make her stop. When they were well away, she slowed to a walk. Smoke was a fast horse who loved to run, and Ketty longed to race to Crane's side, but they had a long way to go. She couldn't afford to wear out her only horse. She didn't even know what kind of help Crane needed. Yrae had made it sound urgent, but he would have known it would take time for Ketty to reach Deep River. She had to trust whenever she got there would not be too late.

Ketty rode through stripes of bright moonlight and deep shadow on the forest road. The cold kept her awake, though she caught herself nodding and Smoke slowing from time to time. A short gallop woke them both up. Ketty ate and drank. The moon was setting by the time she left the forest, shedding enough light to reveal the signpost at the road to Deep River. She would have known even without the sign.

As soon as Ketty started down the new road, she almost turned back. Where did she think she was going? A gentle, almost irresistible pressure pushed her away from ... Deep River. Away from Crane!

You called me, Yrae. You can't keep me out.

She gave Smoke her head. They pounded through the darkness and didn't stop until they reached the one house in the village with light showing. It didn't look like the Fogbank, but Ketty knew an inn when she saw one. She dismounted, grabbed the saddlebags, and pushed open the door without knocking.

She entered an obvious common room with two large communal tables, as well as several small tables, cozy for two or three. She sensed echoes of a lively and pleasant suppertime in the quiet, empty room. Kitchen to the right, also empty, and ...

Her insides dropped. Two bodies lay on the floor, one sprawled out, the other thrown over it in grief or protection.

The one on top raised her head. "Can you help him?"

"I hope so." Ketty knelt by Crane and felt for a pulse. She closed her eyes in relief. Unconscious, not dead. His staff lay next to him, beyond the reach of his left hand. She gave the woman what she hoped was an encouraging smile. "Crane is knocked out, but his pulse is strong. You're his mother? I'm Ketty, and I'll help however I can."

"Yes, I'm Stell. How did you ...?" Stell shook her head. "No, never mind. Wizards."

Ketty didn't bother to correct her. "What happened? Was he struck, or thrown, or pushed down?"

Stell covered her face with her hands. A tremor ran through her. She calmed before she looked at Ketty. "I'm ... not sure what happened. I saw Crane, with his ... with his father. Confronting his father."

"They fought?"

"I don't think they touched each other. But Crane's father did something, and the boy folded up, like a puppet. He didn't even fight back."

"His *father* did this? And ran out, I take it." Ketty would have words with Yrae if she saw him again. He'd been doing so well.

"I'm worried about him, too. Will you be able to find him?"

Ketty stared at Stell. After everything, she still cared about the man. "Probably. My horse will need care before I take her out again."

"I'll send for Jagree." Stell caressed Crane's face. "Why doesn't he wake?"

"I don't know. We should get him off the floor, though."

"His room's over here." Stell got up and opened a room behind the kitchen. She turned down the covers on a big bed.

The two of them lifted Crane, Ketty under the arms and Stell at the knees. It was a struggle for two strong and determined but small women. Although he looked thin, he was long, and all bone and muscle. They staggered with their burden to his room and dumped him onto the bed. Stell removed his boots while Ketty retrieved her saddlebags and Crane's staff. The staff did not want her to hold it. That was the only way to explain the mild vertigo when she touched it. She got rid of it the first chance she had, leaning it against the wall near Crane's bed.

She tried to figure out what was wrong with him. There was no sign of injury, but she sensed echoes of a fierce assault, and a residue of magic.

"Why would Yr ... his father attack him?" Almost too late, Ketty remembered to be careful of his name. She wasn't sure how much Stell knew.

Stell closed her eyes. "Crane tried to keep him from leaving."

"But why would he want to leave?"

Stell maintained a calm surface, but Ketty could feel her struggle against screaming hysteria. "He didn't say. He was talking to someone, out there." She waved toward the southwest. "He said, 'Not now.' Does that mean anything to you?"

"Maybe." Ketty held the lamp near Crane's face. He whimpered and squeezed his eyes more tightly shut. She hoped he would wake up and see who had come to care for him, but it was only a reflex. She dug into the supplies in the saddlebags and found a clean bandage. She gently wrapped it around his head to keep the light out of his eyes and used a pain charm to relieve what she guessed was a mighty headache.

While Ketty worked, Stell went out, Ketty hoped to tend to Smoke. That was no way to treat a good horse, leaving her standing in the cold when she'd run so hard.

"For you, though ..." she whispered to Crane.

Stell returned. "Your horse is taken care of. One of the neighbor boys, Jagree, is minding her. Will you go out again soon?"

"When it gets light."

"If I know Jagree, he'll still be there. You might take him breakfast when you go."

"I'll do that," Ketty said. "Try to get some sleep. I can stay with Crane for now."

In spite of the apparent urgency in Yrae's call, there wasn't much more Ketty could do for Crane until he regained consciousness. She was relieved that lying on the floor for hours hadn't done him any obvious harm, though his own bed would be better for him. At least she had been able to help move him. She pulled the covers over him and renewed the pain charm.

The excitement of the night caught up with her. She extinguished the lamp and stretched out next to Crane. It was unnerving how right it felt to rest beside him, even on top of the quilt. She had wanted to be close to him before, but his strong feelings generally and especially about her made it difficult. She didn't want Crane to stay unconscious, but it did make some things easier.

As soon as I'm sure Crane's out of danger, I'll ask Stell for my own room. She closed her eyes and drifted to sleep.

When she opened them again, pale dawn light showed at the window. She was hungry, and remembered what Stell had said about breakfast, if not the name of the person who needed it. She stumbled to the kitchen and found half a loaf of bread and a pot of apple butter. She cut two thick slices and spread them generously. One she ate and the other, she carried to the stable.

Smoke was the only horse there. A boy lay in the straw in her stall, as if he had collapsed there as soon as he finished caring for her. Ketty nudged him awake. "Are you Jagree?"

He sat up, rubbing his eyes. "Uh-huh."

"I'm Ketty." She held out the slice of bread and apple butter. "Eat this. If Smoke is rested and fed, I need to take her out again."

He stared up at her with more wonder than she usually associated with breakfast. The food wasn't even anything unusual. No, but she was. This was Deep River, where strangers never came. Beyond that, she was probably the first girl he'd met who he hadn't known his whole life. Even without a sense for emotions, she could read the admiration on his honest young face. And something else she couldn't name. A kind of light.

"Right." The boy jumped up and stumbled from his bed of straw. "I'd be happy to get your horse ready for you." He bolted the food, then led Smoke from her stall. "She's a beauty."

"I think so, too. So, you work for Stell?"

He shrugged. "I help out at the inn sometimes. The stable is ours — Auntie Stell's and mine. It was my idea to fix it up and use it again."

"I thought nobody came here."

"You did."

She nodded in acknowledgement, but something else had snagged her attention. "Auntie Stell? So Crane's your cousin?"

Jagree smoothed the saddle blanket over Smoke's

back. "He might as well be, our mothers being as close as they are, but I guess Stell's his only blood relation. Never thought about it before." He hefted the saddle into place and cinched it snug. He talked quietly to the horse while he worked. Ketty could believe Smoke understood everything he said. When he was finished, he stood by to help Ketty mount.

"Thank you." Ketty sprang into the saddle without assistance. She studied him for a moment. "How strong are you?"

"I'm an apprentice blacksmith." He flexed an arm that, while thin for a smith, was comparatively mighty for a boy his age.

"Good enough. Get up behind. I may need your help." He scrambled up behind her and clung to the saddle. Ketty chuckled. "I won't bite!"

Gingerly, Jagree wrapped his arms around her waist, and they galloped away from Deep River. He whooped aloud.

"What's wrong?" Ketty called over her shoulder.

"Nothing! I wish I had a horse like this!"

She frowned. To him, this was an adventure — riding at dawn behind a mysterious stranger on a fast horse. Not long ago, she'd had dreams of adventure, too. "Enjoy the ride. I'm not sure what we'll find at the end of it."

"Are we riding to the rescue?"

"I hope so."

Ketty sensed ahead for Yrae. Based on Stell's gesture, she had a guess as to the general direction he'd gone. Now her link to him told her more precisely where he was. She left the road and crossed open country until they were near the dry river channel. She followed it upstream. As the way grew steeper and rockier, she slowed the horse's gait. She hated to lose time, but it was still faster than walking on her own two feet.

"How do you know where you're going?" Jagree asked.

"Magic," she called over her shoulder.

She turned her attention forward again as they rode into pine woods. Smoke slowed to a walk and picked her way between tree trunks. Needled branches brushed against Ketty's cloak. She put up a hand to keep them out of her face.

"This is farther from home than I've ever been before," Jagree said.

After her long ride the night before, it didn't seem far to Ketty. An hour on horseback; maybe two or three on foot. Not somewhere Jagree might come every day, but it struck her he had never visited these woods to explore or have a picnic. Another example of Yrae's enchantment at work.

"There he is," Ketty muttered. "Whoa, Smoke."

They dismounted and approached the figure sprawled on the ground near the riverbank. Long, tangled hair spread out around his head, and one hand gripped a tall staff.

"Who is he?" Jagree whispered, confronted with his second stranger in one morning.

"I can't tell you. Best you don't tell anyone you've even seen him." Ketty knelt and examined Yrae. He breathed slowly and his pulse was weak. At least he had a pulse.

"All right," Jagree said. "Is he ... dead?"

"He's alive, barely. It won't do him any harm to move

him, though. Here, help me get him onto the horse. You take the head, I'll take the feet."

Together, they lifted the unconscious man. His hand did not open; the staff came with him. He was as long as Crane, and heavier, but Jagree was strong for his age. They heaved him over the horse's withers. Ketty climbed into the saddle and held him in place, while Jagree took the reins and led Smoke back to the Blue Heron. Ketty devoted herself to the unconscious Yrae, whispering strengthening spells and sensing for any hidden damage. She found no physical injuries. His wounds were magical. She suspected he had drawn on his considerable power until there was nothing left. Why would he do that?

It was a long walk. To his credit, Jagree didn't ask questions. He was clearly happy just to be with the beautiful horse, even on such a scant breakfast.

The sun was high by the time they arrived at the Blue Heron. As if by magic, there was no one out anywhere near the inn. Jagree helped Ketty carry Yrae inside. Stell hurried from the kitchen to meet them.

"Here, put him in my room."

Ketty left her with Yrae and escorted Jagree to the door. "Remember, not a word to anyone."

"Not one word." He took Smoke's reins to lead her back to the stable. He turned with a huge grin on his face. "I'll spend tonight in the stable. Who knows what might happen!"

Chapter 41. Darkness

Darkness. Silence.

"Am I dead?" Crane tried to sit up. An explosion of pain burst inside his skull, white-hot sparks against the darkness.

"You're alive. Don't try to move." A muffled, feminine voice. Familiar, but Crane couldn't place it. The part of his mind that knew names and faces still slept. A cool cloth touched his forehead. A gentle hand brushed his cheek. "Drink this."

Crane obediently sipped from the cup at his lips, something hot and bitter. He spat it out, immediately regretting the effort as his head pounded. "Wha ...?"

"For the pain and to help you sleep."

"I've *been* sleeping." His own voice also sounded muffled.

"No, you've been unconscious." If only he could see her face! "You need to sleep so you can heal. It was ... a fierce attack."

"I remember." How could this person know? Mama was the only witness, and this was not Mama. Nor was it Aunt Sudi, the only other person likely to care for him. Crane reached for the cup and forced himself to drink. The vile stuff relieved the pain in his head. Pieces of memory began to fall together. "Where am I? Why is it so dark?"

"You're at home, in your own room. I guess it's nearly midnight."

"Is that why I can't see anything?"

"No. I bandaged your eyes."

"What's wrong with them? Am I blind?" Crane touched the bandage with alarm. The smooth fabric also covered his ears. At least that explained why everything sounded muffled.

"Your eyes are fine, but sensitive. Even lamplight will make your headache worse. Don't worry, we should be able to uncover them by morning."

"And my ... the other man?" Crane asked in a choked whisper.

"He's in the next room."

"He came back?"

"You might say that. Your mother's with him."

"What!?" Crane struggled to rise, only to suffer another painful shower of sparks. "I was wrong — he's not our friend! I have to help her before he does her harm." But what kind of help could he offer when he couldn't even sit up?

"Hush, lie still. He's no threat to anyone right now."

Clumsily, he caught the hand that wiped his forehead. "Who are you?" She kissed his fingers and pressed his hand to her cheek. "Ketty?" He didn't dare believe it. Tears welled up. The effort of holding them back hurt his head. Sobbing would be more painful. He wept silently. The tears soaked his blindfold and trickled into his ears.

"Why so sad, Crane?" Ketty pressed her forehead against his. The pain dropped away to almost nothing. "Why now?"

"I've failed! Why did I even bring him here? I've made everything worse. I've put Mama in danger, and you, and the whole town."

"That isn't true. Everything's going to be all right."

He wanted to accept her reassurance, however unlikely. His thinking had cleared enough to reveal another problem.

"You can't be here. I must be dreaming."

"You're not dreaming. Before I went to bed last night, I sensed something ... terribly wrong. A voice said, 'Help him.' I took the swiftest horse in the stable and rode here as fast as I could."

This took Crane's mind off his worries for a moment. He smiled slightly, though his head throbbed again. "Whose horse did you steal?"

"*Borrowed.* Smoke belongs to Nari — you know, my father's friend. I left a note for her. She won't mind staying an extra day or two."

"Must be some horse, to run all night."

"Mostly we walked and trotted, but sometimes I had to give Smoke her head."

"Yrae's Curse didn't keep you out?"

"It tried. Nothing could have kept me away if you needed me."

Crane's mind filled with images of that desperate, late-night ride, and Ketty's determination to reach him, to *help him*, no matter what. He appreciated what she'd done for him, but he wasn't in any shape to read other people's thoughts. Even his own thoughts tiptoed gingerly. He tried to raise a wall to block any more from leaking through. Nothing happened except a nauseating stab through the eyes. He rolled over and heaved, though there was nothing to bring up. He couldn't remember when he'd last eaten and couldn't imagine when he'd next want to.

Ketty wiped the bile from his lips and helped him lie back. Her hand on his forehead soothed the pain, and no more stray thoughts seeped into his mind.

"Is ... is Mama all right?"

"She's holding herself together by force of will. She was more frightened than she cared to admit, and she's still worried about both of you. When I arrived early this morning, she was on the floor with you, though she couldn't rouse you or move you. I think she'd been there since you fell. Once we got you settled, she begged me to go after your father, too. So as soon as it got light, I went. I found *him* out in the woods near a big mud dam."

"That's a long walk in the dark."

"He must have flown as an owl, or something."

Crane lay quietly, trying to understand what had happened. He soon abandoned the effort. "Where's my staff?" He struggled to sit up. He dropped back with a groan as his head throbbed.

"Shh, it's here, close at hand." As he thrust out his left hand and pawed wildly, she chuckled. "Sorry, other hand." She took his scarred right hand and guided it to the staff.

He took comfort and strength from the familiar grip, and relaxed. "I felt something. Before I blacked out, the ground moved."

"The mountain woke. But now you must sleep."

"Will you be here when I wake again?"

"Don't worry. I'll stay until you're well."

Chapter 42. Aku's Mess

Weak light filtered through Crane's blindfold. He turned his head, braced for splitting pain. When no explosions occurred, he pulled off the cloth that covered his eyes. The pale light of early morning crept in at the windows, barely enough to see by. He tried to roll onto his side. Something weighed down the quilt. Beside him, Ketty slept on top of the covers, her hair a bright tangle around her relaxed face. Crane watched her sleep awhile. It wasn't how he'd hoped she'd end up in his bed, but he'd take it. She came when he needed her.

As he inched from beneath the covers, she stirred and rolled over without waking. Crane was relieved to find himself still in his clothes. It saved both the trouble of dressing now, and the embarrassment of knowing he'd been undressed by his mother or Ketty. He flicked his hand at the lamp. Nothing happened — no warmth of power flowing from his core to his fingers, and no flame on the wick. He whispered the fire spell aloud and tried to draw on his power. Queasiness rolled through him. The feeling passed quickly, but the lamp remained stubbornly unlit.

His heart hammered. He'd been working that spell with control and confidence for months. Lighting a lamp was nothing. He barely had to think about it.

Crane forced down the rising panic. *Worry about this later. There's something to do that won't require magic.*

He sat on the edge of the bed, kicked aside a pair of felt slippers and poked around with his foot until it found one boot, then the other. He pushed his feet into them, gripped his staff, and stood. A wave of dizziness washed over him, but he held the back of the chair with one hand and his staff with the other until it passed.

Crane crept out of his room and found his cloak hanging by the front door. He draped it over his shoulders and stepped outside. The curse weighed on him more heavily than ever. A slap of cold morning air braced him. He continued toward his goal, one hand on his staff, the other on the outside wall to support his unsteady legs. Just inside the stable, he stumbled against something lying on the floor.

"Ugh!" It rolled to a half-sitting position. "Who's there?"

"Crane. Who's that, Jagree? What are you doing

here?" Crane didn't wait for an answer. "Quickly, saddle Ketty's horse."

Crane sank exhausted onto a bale of straw and let his staff drop to the ground. He was not nearly as well as he'd believed back in his room. It was good luck finding Jagree there. Crane doubted his own strength extended to saddling a horse, something he had never done before. The dusky light in the stable was a relief to his aching head, even with the strong scents of oats, straw, horse sweat, and manure.

"And it starts again," Jagree mumbled. He rose, scratched, stretched, and set about saddling the horse. "But only because it's for her. Where's she riding at this hour?"

"She's not. I am." Crane heaved himself to his feet. "Help me up."

With a protesting boost from Jagree, Crane scrambled into the saddle. Jagree handed him the reins. He pointed his thumb at the staff. "Do you need this?"

Crane hated to leave his staff, even for a short time. It was part of him now. And he had not forgotten Yrae's first piece of advice. "I'm not sure how to hold it and stay on a horse at the same time."

Jagree laughed. "That's easy. Look, the saddle has ties on it to attach whatever you need." He picked up the staff, bobbled it but didn't drop it, and passed it into Crane's hand as if he couldn't get rid of it quickly enough. "Hold it right there while I tie it in place."

He secured it so it wouldn't drag on the ground or interfere with the horse's legs. It was in easy reach if Crane needed it.

"Do you know how to ride?" Jagree asked.

"I guess I'll find out."

Mama didn't own a horse and had never known the need for one. Anywhere Crane needed to go, he walked. He had dim memories of sitting behind Elic on a pony once, and of sliding off. In theory, he knew how to talk to animals, which he hoped counted for something. He spoke quietly to the horse. She turned to look at him and walked sedately into the road. "Faster!" Crane said, and "Whoa!" as his mount nearly left him behind.

"Grip with your knees!" Jagree shouted.

Crane barely had time to follow this advice before Smoke trotted out of the village. He clung on, calling directions to the horse. She followed them as if she understood, though whether this was due to his magic or her intelligence, he couldn't say. One way or the other, she knew exactly where to go.

Stell woke from a doze, uncertain what had roused her. Maybe a door closing, though it was early for anyone to go out. She straightened in her chair and massaged her stiff neck. *I'm getting too old for this.* It was a long time since she'd spent the night at a bedside. Since Crane's accident.

Stell's faded dresses looked fresh in the new light of the rosy sunrise. Stell felt younger herself as she gazed at her charge, resting peacefully in her bed. She had recognized him instantly as her vanished lover, even with his lined and bearded face. It seemed impossible he should be there, just like that, after so long an absence.

Crane had worked a miracle.

He had never said he was going to search for his father. His quest had been something quite different — finding Yrae and breaking the curse. What had become of that aim? Though she paid little heed to the old curse, Stell thought she would have noticed something as momentous as its end. Crane had been so determined to do something about it. It was hard to believe he would abandon his goal, though stumbling on his father would have distracted him. Enough to give up searching for Yrae? Or had Yrae defeated him?

Stell studied the sleeping man and considered a third possibility. Who was he, really? She had loved him as a young man. She had no way of knowing what kind of man he had matured into. Though relaxed in sleep, he looked older than his forty some years. Stell didn't care about his looks. Her heart hadn't changed. But the years had been hard on him. Had they been as hard on his heart?

She stood and stretched the stiffness from her back and shoulders, then stepped to her dressing table and looked at herself in the hand mirror. She didn't look as bad as one might expect after a night spent sitting up. She drew her brush gently through her tangled hair. She gasped and dropped the brush with a loud clunk. The man's reflection watched her, his blue eyes meeting hers in the glass.

"Good morning." It was the voice from her dreams, like a deep bell. "I didn't mean to frighten you."

She composed her face and turned toward him. "I didn't know you were awake. How do you feel?"

"Like I should be dead." His brow furrowed as he

glanced around the room. "Where am I?"

"The Blue Heron, in Deep River. I ... I don't know whether you remember me. My name is ..."

"Stell. How could I forget? Whose room is this?"

"Mine, now." She resumed her seat at the bedside. "It was my father's, the last time you ... visited."

His frown deepened. "I shouldn't be here." He tried to sit up but dropped back against the pillow.

"Don't worry." She patted his hand. "I'm not a child, and I say who comes or goes here."

He flinched away from her touch. "Your father. He died, didn't he?"

"Yes, not through any fault of yours. I never got to thank you for healing him. You did, didn't you?"

"It was the least I could do. It doesn't begin to make up for —" He cut off his speech as the door opened and Ketty walked in. "You did come!" His face lost its worried look, and he smiled for the first time.

Stell wished he would smile like that for her. "You know Ketty?"

"Yes, I've saved his life before," Ketty replied. "Stell, do you know where Crane is?"

"No, I just woke up myself. Isn't he in his room?"

Ketty frowned. "That's where I came from. Where would he go? He's in no condition —"

Jagree appeared in the doorway behind Ketty. Stell had never seen such a crowd in her room. "Good morning, Auntie Stell, Ketty, ... sir." He peered over Ketty's shoulder to get a look at the man in the bed. "Ketty, Crane took your horse. I thought you'd want to know."

"Did he say where he was going?" Ketty asked. Jagree

shook his head. "What does he think he's doing?"

"I think I know," the sick man murmured. "When he gets back, tell him I want to see him."

Ketty nodded and left the room. Before he followed, Jagree glanced back at Stell and her guest. "Your secret is safe with me." He put his finger to his lips, then stepped out and closed the door behind him.

Stell studied the man in her bed. He was certainly Crane's father. How could he also be the man who had attacked Crane? If that was what she'd seen. It was all so confusing. "You want to see him. Will he want to see you?"

Once again, Crane followed the dry watercourse to the mud dam. The landscape was so familiar, he could believe he'd never been away; so altered by the change of season, he must have been gone longer than a few months. Overhead, the glowing net of Yrae's Curse hung, taunting him. He doubted the curse would go away when he turned eighteen. Why should he trust Yrae's word on anything? Thanks to him, Crane could see magic, but he could no longer do it. He would never break the curse now.

As he neared the pine woods, he raised his eyes to the mountain, shining in the early light as he'd seen it many times before. A dark smudge marred the glistening summit.

"You had to have your little say, did you?" he said to the distant peak. "You couldn't sleep quietly until he got back. You had to make a mess."

A continuous roar struck his ears, louder as he approached the dam. He reined in the horse and started to dismount, then thought better of it. "You're a good bit steadier than I am this morning." He patted the mare's neck. "Let's take a closer look." Smoke picked a careful path through the sparse woods until they were near the river.

The sparkling stream Crane remembered had become a roaring torrent of mud, tree trunks, and boulders. It pushed against the dam, but the barrier held. Crane rode closer to the dam. Glowing strands of magic bound it together and built it up. He gazed downstream. Far away, tiny and fragile, Deep River sat on the bank of the dry riverbed. He looked again at the grinding flood and remembered the Legend of Aku's Tears. Yrae had reinforced the dam and saved Deep River, after a brutal attack on his own son. What did it mean? Crane wondered about the fate of those unknown people farther down the river, and of Chamokat and the other Mountain Folk. Had there been any warning? Did the safety of Deep River mean destruction for other villages?

These thoughts haunted him all the way home. Ketty waited in front of the inn, mouth set, hands on hips. Crane slid wearily from the horse. He untied his staff from the saddle and leaned on it.

"You shouldn't even be out of bed." Ketty took his arm and steered him inside. "Where did you go?"

"You know where. I had to find out what was so important." He squeezed her hand, and her expression softened.

"He's awake." She gestured toward the closed bedroom door.

"That's Mama's room. Why is he there?"

"I didn't want to drag him up the stairs. Now come on, he wants to see you."

Crane stared at the door. "No."

She studied his face. "You're afraid. Why?"

"In case you didn't know, he tried to kill me."

Crane turned away and stumbled to his own room. On top of feeling ill and weak, his legs ached from riding. He fell into the bed and lay there, exhausted. Too exhausted to sleep. His head took up its dull pounding again.

The magic was gone. He had finally begun to develop his power, and now it was gone. "It was all I had. Why leave me with nothing? Why not kill me?" he whispered. "I've failed Deep River, I've failed Mama. The curse remains and I have nothing left, nothing that matters."

Voices filtered through the wall, one deep and two higher pitched. Crane couldn't understand the words. He pictured his mother and Ketty with Yrae. They had taken *his* side, while Crane was left alone. What would Ketty think when she learned he had lost his power? Would she want to be his friend if they no longer had magic in common?

The door opened and she walked in. "He wants to know how his mountain is."

"She has a dirty face. How ... how is he?"

"Worse than you. You would have recovered on your own, in due time. He could have died. Imagine, he had just recovered from illness, and hiked for three days, in this cold, no doubt controlling the weather all the way.

Why on earth did you go that way when it's so much longer?"

"He wanted to." Crane's throat clenched as he remembered how excited he had been, traveling with his father, continuing to learn from him as they journeyed.

"Then he turned right around and flew up to the dam. You told me he could quiet Aku from close by, but to restrain that much power from this distance, and strengthen the dam, too ..."

"It was as close as he could get." Crane considered his father's behavior as they had neared Deep River. "I don't think he felt her waking until we were almost here."

Ketty shook her head. "He's lucky to be alive."

"It's not luck. It's you."

She accepted Crane's compliment with a flicker of a smile. "Will the dam hold?"

"I don't know," Crane said. "He said it needed to be strengthened. I hope it's good enough."

"Maybe you'll get your river back someday," Ketty said. "For now, the dam is keeping your little town from being swept away."

"I still don't understand how you knew to come here." Crane was so tired, it hurt to think.

"He called me. I didn't know he could do it from this distance, but I heard him clearly."

"Yrae called you? Why?"

"For you." She took his hand and held it. "He didn't mean to hit you with such a strong spell."

"He overdoes everything."

"He couldn't stay to help you and quiet the Mountain, too. So he called me. Of course, he didn't know he'd also need my help."

"It sounds like you're his best friend now."

"He did what he thought he had to," she said. "Even your mother sees that."

"I'm not sure I trust her judgment. But don't you blame Yrae for your mother's death?"

She regarded him quietly for a moment. "We've talked about that. It's over."

"Oh, just like that. I see." He pulled his hand away.

"Crane, I've saved the man's life twice now! That creates a bond. And even if I hadn't ... Well, he's interesting, don't you see? He's ... complex. And his gift, it's mature and developed and ..."

"You love him, don't you?"

She gazed back at him. "And you don't?"

He turned his head away and didn't answer, except to groan at the pain. Finally, he whispered, "He's put a spell on both of you, you and Mama."

"You're wrong. He doesn't know how to think of anyone except himself, or even how to be with other people. He's not easy to get along with, as I'm sure you've noticed. I thought your emotions were overwhelming. He's so full of sadness and regret, it's hard for me to be in the same house with him. But, Crane, he's the only person I've ever known who does what we do more than halfway! I admire that."

He rolled back toward her, moving his head slowly and carefully. "So, is that what you talk about? Magic?"

"No. Mostly, we talk about you."

Chapter 43. Strengthening Soup and Fatherly Advice

Stell rapped softly on Crane's door. He didn't answer. She knocked harder. Still no sound from within. Could he have sneaked out again? She pushed the door open and peeped in.

"Crane?" she whispered.

Lying in his own bed, he was as far from her as he had ever been. He didn't open his eyes or stir. He lay on his back, motionless as death. Her heart plunged. What if he *was* dead? She didn't understand what had happened to him. Something terrible. He had recovered enough to go out on his own. Perhaps he was still in danger, in spite of that. Or because of it. Nothing would surprise her now, though how unfair would it be for him to return from his perilous journey, only to die in his own bed. Especially when he had brought his mother a precious gift.

She bit her fist and watched the quilt rise and fall with his slow breathing. She let out her own breath in a long sigh. It was only sleep. Ketty had probably given him something after his foolish ride, some potion to help him sleep.

Ketty was another mystery for Stell to ponder. She didn't know who the girl was or where she'd come from, though she gathered Crane had met her on his journey. She had appeared out of nowhere when Stell needed help. She knew more remedies than seemed possible in one so young. Stell didn't know her but felt she could trust her.

She backed quietly from the room and closed the door. "It's been a whole day." She couldn't keep her worry to herself. "Shouldn't he be awake by now? Shouldn't he eat something?"

Ketty looked up from sweeping the hearth. She wiped her forehead with a sooty hand that left a dark smear. "Sleep is what he needs most now. I can help some, but sleep is going to heal him."

"So he *is* hurt!" Stell hurried to Ketty's side. "I saw what happened. I didn't think he hit Crane." She glanced toward the best room, where the older wizard now lay.

"He didn't, or not with fists," Ketty said. "His attack left traces of some kind of magic, though I don't know what spell he used. It sapped all Crane's strength. He probably feels like he fell off a cliff, but there's not a wound on him."

Stell sank into her rocker. "I wish I could *do* something. When he was little, I could always make him better. Even when he burned his hand, I could change the dressing and tell stories to cheer him up. But this ..."

"Don't worry. Crane's young and strong. He'll recover quickly, I'm sure of it. He'll wake again soon. Then you can pamper him all you like."

Stell gave a weak laugh. "I feel guilty. I've been spending most of my time with the other one."

"He may need you more than Crane does. It's been a long time since he had anyone to take care of him. He'll sleep a lot, too, but love is going to heal Yrae."

Stell sprang from her seat, trying to look indignant. "Now, what makes you think I ..." She blushed at Ketty's skeptical expression. "Is it that obvious?"

Ketty smiled. "Your secret's out. So you knew who he was?"

Stell returned the smile. "I guessed from things he said, and now you've confirmed it." She could hardly believe she had shared her secret, and with a stranger. Even Sudi didn't know what this girl had seen on her own. "I'm not sure he wants my love. He's friendly enough, but ... distant."

"I've never met a prouder or more stubborn man. He doesn't know what's good for him. He pines for you."

"He told you that?"

"Not in words. I can feel what's under the words. He adores you. But you may have to trick him into admitting it."

"I couldn't! It's nice to know, though." Stell smiled,

then grew serious. "I don't think we should tell anyone else about him. Not yet. What he did to Deep River ... well, I suppose I understand, and I can forgive him, but I don't know about the others."

"I won't tell. If anyone asks about him, he's called Yubi, and you never saw him before. Well, they'll probably guess he's Crane's father, so you have seen him at least once before. They don't need to know the rest of it." Ketty rose from the hearth and wiped her hands on her apron. "I've started a pot of soup that should be good for both of our patients, whenever they wake up. I put strengthening herbs in it. It's simmering off to the side, out of your way, so it'll be hot for them."

"Goodness, you always know what to do! You'll make a wonderful mother someday."

Now it was Ketty's turn to blush and look away. "Do you need anything, or will you be all right if I go out for a walk?"

"Go ahead, get some air. Bundle up, though. It looks windy." She watched as the girl pulled on her cloak and boots and stepped outside. "There, now I have something to do. I'll wait for one or the other to wake, and then I can take him soup."

Crane woke to a tap on his door. For a moment, he didn't know where he was or what day it might be. "Ketty?" he called hopefully.

"No, only your mother." Mama entered with a tray. She set it down and sat on the chair by his bed. "I'm glad to see you awake. I missed you before. So, how's my boy?"

It was a simple question, but he had to think about his answer. He was weak and tired, as if all strength and emotion had drained away. He was alive, and back home. That was something. He could move his head without suffering, and he no longer felt ill, though not yet completely well. The loss of his magic didn't seem quite real yet. Not real enough to talk about.

"I feel ... empty."

"You've been through a lot."

He had to smile at this gross understatement of the trials he had endured in the past few months. But she had been through a lot, too, and not only in recent months.

"You'll be well soon, dear," Mama continued. "You just slept for a day and a half."

"No wonder I'm so hungry."

"Here, this soup ought to help fill you up." She helped him sit up and sat by the bed while he ate. "I like that Ketty. She knows her way around an inn."

"Mama, you didn't put her to work!"

She laughed. "No, Ketty did it herself. She said she needed sensible work as a break from caring for you two. How did she put it? 'The only patient worse than a cranky old wizard is a cranky young wizard.'"

Crane chuckled, then winced as his head throbbed dully, a shadow of his former pain. "I'll try to be more pleasant."

"She seems fond of you," his mother went on. "Any chance you could persuade her to stay?"

"Not likely. She has her own life. I'm glad you like

her, though. What about you, Mama? I've been away ... how long?"

"Almost three months."

"Is that all? And yet, I accomplished nothing. Then I come back after all those months, and I haven't even asked how you are."

"I'm quite well, thank you." She chuckled. "You don't even know about my project."

"What kind of project?"

"Jelf asked me to write down all the stories I know, the old ones and my own, too. He wants to keep them in a book to have in the Hall. Think of it — me, writing a book."

"Jelf asked you?" Crane was more interested in that part of the project. What had overcome Jelf's reluctance to see the woman who resembled his lost wife?

"Yes, one evening a week or so after you left, he came in for supper. He hadn't been to the inn since Aunt Teel died. He was a great friend of my father, you know, and married my mother's sister. I didn't know how much I'd missed him until he walked in that night." She smiled, eyes twinkling. "He said he'd had a dream you were in the Hall, asking for a book, only it wasn't like a regular dream; it was more real. And when he woke up, he had to come tell me about it."

"A dream I was asking for a book? That must have been the night when I ..."

"When you what?"

When I met Yrae, he thought, recalling the terror and thrill of that night, blunted now by disappointment. "The night I dreamed about Jelf."

Mama wore a puzzled frown for a moment, then went

"I know!" Understanding dawned. "You were too far away to do anything from here. I get it." Crane shut his eyes and took a deep breath, hoping to steady his voice. "You keep telling me how strong I am, yet when I might help you, you fight me. Did it ever occur to you to ask me for help that night?"

"You couldn't help me because you can't fly!"

"Because you wouldn't teach me!"

"I'm sorry," Yrae whispered. "I never stopped to think. I never have."

"And it nearly killed you."

"Maybe it's I who need you, son."

"And maybe you're afraid I'm better than you."

Yrae didn't answer, though he gave a tiny nod as if he agreed. "So, will you come with me?" he asked at last.

Crane gazed back in silence for a moment before answering. "I can't decide now; I'm too ..." He pressed his lips together and shook his head, unable to finish the sentence. He stood abruptly and stumbled from the room. His father made no move to stop him.

Chapter 44. Returning Health

Ketty lifted her face to the strong breeze. She had come to Deep River for one reason, to heal her damaged friends. But it was a relief to escape the confining sickrooms. Time alone in the fresh air strengthened her as well as any tonic.

Ketty had judged the surroundings dismal at first. As she explored each day, she came to relish the unfamiliar landscape. She surveyed the rolling, treeless prairie around her with growing affection. She could almost picture living here. Nearby, cultivated fields lay dark and snow-speckled, while in the distance, pale pasture grass fluttered in the wind. Nothing grew now, but Crane was

"Are you Old Crane now?" she asked.

He chuckled. "Let the boy keep his name. He wears it better than I ever did."

"Not Yrae, I hope?"

"Certainly not! Yrae is dead and gone, and good riddance."

"Ketty said to call you Yubi. I don't care for that name."

"Nor do I. It was the best I could do on short notice."

"Goodness, don't you have a name you didn't make up yourself?" Stell snuggled up to his side. "What did your mother call you?"

"I ... don't remember." It wasn't the first time he had tried to recall. The best his imagination provided was a gentle voice and a lovely smile in a dark, gray-eyed face. Her words remained beyond the edge of memory. "Soorhi called me 'poor little fellow', until he changed over to 'long-legged crane'. Just when I had to leave him. I don't recall my mentor ever calling me anything except 'boy'. Perhaps I don't have a name for you to use."

"That's so sad! It explains a lot."

"What does?"

"You don't know who you are." Stell reclined on the pillow. "I named my son — *our* son — Crane because I wanted him to have something of yours. There's only one thing to do. I gave away your name, so I will give you a new name of your own."

"Well, if it matters that much to you ..."

"It isn't for me. Poor little fellow, indeed!" Stell sighed and lay quietly. She went on, almost to herself. "How do we get our names? They're given to us, by our parents or someone who cares. My papa was Stoli, my mama was Telna. They combined their names and called me Stell. Crane's friend Elic gets his name from a grandmother, Elika. You must have had a name like that once, but it was lost before it meant anything."

"Names don't have to mean anything, do they? They're just … names."

Stell patted his chest. "They take their meaning from who speaks them, and how."

"The name I chose for myself was usually spoken with hate or fear or suspicion."

"That's why it won't do." Stell continued in a softer voice. "I know what it's like to have a reputation. I've heard my name sneered."

"I'm sorry." He had been apologizing a lot these last few days. It was better than solitary regret, but how would he know when he was done?

"Hush, I'm not finished. I've heard it more often spoken warmly, with affection, with kindness. So I'm not ashamed. I have no secrets."

"Not even me?"

"I was protecting you, not myself. I was never ashamed, then or now. But I couldn't let anyone try to hurt you more than you already were."

"Stell, you are a wonder. My spell kept people from asking about me. It couldn't prevent you from talking. I'd done enough to you already. Yet you never told?"

"What good would that have done? So, no, not until Crane was old enough to understand. I didn't know I was telling the only one who could do anything about it." He kissed her, grateful she had chosen to give Crane their story. She thought for a moment, then said, "I'm going to give you a name that means something already.

You've lost so much time."

"All right, I'm ready. Who am I?"

"You are Knot."

"I'm not what?"

"Your name is Knot."

"My name is Naught? You are a tease."

"And you are too clever for your own good." She slapped him lightly on the shoulder. "That's your name: Knot. Like a knot of rope, you are complicated and twisted and strong; nearly impossible to unravel. Like a knot in wood, you are stubborn and tough. And my heart and life are bound to yours."

There was no joking about that. How had he won such loyalty from such a woman? He had to smile about the name, though. It said as much about her as it did about him. He tried it on for size. "Knot the Wizard. Knot of the Mountain. I like it. Blunt, but tricky."

"Like you."

"My dear, thank you for this gift." He let out a deep, contented sigh. "You're the same as when I first met you."

She laughed. "I've gotten old and soft."

"I'm not so dashing myself, these days. You're still younger than I am."

"Am I?" she asked. "How old are you?"

"I don't know exactly," he admitted. "I must be getting close to forty, though I suppose I look older."

"Let's call you thirty-eight," she said.

"So young!" He caressed her hip under the quilt. "I like you soft." She wasn't the girl who had first captivated him. She had a woman's shape now, and a woman's mind, which he liked even more. "Besides, I'm not talking about your age or your looks. *You* are the same: kind and generous and good-hearted and beautiful. If only I'd had the sense to stay with you."

"And what would you have done in a place like this? You would have left me eventually, I'm sure. I can't imagine you settled down."

"I did settle down. Do you know how often I've thought of you in the last eighteen years?"

"Not as often as I've thought of you. These last few days ..."

"When I've been ill and complaining."

She continued as if he hadn't interrupted. "Just hearing your voice again brought it all back."

"I'm sorry."

"Don't be. So often, I wished you would come back, if only to have one more night together; to have a chance to tell you everything I couldn't say the first time."

"Did you?" Knot asked. "I've wasted years regretting that night."

"Do you still, now that you know your son?"

"I don't regret the outcome. Nor my time with you. But my cowardly exit? I could have done better."

"Even so, I thought I loved you," she said. "What did I know? I was just a girl."

"Ah." So that was how it was.

"Now, though ..." She covered his mouth with hers before he could speak. And as the moonlight crept up the wall, all regrets were forgotten.

Stell lay in Knot's arms, warm and relaxed, floating somewhere between sleep and waking. She didn't want to leave him, even for sleep. "Tell me again about the giants," she murmured.

"Aklaka," he corrected. "They're only a little taller than we are. Well, a lot taller than you."

"And they're not ugly monsters?"

"The best-looking men resemble Crane," Knot replied. "The worst-looking ... well, I guess they resemble me."

"Then they are beautiful people indeed," Stell sighed. "What about the women?"

"I kept away from them. Aklaka don't trust our magic, and I didn't have enough words for wooing. Anyway, that's not why I was there."

Stell nodded, more awake now. "I didn't know so many of my stories were true. I'm glad they had a good place for what you needed, though I'd rather have had you here. I suppose you'll be going back soon now that you're well again."

"Mmm," Knot murmured, drowsing. "I could stay."

"But not for long." Each time she visited him in recent days, she had seen how his gaze strayed to the window. "You already miss your mountain."

"Yes. I will miss this, too." He gestured with one hand, a subtle motion that included Stell, the room, the moonlight.

"You'll always be welcome here. You always were, if only you knew. I love you, Knot."

"How do I know what you mean?"

"You have to listen."

"I can't believe you waited for me, all these years."

"I didn't *wait*, exactly. I've had a busy life."

"But you never married. I'm sure any man would count himself lucky to have you as wife."

"I've had a few proposals, it's true."

"And you rejected them, though you had no reason to believe I'd ever come back."

"Marriage wasn't what I wanted anymore. I didn't need it, with the inn to support me."

"Weren't you lonely?"

"Ha! With a child to raise, and a roomful of supper guests? Hardly ever. It's funny, though — when I was young and Papa wouldn't let me marry, it was all I wanted. I was a terrible flirt. I might have married any one of my favorites, and happily. Then you came along, you magical, mysterious fellow, and how could any of those Deep River boys hope to compete?"

"You barely knew me!"

"I knew enough. You had already spoiled me. I couldn't bring myself to settle for anything less."

They lapsed into silence. Stell could barely believe she had finally told him these things. He hadn't spoken as much of his feelings. It was probably harder for a man who had lived alone so much of his life. She knew without hearing the words he returned her affection.

"At least one of you loves me. Crane hates me again."

"He does not. Didn't he send you one of his apples? He's angry and hurt, that's all."

"And rightly so. I would change my actions if I could. I seem to do only wrong in this place."

"That isn't so." Stell kissed his whiskered cheek. When was he going to stop berating himself? "You could go to him."

"He wouldn't hear me."

"Stubborn old man! Shall I talk to him again? I so want him to make peace with you."

"What man was ever at peace with his father?" Knot asked. "He's strong; stronger and better than I am."

"He gets that from me."

"I believe he does. He's better off without me. He'll find his own way."

Chapter 47. Full and Empty

After days of weakness and misery, Crane woke on a cold, frosty morning feeling better than he had in months. Instead of the long, gradual recovery Ketty had warned him to expect, full health had returned overnight. Only two days ago, he had been unable to walk past the inn's front porch. Now the weight of illness had lifted. He didn't even care whether he regained the rest of his power. He could be happy with illusions, as long as he felt this good.

It was early — barely light out — when Ketty knocked and entered, carrying a breakfast tray.

"Good morning! Do you know what day it is?" She set

the tray down and perched on the side of the bed.

"No. Should I?" Crane sat up and grinned. Here was the source of his well-being. The sight of her made him feel even better. Without waiting for an answer, he reached out to pull her close, then withdrew his arm. "May I please kiss you?"

"Thank you for asking." Ketty leaned closer. "Yes, you may."

He pulled her close and gave her a long kiss. She received it gladly, unlike the kiss he had forced on her in Misty Pass. A lifetime ago, it seemed.

Ketty pulled away at last, but not too soon. "You're getting good at that. You must be fully recovered."

"Better than that. I feel like ten men! Let's do something today."

"Yes, let's." She smiled and went to the door, bolting it firmly. She returned to the bedside, stepped out of her shoes and to Crane's amazement, slipped off her dress. "I don't need ten. One will do, if he's willing."

"Oh, he is very willing," Crane whispered.

Crane had never seen a young woman in nothing but her underclothes before, so that was an education right there. She got under the covers with him, and together they explored down to the skin and beyond. For a sweet, brief eternity, time had no meaning for Crane. For once, he was precisely where he wished to be, with no heart for anything else. Magic meant nothing, his father meant nothing, the future did not exist. Afterward, he floated on a blissful cloud, far from all his troubles. Reaching drowsily to caress Ketty, he touched a warm, empty indentation in her pillow. He opened his eyes.

Ketty sat up with her knees drawn to her chest and

the quilt tucked under her chin. She gazed into the distance but turned to look at Crane when he shifted position.

"Happy?" she asked.

"Mmm," Crane mumbled, dazed by the experience. "That was ... better than magic."

"I'm glad." She leaned over and kissed him lightly. "For me, too. Must be why people keep doing it."

He could hear her thoughts — not enough to make sense of them. He gathered she was of two minds about what they'd done. He successfully blocked her thoughts, a good sign of his returning power.

She flopped back down next to him and stroked his face. "Happy birthday, Crane."

"Birthday. Is that what today is?"

"It is, and I'm glad I could celebrate with you before I go."

"You're leaving? Even after ..."

"Well, it's not my horse, is it?" She winked. "You're well now, and I have other work, and my midwife training."

"And your game?" he asked.

"I'll put an end to that first thing," she said. "But if I don't go soon, the road might be closed for winter."

"You'd have to stay here. Is that so terrible?" How could she speak so lightly of their parting? "Stay. A little while, anyway." He tried to smile, to sound playful, but his throat clenched. "You're not sorry, are you?"

"No." She sat up again. "It ... wasn't what I expected."

He sat up next to her. "Did I hurt you? If I did, I'm sorry. I tried to be careful."

"You didn't hurt me." She frowned and pressed her

hand to her head.

"What is it?"

"When I'm with you, I feel what you feel, remember? This ... didn't help. Now your feelings are all mixed up with mine, until I can't tell the difference! If I stayed with you now, I'm afraid you'd ... I don't know ... swallow me alive." He turned away, sullen. She laid her hand on his shoulder. "You wouldn't mean to, but we both have so much to learn. Give me time to learn to use my power and protect myself. You can come see me later on."

"What if ..." He couldn't finish.

"What if there's a child? Don't worry about that."

"You wouldn't ... get rid of it?" Crane didn't know the details, but he'd once overheard Mama and Aunt Sudi discussing such a thing. If Ketty didn't already have the knowledge, she would know where to find it.

She smiled gently. "No, I wouldn't, not with any child of yours. It doesn't matter. There isn't one. I can tell."

She could tell? So soon? If she was telling the truth, she had more power than he'd suspected.

"I wouldn't abandon you," Crane said. "I'm not my father."

"You couldn't even if you tried. Not now, anyway. I'll always know where you are." She sighed. "I promise I'll find you. Someday."

"Unless I find you first."

Ketty smiled. "Not too soon, all right?"

"I'll try to be patient," Crane said. "When though? In the spring?"

"Probably later than that. I'm already looking forward to the adventures we'll have, an itinerant wizard and healer!"

At this talk of wizards and adventures, Crane jumped out of bed. "I've been such a fool!" It was cold in the room. He dressed quickly and picked up his staff. "He can still teach me. And together, we can find ... some people."

"But Crane —" Ketty reached for him.

He kissed her quickly. "Wait here. I'll see you before you go." She shook her head, half smiling. He grabbed the bread from his breakfast tray and hurried out of the room.

Even in his rush, Crane noticed the kitchen was quiet. If Mama hadn't been up baking, that explained why his room was cold. And why his breakfast included yesterday's bread. It wasn't like her at all, but if anyone deserved to sleep late, it was Mama. He tiptoed past her room and up the stairs. He tapped on the door of the best room. To his surprise, Mama's voice called, "Come in." His surprise increased when he found her lying alone in the big bed. There was no sign of his father.

"What are you doing here?" he asked.

"What do you think I'm doing here?" She stretched luxuriously.

"Mama! Did you sleep here?"

"What if I did?" She smiled, and her eyes shone. "I was not wrong about him."

"Where is he?"

"He left at first light. I asked him to wait, but he thought it would be better if he didn't see you. He was in a great hurry, now that he's well again. He couldn't even take his knapsack — just put on layers of clothes, filled his pockets with food, and turned into an eagle, right there in the window." She gazed with frank admiration at the window in question.

"I can't believe this! He left you again! He left *us* again!"

"Calm yourself, son. It's not what you think. He'll be back."

Crane wanted to believe her. Could they trust the word of such a man? "Where did he go in such a hurry?" With his own health restored, Crane couldn't begrudge his father an equal recovery, but to leave without even saying goodbye ...

"He's flown back to his mountain. It can't get along without him, apparently. Imagine!" She laughed, as if it didn't bother her at all.

"What makes you think he'll be back this time?"

"It doesn't take magic to read a man's eyes. Or maybe I'll go to him when the weather gets warm."

"You, go to him? Mama, you've never been anywhere!"

"Then isn't it about time? A mountain holiday would suit me."

"I can't listen to this!" Crane stomped out of the room. How could she be so calm and cheerful when Yrae had abandoned her again?

Even the large common room couldn't contain his storm of emotions. He snatched his cloak off the peg and stepped outside, banging the door shut behind him. The cold morning air shocked him back to reality. His anger and energy drained away as he sank onto a bench by the front door.

What have I accomplished, for all my trouble? he thought bitterly. *Found my father; lost him. Found a girl who isn't afraid of me; can't keep her. Perhaps the curse is on me, after all. I'm back where I started, but how can I stay here, now?*

His throat ached and his eyes burned with tears that refused to be shed. Aunt Sudi's little black and orange cat trotted across the road and leaped up beside him. She put her paws on his shoulder and rubbed her face against his. He stroked her fur, taking comfort from the soft warmth.

"Embers, what am I going to do?" The cat stared and purred. She jumped down and trotted along the road. "All right, yes. I can finally visit Elic." Crane got up and followed. It was better than thinking. The sky above him was a cold, flat gray. The road was frozen mud, gray with frost. The whole world was empty and gray.

Crane walked until he reached the east edge of the village and stood in front of the school. A hoarse voice croaked, "Crane!"

Startled, he turned toward the voice. Jagree's magpie perched in the bare branches of Elic's apple tree. "Ek!"

"That's right," Crane told the bird. "I've come to see Elic." Here was one thing he could make right.

Chapter 48. A New Path

Ketty dropped back onto the pillow and listened as Crane climbed the stairs to the best room. He wouldn't find his father there. She'd tried to tell him, but he wouldn't listen. She hadn't seen Yrae go. She knew the moment when he left the Blue Heron and took his pummeling emotions with him. She would have liked to say goodbye, but that was probably the best way for someone like him. She suspected she would meet him again someday.

The sound of voices filtered from the room above. Ketty smiled when she heard Stell's. She had taken her love to Yrae before he left. It would do them both good. Ketty got out of bed and put her clothes back on. She ate the rest of Crane's breakfast. She could fix him another if he was hungry.

She recognized his footsteps pounding down the stairs and across the common room. She recognized his anger and despair, too. What now? She waited for him to come back and explain. The next sound was the front door slamming. No point in waiting any longer. She left the room.

At the same moment, Stell appeared at the top of the stairs. They shared a knowing smile.

Ketty met her at the bottom of the steps. "So, he's gone?"

"Looks like they're both gone." Stell shook her head. "Crane's all upset, and I couldn't make him understand. But Knot couldn't stay here. He has his own work to do."

Ketty didn't have to ask who she meant. "New name — that's good."

Stell smiled. "He seemed to appreciate it."

"I hate to leave you all alone, but I've got to be going, too. I'll miss you."

"Oh, Ketty, it was wonderful to meet you. I'll miss you, too." Stell pulled Ketty into a motherly hug. "I hope we'll meet again someday."

"I'd like that, with or without Crane."

Crane strode down the path to Elic's cottage. Sunnea had said Elic was sitting around in the dark, but the shutters on this side of the house were all open, and a lamp burned inside. A thread of smoke drifted from the chimney. Crane stepped up onto the narrow porch and raised his fist to knock. Before he touched the door, it swung open.

Crane and Elic stared at each other. Now that he was here, Crane didn't know what to say to his best friend. It felt like a lifetime since they'd camped beside the river.

Without a word, Elic fell to his knees and pressed the back of Crane's scarred hand to his forehead.

This bizarre gesture annoyed Crane even more than Elic's refusal to visit him. "What are you doing? I don't need one of your jokes right now."

Elic looked up at him, his eyes wide and alert. The thoughts that leaked from his mind to Crane's were confused and full of fear, utterly lacking in mischief. "I'm sorry. I never met a powerful wizard before. How should I act?"

Crane pulled Elic to his feet. "You haven't met one yet." It came out rougher than he intended. He tried to smile, though he was close to tears. He'd lost so much. At least he had his friend back. "It's good to see your face again. I ... dreamed you were in trouble."

"I was, but that's over now." Elic whooped and pulled Crane into a crushing hug. "Welcome home. I was afraid we'd never see you again. I thought ... well, never mind." He stepped back, holding Crane at arm's length to study him. "In that old cloak, you look like a real wanderer. And the staff suits you now. You're a greater wizard than I knew."

Crane frowned. "I didn't do anything."

"You must have defeated your enemy."

"I didn't defeat anyone. Perhaps he never was my enemy. I served him and brought him here so he could make a fool of me."

"I'm sorry to hear that, even if it doesn't make any sense." Elic grinned. "You're home, safe and sound, and that's what matters. I heard you were ill."

"I heard the same about you," Crane said. "Sunnea came to see me."

"She told me. Did you enjoy the apples?"

"They were good medicine." Crane managed a real smile this time. With enough practice, he might remember how to be happy again, the way he was when he first woke up. "Thank you for sending them. I hoped to see you."

"I wanted to come, but ... it's hard to explain. Maybe I expected too much of you."

"I expected too much of myself." Crane sank into one of the comfortable porch chairs, and Elic took the other. Crane reached out and flicked the earring on Elic's left earlobe. "So, are you still planning a spring wedding?"

"I guess. If she still wants to."

"What do you mean, *if*?"

"I might release her from our agreement."

"Why? She loves you. She's been trying to help you."

"I'm beginning to understand how much." Elic got up and paced. His racing thoughts hinted at what he'd suffered when he returned to Deep River — the curse a heavier weight than it had been before, a soul sickness, with no Crane to lighten the load or listen to Elic talk about it. He blamed Crane, at least in part. That stung, though Crane blamed himself at least as much. "Things have changed. I'm not the same person I was."

"You're not the only one who's changed. Does she want to break with you?"

"I don't think so. But she's so innocent, and fragile ..."

Crane shook his head vehemently. "Nonsense! She's strong and brave."

"So, she's your friend now?"

"She is. It's up to you to make her my sister. Set the date. You'll see."

Elic smiled. "When the apple tree's in blossom ..." He gazed at the bare branches.

"That's so far off," Crane said. "I'll be sorry to miss it."

"Why, where will you be?"

"I don't know. I can't stay here."

"You just got back. You were going to be our wizard."

"Hasn't Deep River suffered enough wizardry? You're better off without it. Without me." Crane's scowl was back.

"Crane, why are you so unhappy, on this day of all days?" Elic gasped. "You ... don't know?"

Crane shook his head. "Don't know what?"

"The curse — it's gone!"

Crane stared at Elic. He understood the words, but how could it be true? Wouldn't he have known? True, he didn't feel the weight of it. He rarely had, except when he was ill. He stood and stepped off the porch to gaze up at the sky. Only sky, without any magic shimmer.

"It's gone," he echoed. At that moment, a sunray beamed through a gap in the clouds. "He wasn't lying."

Crane closed his eyes and spread his arms, letting the sunshine melt his fear and sadness and anger. His quest, in a roundabout way, had succeeded. Would he ever know what the necessary thing was? It hardly mattered. Now something new beckoned. He didn't know all the details, but he was a wizard now. He would find his way.

Not to his father, though. Yrae was trapped, and if Crane went back there, he'd be trapped, too. If anyone were to free his father, it would be Mama, not him. He could go on his own to the mountains now and find those people his father had spoken of. The Aklaka. Learn their wisdom. He let his imagination fill with the elegant crane he'd seen on his journey, whispered words he'd memorized on a hot summer afternoon, and took to the air on wide white wings.

The End

About the Author

Karen Eisenbrey lives in Seattle, WA, where she leads a quiet, orderly life and invents stories to make up for it. She's the author of the Daughter of Magic trilogy (*Daughter of Magic*, *Wizard Girl*, and *Death's Midwife*), the St. Rage series (*The Gospel According to St. Rage, Barbara and the Rage Brigade*, and *Far from Normal*) and *Ego & Endurance*. She also sings in a church choir and plays drums in a garage band. Find more info on Karen's books and short fiction, follow her band-name blog, and sign up for her quarterly newsletter at kareneisenbreywriter.com

Special Thanks

... to Benjamin Gorman for starting a publishing company that so perfectly fits my writing; and to M. K. Martin for her astute editing.

... to the whole Not A Pipe family of authors for their support, encouragement, and example.

... to Angelika, Keith, Maureen, Nan, Steve, Tabitha, and Yvonne, my invaluable beta readers.

... to John and Isaac, who inspired much of this book through their reading choices, random comments about magic systems, and just by growing up in my house.

... to Keith (again), my example for doing the creative work that needs to be done in spite of everything else. He has read countless drafts (of this and other projects), listened to me fuss over ideas, welcomed the host of fictional people who live in my head, and kept a roof over our heads all these years. I couldn't do any of it without him.